AFTER MIDNIGHT STRIKES

J. DARLENE EVERLY

WISHING WELL BOOKS

Hardcover: ISBN 978-1-954719-38-5
Paperback: ISBN 978-1-954719-37-8
Ebook: ISBN 978-1-954719-36-1
First paperback edition May 2022.
Edited by Jupiter Alley.
Cover art by Miblart.
Layout by Wishing Well Books.

AFTER MIDNIGHT STRIKES

J. DARLENE EVERLY

CINDERS IN MIDNIGHT GLASS 4

For the ones who fight when they need to

For the team at Miblart and all other Ukrainians fighting for their lives and their country

For the Ghost of Kyiv

Ghosts never die

INTRODUCTION

After Midnight Strikes is the fourth book of the six in the Cinders in Midnight Glass series. The fifth book, After Glass Shatters, is coming in September! If you would like to be the first to hear about the next books in the series, get an exclusive prequel to this story and more free books, as well as see what else the author has written and is writing, please go to jdarleneeverly.com and sign up for her newsletter.

CHAPTER 1

LAST CHANCE

Cinder

"Why here?" I whispered, my breath fogging in front of me in the chilled air.

In the time we spent on the coast, in the time it took for everything I ever wanted to fall into my arms and to lose it all again, winter wrapped its frost-covered fingers around Bridgeton and the surrounding areas, strangling them.

Just this side of the city, beyond the last opulent street and over a massive bridge headed toward the western end of the country, the squat tavern building looked like I felt. We were both shabby at the edges, frosted over in our relative uselessness.

At least some people were thankful for the tavern's existence, even if only in the vague way that they were happy they didn't have to pay city prices for a room and a meal.

But no matter how much it surprised me that Tristan even knew this low-rent place was here, there was proof of his presence in his horse standing in the stall next to the one the barn attendant closed mine into.

Paying the stable attendant, I turned back to the building and tried to imagine a way that Tristan wouldn't just pull rank as King, and order me to leave him alone.

Or maybe he would order me to kill myself. That way he could avoid being the one at fault for my death as far as the guard was concerned, and still manage to get what he wanted.

Tucking in my arms, crossing them over my chest, I shivered and hunched as I made my way across the courtyard to the tavern.

For some reason, when we spoke of taverns and our common pursuits at them, I expected he frequented places with more class than the ones I talked about.

But…

I stopped in the middle of the yard, the threat of Corvids hanging over me dashing from my head for a moment as I looked up at the windows of the second story.

Was I about to walk into a building where Tristan was busy drowning his wishes for my death as a traitor in another woman?

Uncrossing my arms, dropping them to my sides, curling my hands into knuckle-popping fists, I stalked toward the front door, snarling into the ice-tinged breeze.

The crackling of the lawn beneath my boots sent an echo of the snapping rage inside my head into the wide world.

But when I slammed open the front door, he wasn't with someone else.

It didn't matter that he was in a heavy cloak with the hood up, shadowing his face. Nor did it matter that he looked every bit the average, shady traveler, road-dusted and rumpled, even if his clothes were a touch better quality than they should have been.

He could hide his identity from the rest of the world, but my eyes went right to him. My entire body was aware of him in a way it wasn't of anyone else.

Somewhere between my awareness of an opponent in a battle, and the way I thrilled to his presence when we were alone in bed, it was like part of me sat there with him even before I opened the door.

It wasn't *his* back to the wall with a meal in front of him, and *his* eyes on me from under the edge of the fabric of his hood—they were part of me. *He* was a part of me.

Because I was his. And he was mine.

All I needed to do was remind him of that. And not rip out what was left of my heart in the process.

Easier said than done.

Closing the door behind me, all the fury that walked inside with me flitted back out again before it latched shut.

The people in the room looked up only long enough to register my presence, decide I wasn't going to start problems, and then go back to whatever they were doing.

But Tristan stayed frozen, staring.

I swallowed and made my way across the room to him, every single step filled with the growing weight on my shoulders from being in the same room with him.

Once, being near him was like some kind of trick to make me believe life was good. Now, it was proof that, while life had the capacity to be good, it didn't mean I was allowed to partake of any of those parts of it.

He reminded me of the blood on my hands.

Just sitting still and watching me with eyes as cold as the air outside, he managed to cause an echo of the words he said in the cells of Sandstone Castle to run through my mind.

Part of me wondered if I would ever forget that he would have hanged me as a traitor if not for my connection to the guard.

By the time I stood close enough to pull out the chair across from him if I wanted to, I managed to shove that day, his words, and the fact that I deserved them, far away from me, and hold onto something else I knew to be true.

No matter what happened in that dungeon, no matter what he said, no matter how many more times I might have to put up with him saying it all over again, we belonged together.

I knew it before he ever told me he loved me.

I knew it before we ever kissed.

I knew it long before I was willing to admit that I loved him, too.

On my way from Breakwater, through the long hours of an entire night, day, and into another night, I tried to think of the moment it became true.

Every single time I looked into his eyes in my memories as he said beautiful things to me, it seemed like that knowledge was already with me. Memories I held onto while I tried to stay warm riding through the winter-covered world.

No, the moment I knew we belonged together happened long before I was willing to admit.

Even through all those hours, and standing before him now, while I waited for his ever-changing eyes to react to me in some way that might show me he felt the same, I couldn't pinpoint the moment.

A million little things, tiny memories, passed through my mind, and none of them were the moment it happened.

The monumental memories—like the look on his face when he kneeled before me naked in the light of sunrise to propose— were etched on the insides of my eyelids. Ready for me whenever I needed to call on them to remind myself that this was real.

No matter what he said.

But they weren't when it happened either.

They were the warmth I missed that he once gave me, keeping me from freezing in place and never moving again.

My memories were a lot of things.

They just didn't answer my question.

I opened my mouth a fraction, almost asking him the question out loud.

When did we fall in love, Tristan?

At what point in my cold and guarded nature did you see someone you loved and wanted to spend the rest of your life with?

Because I didn't know when it was that the heat of him turned me from a block of ice into a burning star. But I knew it was his influence.

I broke from my brother because I loved Tristan enough to see.

Somehow, someday, I was going to convince him of that.

First, though, I had to avoid punching him in the face for not believing.

DAMN IT

Tristan

"Why the fuck are you here?" I asked. Well, more like snarled. But she was the last thing I needed or wanted.

My blood heated with the white-hot need to destroy something just as I was destroyed by the person standing in front of me.

"Because you're stupid enough to be here," Cinder said, matching the hostility in my voice with the venom in hers.

Just hearing her voice sent the hairs on my arms rising as I pulled my eyes from hers and scanned the tavern's scant crowd.

A couple of only slightly unsavory looking patrons were turned our way.

"Not an answer." My voice was quieter this time, hoping they would stop looking at us. Neither my hood, nor hers, were enough to make me comfortable with people looking too closely. "There's no reason for you to follow me."

She snorted a short laugh.

"Right. You can try to convince someone else of that," she sat down in the chair across from me at the small table, crossing her arms and leaning forward, "but I know you."

"Gives you an advantage. I don't know you at all." I turned away from the hurt that passed over her face, and continued eating, although my food turned bitter in my mouth. "You seem comfortable having your back to the room. Know anyone in here?"

"The number of people I really know, I can count on two hands. And, knowing how to protect myself should one of the people behind me try something is different than being comfortable sitting like this."

Cinder turned toward the bar, and lifted a hand in some gesture I didn't recognize. The bartender nodded.

"What did you just do?" Questioning her every move was going to be exhausting. Why didn't she stay back? Why couldn't she leave me alone?

"Ordered what you're having."

"By hand gesture? Exactly how many taverns have you been in?"

She turned that gaze back to me, but there was no hurt there now. There wasn't anything I had ever seen from her. Now she looked like she was my tutor, and was disappointed in my work on a test.

"Enough. And before you ask the next question in that stupid checklist of yours, I won't be elaborating on how often *that* happened because you made it clear you don't care. And, therefore, it's none of your business anymore." She raised a brow at me and shook her head before she went back to staring at a spot on the wall above me.

After everything, Cinder really thought I cared how often she went to bed with people at taverns?

That damn heat, the searing and burning in my veins, came

roaring back. I curled my hands into fists. Just one more reason to find a way to get her out of here as soon as possible.

"Funny," I said, taking a bite and watching out of the corner of my eye as she narrowed hers at me.

"What's funny?" she asked after a time as if she didn't want to know.

"Sitting here in this inn, I finally realize, I should have known the truth when you told me that story about your habits at places just like this." I shook my head and she set her jaw.

"The same habits you have at taverns, you mean?" She had nothing but contempt in her voice. If anyone around us listened in, they must have thought she found this to be a bad joke.

Maybe it was something like that.

"No. I mean that you shared a bed with me how many times before you decided to fuck me to solidify your claim?"

"How many times were we alone, Tristan?" she asked, her voice a sigh like I was a petulant child she needed to scold.

"You really must think I'm disgusting if you waited so long." I took another bite just to stop grinding my teeth.

"Not then, but I think you're acting pretty fucking gross right now." She leaned forward, her hand on the table in a tight fist. "I was fighting against loving you. But I was too late. You fucking mattered too damn much for me to be able to even kiss you without the pain of knowing I couldn't tell you the truth, that I fell madly in love with an idiot."

"An idiot? Nice."

"Someday, when you look back on this moment, you'll agree with me that you're being fucking stupid right now."

"Oh, I think it's safe to say I have been stupid for far too long."

With a roll of her eyes and a shake of her head, she leaned back in her chair, and I returned to my meal.

I ate, she sat, and neither of us spoke.

Not even a few days ago, I would have said I knew what she

was thinking when she lapsed into silence.

They were all lies.

All those looks. All those quiet revelations. All just careful manipulations to get me to marry her so she could take the crown for her brother.

Soon, Duke Ash Ahmya of Lehar was going to pay for that.

Rath would make sure of it. If he didn't get to him first, then I would gladly make him pay.

But, in the meantime, I needed her to go away so I could finish what I needed to do.

Her food came, and she ate half the plate faster than I thought possible before she took a drink of her ale, wiped her mouth, and directed that gaze at me again.

My entire body stiffened in response.

"Listen," she said, her voice like a defeated sigh, "I know about the kids. Let me help you get them back."

"Why? So you can be a hero to more people? You already made it so I can't kill you. You can put down the act," I whispered, shoving one of my last bites in my mouth before I could yell or say something that might give us away.

"They should be where they belong." Her voice gave out on 'belong,' and I forced my grip to loosen its hold on my cup before I snapped it in half.

Grinding my teeth, I squeezed my eyes shut for a moment. I couldn't look at her when she said things like that, when she turned my own words on me.

She just shook her head, and went back to eating, acting like I wasn't even here.

It was for the best.

Telling myself that while my throat tightened on a roar of rage, and the temperature of my blood climbed even higher, made the word 'lie' louder in my mind, ratcheting up my anger. She turned me into a monster feeding on itself.

"We should get back on the road tonight," she said after

downing the rest of her food, "get there as fast as possible, and rest when we're done."

"No." Admitting weakness to her wasn't what I wanted. But as blurry as my vision already was, and as much as my hands didn't want to do what I told them half the time, I didn't have a choice. "You can do stupid shit like that. But I need sleep, or I'll be in trouble. And then, so will they. My horse needs a rest, too. I don't want to stop, but I've been going for two days straight. And I can't keep doing it."

"Fine. Then sleep on your horse, and I'll pull you along. Going slowly by horseback is still faster than staying still."

She actually seemed serious.

But instead of answering that idea—which could kill the horses and leave me totally at her mercy in the middle of the night on a lonely road—I shook my head and wiped my hands and mouth.

"Tonight, I'm staying here." I got up from my seat, and she pushed her chair back, her hands still on the table.

"How many times am I going to have to save your ass before you trust that I'm not going to kill you?"

I stared at her, at the face I still loved no matter how much I didn't want to, at the scar I once thought made her more beautiful and showed off her true character...and I saw something different now.

All of that still crossed my mind every time I looked at her, but the very next things that ran through me were fury and distrust.

Her face was now a mask covering threats and lies, the scar revealing not her true character, but her true wishes.

To hurt.

To kill.

Just like the poison that caused her wound.

I didn't have possession of the words to explain to her.

Whatever part of me still hoped it wasn't true—that she

really did want to save my ass and not kill me—wouldn't let the rest of me tell her I would never believe her. The trust I had in her died with the prisoner in the dungeon of Sandstone Castle. And I couldn't admit it out loud.

Instead, I turned away from her, and trudged upstairs to my room for the night.

Maybe in the morning she would be gone.

But moments later, as I took the last step to the top story, the sound of her footsteps on the stairs behind me told me I wasn't that lucky.

How she found me, and followed me all the way to this tavern from Breakwater without alerting me to her presence, I didn't know and couldn't guess.

Although it did make me hold tighter to the saddlebag I brought with me and the things inside.

My room was in the corner at the end of the hall, as I requested when I came in.

Unlocking the door, I waited until I saw Cinder go into her room next to mine, just so I knew where she was.

Being aware of her was not new. But this kind of awareness, the same kind I had for crows in the skies when we were in the middle of the battle on the last ship—this hurt.

Rubbing at the spot on my chest that ached, I locked the door to the small, dormered room behind me after I walked in and tossed the saddlebag on the bed.

No cloud of dust puffed out of the bed, so at least this room was clean.

Shaking my head, trying to clear my vision as it started to narrow, I somehow had to keep my eyes open. For a little longer. And get this done.

My saddlebag had the roll of exactly what I required in it.

The last thing I needed was for her disdain of walls to bother my ability to sleep. The world around me was challenge enough to that.

CHAPTER 3

LIGHT

Cinder

I couldn't breathe.

Leaning against the back of the door, my arms and legs shaking, I hiccupped and stuttered the air into and out of my lungs.

How was I going to do this?

In what fog of delusion did I ever think I could do this without breaking?

Just being around him, close enough to touch him, to...try and get him to understand was too hard.

This stupid plan?

Not just following him, but traveling with him?

Finding the kids with him?

Probably saving him again if history repeated itself?

Every single second of it meant I had to be near him, smell that scent I wanted to surround me as it teased by on the air, see those hard eyes I wanted to soften in my direction so badly it was worse than hunger, and feel his presence when I couldn't get close enough to touch him.

No choice. I had no choice but to force the re-breaking of my own heart every minute of every day I was with him.

All to protect him.

Someone who wanted me dead.

I was only alive because it wasn't politically advantageous to kill me. He said that. He made it clear.

He thought I was a traitor.

My King wanted me dead. Even worse than that, the man I loved wanted me dead.

Wrapping a hand around the ring hanging from the chain around my neck, I took another deep breath, and shoved it all to a far corner of my mind.

No matter how hard I tried, my heart ached in a way that made me rub my chest again. But if I didn't think about it too much, I could at least keep going, keep moving, keep doing what needed to be done.

Turning to the room, I took in the small space, the angled ceiling, the bed that actually looked clean with the quilt of soft colors, and the dormer window.

At least with the dormer, the next step would be easy.

Even though I wanted to keep going, to just ride through my exhaustion and trade my horse in for another when I needed to, Tristan couldn't. He never trained to, and I couldn't blame him for stopping.

But if this was going to be a habit of his, this staying at inns and renting rooms above the taverns we stopped at, I would need to steal another purse.

On my way in, once I knew where he was and which direction he was heading, I broke into the first wealthy looking house I found, and stole a purse from the cloak by the door so I would have something to buy food with.

It had less in it than I would have wished, but hopefully the person I stole from wouldn't miss it as much as a larger amount.

Going to the window, I shook out my hands and blew air through my pursed lips.

"Fuck," I said to the empty room as I opened the window, just thinking about seeing him again made it more difficult to think, to do.

But once I swung my leg up onto the windowsill, my mind finally snapped into focus.

Jocelyn once said while I was training on a climb, that we trained for our mind more than our bodies. If I trained enough, my mind would quiet, and the training would take over in the times I needed it to.

She was right. As usual.

Now, making my way out onto the roof was easy. Not just because these kinds of roofs were easier than almost any other, but because my heart didn't distract me from the work. For once.

Riding a horse didn't present the same level of distraction.

Tristan's window wasn't far from mine, so in a few steps I was at the side of the dormer to his room.

But crouching down and swinging around to look in, to check on him, I came close enough to his face to feel his breath on my lips.

For a second, just one blissful second, he looked at me like he used to.

His eyes softened, and one corner of his mouth twitched like he was going to smile. The hazel of his eyes was warm and deep enough for me to disappear inside.

My heart thudded, and the blood in my veins hummed. Warmth spreading through me.

But then it was over.

Steel entered his gaze, the corners of his mouth tightened, and the hazel froze over like a field of grass in an early frost.

Tristan shoved his hands out his open window, snagging a

roll of fishing line on one of the nailheads of the window surround, wrapping it across and finding another, creating a crisscross similar to what was all over Breakwater.

I pulled my face back and out of his way.

"Good," I whispered, "you're safe."

"Right," he said, not looking at me as he went about securing the window, "I'm sure you're upset that the walls will hold tonight, even against you, and you won't get a chance to finish me off."

"No, Tristan." I took a step back, giving him more room, watching while he still had the window open and was at further risk. At least that's what I told myself I was doing, just protecting him.

He humphed through his nose, focusing on finding another rough spot of wood or a nailhead to wrap his line around.

"I'll just keep saying it until you believe me." My voice was barely there, a muffled hint on the wind. But it was as much a vow as anything I ever told him.

Pausing with his hands still halfway through wrapping the line around a nailhead, he shuddered, his jaw tight.

But all I got was a glance before he cut the line with a dagger and shut the window, throwing the lock and adding a bar wedged between the two sides.

With the glass between us, he finally looked at me.

No amount of training could ever prepare me for being on a roof with his eyes on mine, when nothing in them said he ever loved me.

A wave of dizziness washed through me, and I grabbed the edge of the thatching covering the dormer.

He turned away and turned out the hellfire powered light, leaving me to stare into the black eye of the darkened window.

I allowed myself a moment to get my head back, and turned around to return to my own room.

Tonight, my only goal while I slept was not to see him in my mind. I needed to leave my own light on.

16

CHAPTER 4

READY

Tristan

Saved by exhaustion.

That's what last night was.

I was so close to tossing and turning all night. Even though my eyes didn't want to stay open, my mind ran in circles and twists and turns. Every thought centered on her—just a wall away.

Fucking walls, I thought as I picked up my boots, holding them in my hand, trying to make zero noise in the process of leaving.

Normal people used walls to help protect themselves. That wasn't something I could rely on anymore. Not when Cinder was around. I believed there was nothing that could protect me entirely from her anymore.

The best I could do was get this done. She might not kill me until we got the kids back. Then I could keep myself surrounded by people at the palace until….

Until.

Every time I got there in my mind, trying to think ahead, I came up to that word, and I didn't know what came after.

Not anymore.

My entire life, there were few actual question marks about my future. But to know, to try and accept that 'until' meant 'until she succeeded and killed me,' wasn't something I was prepared to do.

Part of me wasn't sure why.

I went from knowing everything about my future, our future together, to having no idea so fast that I still couldn't figure out what I felt about the change other than the rage.

Opening the door, slowly and incrementally so it didn't make any sound, I stepped out into the hallway.

She was already there, leaning against a wall, her head tipped down, one foot rested on the wall behind her, brimming with weapons, and all in the same black outfit she wore when she got soaked during the last battle.

It didn't matter that her dark hair was clumped and dirty, lifted off her face in the front because it dried in the wind of her riding. It didn't matter that her cloak was road-dusted, and she smelled vaguely of horse. She looked feral and wild.

My heart hammered in my chest, my lungs constricted, and my arms ached to hold her.

Cinder looked up at me through her lashes, her head down and that curl to her shoulders still there, as if even alone in a hallway, she braced herself for a blow.

My breath came out in a whoosh.

Rage.

The heat in me rose, made me want to lash out.

But it wasn't directed at her. It made me want to punish myself.

Even now, looking at the way her shoulders were set, so

different from the unrelenting, unquenchable, impossibly strong flame she used to be, made me hate myself for hurting her.

I laughed, a low, brittle sound, and shook my head before I slipped on my boots, leaning against the closed door.

She was going to kill me, and I was mad at myself for how she made herself small.

"Just go," I said, hoping for once she would listen. "There's no reason for you to follow me."

"Yes, there is." She pushed herself off the wall, looking down the hall and away from me in a guarded and ready stance like any minute she might have to fight someone off.

"If I fail, if someone kills me, then you win. Why not just let it happen?" I gestured for her to go ahead of me, and she sighed before doing as I asked.

"Because that would be a tragedy," she whispered. Even though her voice was barely there and directed at the floor in front of her, somehow her words fell back toward me. I heard the same note of sadness and love in them I did when she held me that last night together.

Curling my hand into a fist, I squeezed my eyes shut for a moment to fight off the useless hope that flooded through me.

This was exactly why she needed to go.

Maybe she would hold off on killing me. She didn't know the lead I had on the location of the kids, and Onyx was a big enough country for it to be a problem finding them. But aside from the threat of her presence, it was the way she had of breaking through to the part of me that wanted to believe her that was the most dangerous.

I couldn't allow her to do that to me.

No matter how much the remaining shards of my heart cried to let her.

Just make it to the kids, that's all I had to do for now. And worry about the rest later. Of course, reminding myself of that over and over again grew more difficult with every second in her presence.

After years of thinking ten, twenty steps ahead, and still dealing with twists and shocking moments that derailed all my efforts or changed things in a second, this whole thing was starting to run my mind in circles.

The plan, such as it was, only consisted of the next step.

Stopping at the counter in the tavern, I picked up some basic provisions to keep me going on the road, and tucked them away in my saddlebag.

Cinder stood to the side, her back to the counter, and watched the mostly empty main room of the bar as she bit her bottom lip.

For a second, looking up from my bag, I almost reached for her, to kiss her and tell her we would fix everything.

Just for a second, my body didn't remember her lies.

I shook my head, and turned to the doors, losing the ability to care that it left her open to my back.

Kill me, follow me, hate me, forget me.

Whatever she wanted, I couldn't worry about it until I could get away from her long enough to remind myself of what she had planned.

Outside, I let out a short, humorless laugh.

My horse, prepped and ready to go, stood tied to the post alongside another that Cinder went to and untied.

"Sleep is hard for me to come by," she said, leading the gelding toward the road.

Putting on my saddlebags, checking the saddle itself and everything else to make sure she didn't sabotage it, I tried to ignore what she said.

It didn't mean anything.

Anyone could say the same thing. We were at war. Corvids could attack from the skies anywhere, anytime.

But hearing *her* say it…so many mornings ran through my head where I woke up before her. Mornings where I woke her up with a kiss, or a brush of my hand. Mornings where I carried her to bed, or moved away from her, and still she didn't stir… Mornings where I had time to study her face while she was in my arms.

Shuddering, fighting off the images carved deep within me, I lifted myself into the saddle and turned the horse to the road, kicking her up to speed.

The road was too exposed out here. I should have kept an eye on the skies above me, but I rode hard, giving the horse her head.

Not to lose Cinder.

I knew better than to think I would be able to do that out here where she could see me so clearly.

Just so I had something to focus on, to distract my fool body, and center my mind on something so I wouldn't hurt the horse or myself.

Finally, trees began to reach over the road, the track itself narrowing. Offshoots of the road became nonexistent, and I entered the forest that precluded Mariposa, the first duchy I needed to pass through after making it to the other side of Bridgeton before entering Thirteen Rivers Valley.

Allowing the horse to slow, I looked behind me.

If she was going to do it before we got there, now would be the time.

Here in the woods, no one would see her kill me, and no one would be able to find my body hidden in the trees.

She was coming up fast, her cloak billowing out behind her.

With my heart in my throat, I slowed further.

Did I want to go through all these woods wondering, waiting for one of her perfectly thrown knives to slice into my back, or was I really ready to have her kill me?

It didn't matter whether I was ready, or not.

The moment was here.
She slowed as she reached my side.

CHAPTER 5

PUNISH

Cinder

"Do you need to stop?" I asked, bringing my horse alongside Tristan's, and adjusting my seat in the saddle.

"Get it over with," he said, an odd breathlessness to his voice.

The small hairs on my arms rose, even though I couldn't understand why. Something about the way he said it. My body reacted before my mind caught up.

"What are you talking about?" My voice was hushed and thin, but the horse beneath me still threw his head, tossing his mane and whinnying.

"Look around us, Cin-" he coughed, unable to finish saying my name, which stabbed me deep, making me ache. He shook his head and looked at me, a kind of defeat in his eyes I never wanted to see again. "No one is here. If you're going to kill me, now would be the perfect time."

"Fuck." The air left me in a whoosh, shooting out of my

body, leaving me gasping and shaking my head violently. "No," I wheezed. No other words managed to get through my closed-up throat.

I couldn't keep doing this. Looking at his face, the look in his eyes, it was as if I were seeing a totally different person. Even from this morning.

Now, he was…lost.

And it didn't matter that I denied it, that I had said, 'No.' He still looked shattered.

Tilting my head to the sky, away from his eyes and toward the gray beyond the branches overhead, I finally sucked in a whole breath.

He still didn't say a word, nor did he look away from me when I met his eyes again.

"Maybe I should have told you a long time ago," I said, my voice thin.

But the despair left his face as he snapped his head back like I slapped him, rage filling his eyes instead.

"Maybe?" he asked, his voice like a scythe that slashed through me.

Nodding, steeling myself for the risk I was about to take, I said, "Yes, maybe."

He laughed a harsh, grating bark, and shook his head.

"Your reaction," I said, "the reaction you're still having, even though you fucking know better, means I wasn't wrong to keep it from you."

I set my heels to the horse's sides, pulling in front of Tristan.

Even though I couldn't leave him. Even though I couldn't just ride ahead when I didn't know where we were going, I didn't have to keep talking to him right now. Not when he did this.

Checking behind me a few minutes later, I spotted him following.

Good.

My breathing still stung as my lungs filled around my sharp-edged heart. At least I *could* breathe, and he was following me.

But I didn't want to ride alongside him.

How could he be so enraged with me when it was obvious that I couldn't tell him, or we never would have been able to develop a relationship at all?

Of course…that was probably the point. He didn't want us to have the chance, the history. In Tristan's mind we spent the time to develop our relationship, and that was the crime. Allowing it to happen in the first place.

Tristan, my King, the man I loved, would have preferred I told him the truth at a time when he could have still taken my head from my shoulders, and declared me a traitor for the whole country to judge and hate.

Fine. I shook out my shoulders and shoved everything, every part of me that wasn't an assassin on a mission, every piece of me that wasn't shaped to my brother's specific standards, away from me.

Where it all went, I didn't know, and didn't care.

Maybe it would be gone forever like the life I deluded myself into thinking I would be able to keep.

A laugh burst out of my mouth, and I couldn't stop it.

Even squeezing my lips shut tight didn't stop the inappropriate laughter from bubbling up.

No amount of curling in on myself managed to stop it.

Slowing the horse didn't end the stupid guffaws from shaking my shoulders.

It wouldn't end, and I knew why.

Closing my eyes, allowing the horse to keep its own pace and relying on it to keep to the track, I tried to find the cold place.

What came next if I couldn't shut it down wouldn't be yelling, wouldn't be the swift move of a sword, it wouldn't even be laughter.

At some point, if I let this go on and didn't control myself, the tears would follow.

The last thing I wanted was to cry in front of him again.

No. No more.

I already shed too many tears for him, for myself, and for this entire fucked up life. I needed to keep moving. If I started crying again, I wasn't sure I would stop. And then all that would be left for me to do would be to curl up in a corner, and wait for oblivion to take me.

Finally, the sound of hooves—not from the horse beneath me—made my eyes snap open, and panic race through my blood.

With a tight grip on the reins, I urged my horse to a faster pace, my hands shaking.

Part of me wanted to just go. To keep riding, as far and as fast from him as I could get.

But the rest of me held back, not willing to try and outrun this.

He made me promise.

And I was going to keep that damn promise. Even if he wanted to forget.

Rubbing my one hand on the ache in my chest, I held my breath and looked behind me.

Tristan was close enough for me to see his eyes under the shadow of the hood of his cloak.

"Good," I muttered under my breath, facing forward, and settling more comfortably into my seat and the rhythm of the horse.

My leg muscles, still worn out from the riding of the days before, yelled at me for posting up to save my ass some pain.

Even better.

Aching muscles was a good thing, as far as I was concerned.

Pain taught lessons.

Ash was right about that much, even if he was wrong about

how it was a teacher. And this pain was at least the kind I knew would teach my muscles strength. It was something to focus on to avoid thinking about the ache in my chest that only managed to teach me sadness.

I reached deep into my memories, and conjured up one of the old songs my mother used to sing around the house.

Running the song through my head, I started to hum.

Just to fill the space where Tristan's love used to be. But it made me miss my mother too much. I let the last notes of the song fall silently through my mind before I went back to being in this place and this time. And just as alone.

Somehow, I had to focus on the kids. To focus forward and keep moving.

My most important mission rode his own horse right behind me, but if all I could think about was him while we went forward in silence, that mission was already a lost cause.

In this one, I couldn't allow myself to fail.

Ash wouldn't punish me this time.

My future would.

And she was much more dangerous.

SOFT

Tristan

She slowed up again.

I expected her to take off at a gallop, pulling far enough ahead of me that my chest didn't ache so much. Just like she did the last few times.

Cinder was a good rider, but her inconsistent speed for no discernible reason in the hours we had already spent traveling had me looking to the skies and the trees around us on a regular basis, afraid I was missing a threat.

This time, though, she came to a complete stop, swung one long leg over the horse's head, and slid to the ground.

Maybe I should have kept going, riding past her and onto the next inn or tavern. Wherever place came next on the road ahead of us.

But I slowed, too.

I could blame the curiosity that had me looking around, and trying to understand why she stopped. But it was just as likely to be the way the hairs on my arms stood on end, and my blood heated at the thought of her being attacked out here while she was alone. No one would hear her.

She thought she was invincible. She was a good judge of threats, but that was only if she registered someone as a threat at all. Half the time she didn't seem to think enough about people as a whole to understand that more than swords could be weapons in the hands of someone who wanted to hurt you. No matter how difficult you made it.

Cinder was proof enough of that.

Even though my brain knew better than to waste time worrying over the welfare of someone who wanted to kill me and steal my throne, my heart told me that it might never beat properly again if I rode off and she died out here.

Reaching her, I looked to the skies and deep into the trees, trying to find any hint of Corvids or the unknown threat in Thirteen Rivers Valley. Maybe they expanded their reach.

Until I knew more about them and their objectives, I could neither rule them out, nor ignore the possibility of confronting them at any time.

"Go ahead," she said, turning away from me, and walking off the road into the trees, "I'll catch up."

"What are you doing?" A normal enough question. Her comment was normal enough, too. But even talking to her about nothing made every muscle in my body tense.

"Sometimes, people have to pee." She looked over her shoulder at me, and shook her head before continuing on her way.

Fine. I was stupid to ask. Even an assassin was human, and needed to take care of mundane, human things.

But this couldn't have been the best place to stop.

The road ahead and behind us curved, leaving this a blind corner to whomever might come upon us.

How could she be so threat-averse sometimes, and not think

through her actions at other times? It was as if she thought when the risk was to herself alone, she shouldn't count it in the tally.

And here I was, sitting still in a blind corner, exposed while I waited.

Then again, she did want me dead. Why would she take my safety into consideration?

I was out of mind to her now. Not even worth a thought.

Once, I would have sworn to anyone that she worried and thought about me as much as I did her. Now, all those assumptions proved to be delusions I made myself believe.

Sounds ricocheted off the trees around me in a way that distorted them, making me unsure of their origin. They left me preparing to grab for my bow.

No matter how prepared I was, the thundering of hooves as a group of riders barreled toward me on the road still surprised me.

They stopped alongside me before I could do more than put a hand to the hilt of the sword at my side.

Arrayed around me in the road on their own horses, the riders wore shoddy, dark gray clothes that looked as if they were once black.

"Hello, friend," a large man said, tilting his head back, and looking down his nose at me.

"Hello." My voice was flat. The way he said 'friend' made it clear that we weren't going to be, but I wasn't sure what these people had in mind. Or even who they were.

Was I likely to be robbed on a road in the middle of the day in my own country? Was that a problem I wasn't aware of in Onyx?

"Don't often see people dressed that fine out this way unless they're in carriages."

The comment was about me, but directed at the five people

around him. None of them seemed to miss the invitation to look closer at me.

Fine clothes…they really were going to try to rob me.

It was everything I could do not to laugh, but I couldn't help the smile that formed on my face.

One of the people at the back of the group narrowed her eyes and swallowed, her gaze darting to her leader.

"Maybe we should just get going," she said, her voice rough and grating, as if it were damaged at some point in her life. "We need to get there before dark."

"No, I would like to talk to our new friend first," the man said, sneering.

"You know how she gets if we're late," the woman said, glancing the way Cinder and I came, as if she expected someone to materialize from the corner in that direction.

"She hasn't been putting up with what we have," he said.

I shook my head.

"Amazing," I said with a scoff that I couldn't hold back.

"What is?" The big one let his horse take two steps closer as he snarled.

"Having a shit day makes you think that menacing strangers on the road is an appropriate use of your time." I didn't bother to hide my hand pulling my sword a fraction out of the sheath at my side.

"More like a shit life because of spoiled, soft things like you."

All I could do was smile wider.

The woman at the back shook her head and drove her horse forward. Two others tried to follow her, but a second later, their mounts reared up and danced in the road.

"Everything all right over there?" Cinder yelled from the other side of the escaping members of the group.

I couldn't see her from here, and I didn't dare take my focus away from the three arrayed before me, even as they looked back and forth between me and whatever was happening where Cinder was.

"Just a little misunderstanding," I yelled.

"Misunderstanding of what kind?" Her voice was hard, like she understood exactly what I meant without me needing to say it.

"One of these people seems to think I'm soft." There was laughter in my voice that I wouldn't have been able to shove away even if I tried. And I didn't try at all.

She didn't try to hide her derisive laughter in response either. It bounced off the trees around us, and it was as if we were all inside a bubble she created with an insult. And she was threatening to pop it with one her spikes.

"None of them have seen you shoot a flying Corvid through the eye." Her voice was full of a sharp kind of joy.

But it matched my own.

Few times in my life was I more ready for a fight than right that second.

A shit day. Couldn't agree more. That was all it took for me to be more than ready to enjoy this fight.

The man at the head of the group, the one who wanted the fight more than all the others, lowered his brow, and bared his teeth at me like some kind of wild animal.

His companions behind him stared at both the bow across my chest, and the fletching sticking up over my shoulder from a quiver of arrows.

"Just because I'm feeling magnanimous," I said, pulling out my sword, turning my wrist, and flashing the blade in a circle that sent a shard of light through the tree canopy overhead glinting off into the world around me, "I'm not going to shoot any of you."

"Good," the stupid one in the lead said. "I'll kill you faster this way."

"The fuck you will," Cinder yelled. The sounds of grunting

and the clash of metal coming from where she was rang through the air. They accompanied the panicked whinny of horses and heat searing through me because I couldn't see her, and she was in danger.

Raising my sword, I yelled a guttural cry as the head man charged me, trying to strike me while his other two friends closed in.

CHAPTER 7

IN MY WAY

Cinder

These idiots were in my way.

One of them pulled their sword when I yelled.

I grabbed the strap of the bridle of their horse and swung my legs and sword up at the same time, blocking their swing with my blade and slamming my feet into their side, sending them toppling over into the road.

His companion rode for me, but I dropped from the horse, letting it buck and run as I rolled to the side, out of the way of her charge.

Surging up, I leapt at her, point of my sword first, and drove it into her side, into the soft place below the edge of her ribs.

A second later, wrenching my sword free as her horse continued on the trajectory she sent it on, even though she was bent forward and limp in the saddle, I turned to the last of their party on this section of the road.

But she was frozen, her eyes wide, and she shook her head,

raising her hands palm out, showing me that she only held her reins.

"Go, then," I said, my voice a snarl, "and find better friends."

I didn't wait to see what she would do. I ran for Tristan and the three people who had managed to get him off his horse, as they had come off theirs.

One of them was only off their horse because dead bodies tended to fall out of saddles. The other two were fighting with Tristan, swinging at him, and forcing him to move faster than I had ever seen him move.

Why was he just using one sword and not his bow? He could at least use a dagger in addition to the sword.

And…was he smiling?

Picking up speed, I ran at them, that ache in my chest, ever-present since Tristan ripped me apart, screaming for their blood for threatening him.

"Stay out of it," Tristan yelled, one hand pointed toward me.

"You just keep insisting on being stupid lately," I yelled back, clanging my sword against one of his attacker's blades as I went by. They managed to turn and block just in time.

The one standing in front of me feinted to one side, and I followed, cocking my head at the move, raising a brow, and waiting for them to try another tactic.

"Didn't I tell you to stay out of it?" Tristan asked.

I scoffed, and my opponent took that as a good time to try for me.

Slamming his sword to the side with my own and stepping past to whirl around at the ready, a smile still on my face, I said, "And didn't I tell you that was stupid?"

"Why can't you fucking listen? Even once?" Tristan's voice was irritated, but he still had that giant grin on his face as he seemed to toy with the man he fought with.

"Fine. You want me to just leave you to someone's blade?" I hurled my sword toward the trees, and shoved the spike back into the sheath on my thigh, holding my arms out wide in the middle of the road, and turning toward Tristan.

"Damn it, Cindy. Look out," he yelled, shoving away the man he fought so the man fell on his ass in the middle of the road as Tristan stalked toward me.

"Cindy?" I hated that name.

The one I had been fighting ran up on me from behind with his blade held high. Tristan darted past me, and slammed his sword into the blade of my attacker.

"Or should I just call you suicidal?" Tristan shot me a glare, and stepped sideways so he could see both the assailants as they circled.

But they didn't advance from either side.

Instead, they looked back and forth between Tristan and I, their brows furrowed. One of them kept working their mouth like words tried and failed to come out.

"Oh, please. These terrible want-to-be rogues can't kill me." I shook my head at Tristan. He knew better.

"You threw your sword," Tristan ground out through clenched teeth. "Or do you have some damn move to disarm two of them like you did me."

"Disarm?" One of the idiots still not attacking us asked.

"No. I wouldn't try that here. It's hard to do right, and normally when I'm fighting someone, we actually want to kill each other." Come on, he had to know he sounded like a petulant brat right now.

"Fine then." He dropped his sword arm down to his side, and stepped right up close to my face, his eyes bright green but colder than hellfire water ever was. "Do it now."

"Stop it." My voice was low, my breath heaving in my chest feeling him this close to me and aware of the heat that poured off him, the first I felt from him since he turned so cold.

"Go ahead. Do it."

"No."

"Why? You want me dead. I should kill you. Do it."

"You two are fucked up," one of the attackers muttered.

"Who *are* you people?" the other whispered.

Neither of them came at us. They seemed too mesmerized by the strange stalemate happening in front of them.

And I couldn't manage to do a thing but stand in front of Tristan and wish for the world to be different. For me to be different.

Just so the hurt would leave those eyes. Bright green and pain filled, I wanted them to change as I watched like they had so many times before. I wanted them to shine gold in the dappled light coming through the trees. I wanted them to shift with the pace of his breathing as he looked at me.

"Tri—" I stopped, halfway through his name, remembering we had an audience, they might attack at any second, and under no circumstances could they find out who he was. "Before you took me to meet the kids the first time, I wrote to Ash and told him we were wrong. Not one time after I met you, after I knew you, was it something I wanted."

He closed his eyes, his whole body shaking.

"I…don't believe you." His voice was a wound, and I was the jagged weapon that shattered as it tore him open.

Clutching at my own chest, the pain that centered there, I choked on the tears that wanted to fall.

"Ash?" asked the man who fought with Tristan.

Looking back and forth between us and his companion, he shook his head.

I narrowed my eyes at him, forcing myself to focus.

"How do you know, Ash?" I asked, careful not to let any of the complicated feelings I had toward my brother show.

"You can't know our King," the other one said, and I laughed, loud and bursting.

"King?"

Tristan raised his head, his jaw tight, his eyes still on me.

"Someone else." The first one said to the other. "She means someone else."

"I don't think I do." Turning away from Tristan, I faced the first one, who lifted his chin, and looked down his nose at me as much as he could.

The man wasn't much taller than me, so the move looked ridiculous. It opened him up too much, but it gave me a chance to study him more closely.

Worn, sturdy clothes, well fed, but sallow, and a mark on one hand that looked like a crow.

"You're a slave," I said, with dawning horror. "He bought you."

At that, Tristan sagged next to me, his sword no longer in a ready grip, even as a muscle in his jaw jumped, and his eyes grew harder.

"He freed us," the man said, his shoulders straightening and pride emanating from him.

I shook my head.

This was why Ash did it. He made them believe his lies, and now they were devoted to him, no matter how deranged and wrong his mission. They believed he gave them the greatest gift.

"You're free because he brought you to Onyx," I said, wanting to tell them this was the real King standing in front of them, who wouldn't let them be enslaved, "which is a free country. There is no slavery here."

"Liar," the man yelled, running at me with his sword swinging toward me in a wild attempt at a strike.

I had enough time to grab my spike and clang the narrow piece of metal against his sword at the same time I slammed my other hand into his arm.

Behind me, Tristan engaged with the other one, the sounds of their blades crashing together ringing through the air.

My first attempt to disarm him didn't work.

He cringed and grunted in pain, but stepped back to try again.

"Just stop. Please. I'll explain. You're free," Tristan begged, not wanting to hurt these people any more than we already had.

The one attacking me didn't listen. He came at me again with a downward swipe this time. Again, I blocked his blade with my spike, and slammed my hand into the spot on his arm.

It worked.

His hand spasmed, and he dropped his sword, sending me jumping backward out of the way of the falling weapon.

"Finally," I said, sliding my spike back into place along my thigh, hoping that now that he was without a blade, we might be able to talk to him, to convince him.

But he attacked again with a wild swing at my face, his still-working, bare hand in a fist.

I ducked. On the way back to standing, I used the momentum to punch him in the stomach.

He bent over, wheezing, and I grabbed his hair with both hands, taking his head as he tried to get his breath back, and slamming it into my knee as I lifted my leg off the ground.

Letting go of his head, I let him drop to the road, knocked out at least for a little while.

Turning around, I found Tristan standing still and shaking his head as the other one jumped onto the back of a horse and rode away.

"I tried to explain, but he wouldn't listen," Tristan said, his voice defeated. "I think it scared him."

"Because all they know of truth is their suffering, and the lie that gave them hope," I said.

CHAPTER 8

FRAGILE

Tristan

I turned around to look at Cinder and my heart stuttered.

What she said made sense of their situation, but the way she said it…for some reason I thought there was more to her words. I just didn't know what.

Shaking my head, I realized the lead man was in a heap at her feet.

"He's not dead," she said, turning her eyes down to him. "But his head is going to hurt so bad when he wakes up, he might want to be."

"Good. We need to talk to him when he comes to." I sheathed my sword, and grabbed the man by the armpits, hauling him up.

Cinder took hold of his ankles without me asking, and we dragged him over to his horse, draping him across the saddle.

"I'll tie him so he doesn't fall, and so he can't attack when he wakes up," I said.

She just nodded, went to retrieve her thrown sword, and get her own horse.

Her brother actually bought slaves. Why?

"Cindy," I said.

"You fucking hate me now, I get it," she said, not turning to look at me, "but please don't call me that. I hate it."

"We need names that aren't ours while we do this."

"Fine. Pick anything other than Cindy."

"Okay, well, Cin, your brother bought slaves?" My hands kept moving, tying the rope, lashing the man to the horse in knots that wouldn't be too tight. He wouldn't be able to get out of them either. But my eyes were on her, where she withered and shrank as I watched and burned to make her stop.

Her back to me, she was at the side of her horse, her shoulders curling in more than ever, and her head hanging down.

"I thought you heard it, what Brix said."

Just that, the reminder of what I did hear, triggered the exact words to ring through my head.

Ah, Cinder. Don't be stupid.

Forcing the words, and the sound of his voice, as far from me as I could make them go, I took the reins of the burdened horse, and went to mount my own.

How could she have supported her brother in buying slaves? She hated Amethyst for trading in them, and Corvid for having them.

And her reaction now...she wasn't okay with it. It was almost as if she wasn't sure it was happening, but just now believed.

Once I was up to speed, riding behind her horse, with the other one carrying our prisoner tethered to mine, I rubbed a hand over my face. All of the delayed sleep of the night before and the expending of energy in the fight left me struggling to stay awake.

We rode down the tree-lined road until the light started to thin.

Cinder slowed her horse, and I followed suit. But when she steered her horse to the edge of the trees and began picking the way through the underbrush, I stopped following.

"You're going into the woods?" I asked.

"If you know of a tavern or inn that would let us bring in a prisoner and question him without calling the guard, let me know."

Fine. That was a fair point, and I was stupid.

Being King, I kept forgetting I was limited in what I could do now without giving myself away. All my time in the palace left me unsure of the realities on the ground in my own kingdom. Was I at risk of becoming so out of touch I would be the terrible King that Cinder believed me to be?

Following Cinder through the woods, ducking low hanging branches, and allowing my horse time to pick her steps, I turned to look at our prisoner. He still seemed to be out.

How hard did Cinder hit him?

She stopped her horse and hopped down at the edge of a circle of ground, devoid of trees except for the remnants of one that looked like it was felled by lightning, the charred trunk laying along the ground at the edge and disappearing into the woods.

I brought my horse to a halt and dismounted, looked around at the clearing, and wondered about the sensibility of a fire.

"We shouldn't have a fire once night fully falls," Cinder said, setting one up and reading my mind, "but we should be okay right now."

She looked up to the sky, and went back to her work.

Taking my bow and knocking an arrow, I nodded and stepped into the trees. Although she wasn't paying attention, and I wasn't sure what I was responding to.

My legs were sore, and it was an effort to place my steps without causing a racket that would scare off anything edible.

But at least the focus meant I didn't have to think about spending a night in the dark with Cinder.

Chewing on my lip, trying to get lost in the act of hunting, I heard the thumping sound of grouse.

Perfect.

Moving through the underbrush, careful not to spook the little bird, I made my way to the spot where I heard it.

There he was, sitting on a log, blending in, only his breathing setting him apart from the wood and the bramble around him.

One tiny fraction at a time, I raised the bow and shot.

A grouse wouldn't give us much food, but it was something.

Taking hold of his legs, I turned to head back toward the clearing and Cinder.

But the tiny shaking of a rabbit, tucked as close to a tree trunk as it could get, made me aware of its presence.

Looking at the grouse in my hand, I tried to judge if it would be enough for Cinder, me, and the prisoner.

Part of me wanted to leave the little rabbit, and just split a small meal between the three of us. But we needed to garner trust with the prisoner, to help him to understand that Ash wasn't King.

I didn't think that could be accomplished with a few bites of bird.

Tucking the feet of the grouse into my belt, I raised my bow again, knocking another arrow.

"Sorry, rabbit," I whispered, not sure why I said it out loud.

Maybe because relegating a life to just a bargaining chip for someone else never felt great, no matter how necessary.

As soon as I let the arrow fly, a groan echoed through the trees, so loud it was close to a scream.

I snagged the rabbit as I ran past it, crashing through the forest by the time I reached the clearing again.

Cinder stood with her hands on her hips, staring down at the prisoner who sat against the burned tree stump, still tied up…Although that wasn't my knot.

"What happened?" I asked, placing the bodies of the grouse and the rabbit at the edge of the fire ring Cinder created.

"Farmer here decided that being untied was a reason to attack," Cinder said without anger, but full of irritation.

"You'll be sorry when my King finds out about this," the man named Farmer said, his voice wavering, his eyes squeezed shut, and his mouth twisting in pain.

"My brother is not a King," Cinder said, her voice like a lash, so hard it sent birds flapping from their perches in the trees around us.

"Brother?" Farmer actually opened his eyes all the way as he asked the question.

"Why don't you talk to him," Cinder said, throwing her hands in the air, stalking toward the animals I killed, and beginning to prep them in deft, swift movements.

She was too close.

Even though she probably wasn't aware at all of our proximity, it took over my brain. I stepped away, going nearer to the captive.

"How long ago did Ash purchase you from Corvid?" I asked, crouching down to loosen and retie his restraints so he would be more comfortable.

"My King freed me four years ago, and I have been a faithful citizen of Ahmya since." Farmer lifted his head in that way he had of attempting to look down his nose at the world that had treated him so poorly.

Cinder made a choking noise that she tried to cover with a cough before she ripped the skin off the rabbit in one swift tug.

"*Duke* Ash Ahmya and his lands of Lehar are vassals of the

King of Onyx," I said, trying for the truth, and wondering if the man was told anything about the way things actually stood.

"Not for long. He's going to take over all of Onyx and Amethyst, and form Ahmya."

That tilt of his head again paired with his words managed to make a shiver run down my spine.

"Amethyst?"

"Yes, after he conquers Onyx and frees it, he and his wife will turn to expand on her lands in Amethyst and free that whole country, too." He turned to the side and spit. "Damn Amethyst bastard who sold me is on the list that will be saved for me to kill myself."

Cinder looked at me, her face ashen, and mouth quivering like she held back tears.

I didn't have the ability to try and puzzle out what her expression meant.

"Wife?" I asked, my voice failing, the word barely eking out of my throat as I looked at the woman whom I had wanted to be mine, and lost to the same plot this man spoke of, one far larger than I imagined.

"Of course."

Farmer looked up at me, his face clearer than before, almost as if speaking of Ash and whomever he married gave the man strength.

I swallowed, for the first time wondering if Farmer was right and Ash would win.

"What about Corvid?" I asked, trying to pretend I was curious in the way someone would be if they wanted to defect to Ash's side. There was little chance I was successful in completely putting on that face.

"Once this war is done, Corvid will be ready for us to take them over." He smiled only for a second before his face twisted in pain, and he returned his mouth to a grim line even as his eyes continued to dance.

"Just imagine," he said, "All those kingdoms under one king..."

Even for a second, having that version of the world in my head made my stomach roil. If Ash managed to do what he planned, if he was successful, it would be one-third of the continent in his hands alone.

What would stop him from waging war on all the other kingdoms, one at a time, until he took it all?

Glancing at Cinder, her hand shook as she put the meat from the rabbit and the grouse on sticks to hold over the fire.

She focused solely on cooking the meat, her shoulders curled further, and she sat on the ground, pulling her knees to her chest.

Cinder's muscles, the well-defined and perfectly formed strength that looked bulky only when she was using them, didn't just soften in that position, they disappeared.

Not one time since I met her had she looked so much like a child.

Even when she played with the Shield House kids, or flew around in the training grounds. Then she was painted in the kind of open and free joy that small children could have, and so few adults allowed themselves.

But now...

Sometimes when the Shield House kids first arrived at their new home, they wore their pain in everything they did, their trauma loud in the way they reacted to the world, or didn't.

Cinder looked like they did when their memories were too haunted.

Instead of a flame, now she looked like the ashes that fell on Lehar.

Gray and diminished.

CHAPTER 9

SCARS

Cinder

My brother actually did it.

Even when Brix told me, I didn't allow myself to really believe it. Not all of it. I couldn't accept it could be as bad as he said.

Tristan and Farmer continued to talk. Tristan trying to convince the man of the reality, and Farmer refusing to listen to reason.

Most of the things Brix told me, Farmer told Tristan.

In addition to that information, Tristan did manage to learn that, until recently, the slaves were kept on the lands of Ash's new wife in Amethyst who was then just someone he knew.

No one in Amethyst questioned her growing group of slaves. It was normal there before some large trade.

At that, I looked toward them, no longer able to stop myself.

Farmer was in pain, that was obvious. His head probably screamed at him, and any movement would make it worse.

Even with that, he remained steadfast in his belief of Ash and Ash's lies. He remained a true believer in the cause he thought he was a part of.

Tristan kept the conversation going, not willing to give up it seemed. And he didn't seem to see the connections I saw as I heard Farmer's story.

Maybe Tristan didn't hear all of what Brix said to me in the dungeon. Maybe he only heard that I was supposed to kill him.

The shock was fresh. If I were only learning just now about Ash buying slaves, I might not have seen it all as a connected whole either.

Finally, the meat was done, and the sky was darkening.

Kicking dirt over the small flames, I put out the fire and carried the skewer of meat to where Farmer sat and Tristan crouched, handing it to Tristan.

"You'll see. King Ash is a wonderful ruler," Farmer said, like he thought this conversation was a chance to sway us to Ash's side. "You should know if he's your brother."

Turning, I dropped to one knee right next to Farmer, my spike in my hand and at his throat.

"Cin," Tristan said, a whispered scream as he surged to his feet.

"What I know about my brother is written all over my skin in scars. He lied to me, too. But I'll be damned if I'm going to listen to anymore bullshit lies out of you on his behalf."

Ash gave this man and the other slaves lessons in kindness along with his lies. He gave them exactly what they needed to become his devoted army, to be willing to lay down their lives for him.

My lessons were in lies, too, but they were accompanied by pain. He gave me exactly what I needed to be his one-woman killing machine, to be willing to lay down everything for him.

The difference was, I learned new lessons.

Part of me wanted to slit Farmer's throat. Because he was

Ash's man. Because he was a threat to Tristan. Because he wanted to destroy my world more than it already had been. But mostly because he reminded me of myself.

Farmer, eyes wide and head pressed back into the blackened bark of the log, didn't move. He barely breathed.

Instead of killing him, I surged away from him, stumbling when I turned in the detritus of the forest floor, and made my way past Tristan to sit down by the dead fire.

Tristan followed me with his eyes. Even after I sat back down in the same position as before, I felt his gaze on me.

What did he see now?

Did he see his Flame? His Queen? A woman he once loved?

Or did he see what I really was?

Nothing. I was nothing except a burning ball of rage and agony.

My brother saw to that…

But that was a lie, too.

I did this.

Willingly, I turned myself into this.

As the light failed and Farmer finally managed to eat something and fall asleep, Tristan made his way through the dark to my side.

How he managed to see well enough not to trip and fall in the utter blackness beneath the trees at night, I didn't know.

Even the moon slept, hidden behind clouds midnight deep.

Tristan touched my hand in silence. The feel of his skin, dusted with grime and the leftover coating of meat from his few bites of dinner, was eclipsed by the heat that came through that small contact. It made me close my eyes on a sensation I wondered if I would ever feel again.

He followed his hand with the skewer, placing it in my palm, and waiting until I wrapped my fingers around it.

"You should eat something," he said. "I got him to eat by having some with him."

I nodded. Even though I didn't think he could see me, he let go and walked away.

Judging by the sound, he went to his saddlebags and laid down on them.

Sitting in the middle of the little clearing, the ghost of the brother I thought I knew on one side, and the ghost of the hope I developed on the other, I stared into the dark and ate what was left of the grouse and the rabbit.

There was no sleep for me that night. Even staring into the darkness that reflected all the worst moments of my life back at me, I couldn't close my eyes.

With the first light of morning, I prepared Farmer's horse and my own.

Maybe Tristan would be gone by the time I got back. But it was a risk I would have to take. I couldn't risk Tristan.

Another selfish decision.

It would be the safest thing for Tristan to be caught by the guard and returned to the Obsidian Palace. But if he was, would I ever see him again? And would I ever be able to save the Shield House kids?

Staring down at the sleeping Farmer, I chewed on the inside of my cheek, and wondered if his brain could afford another knockout.

Trying to move him while he could wake up might alert Tristan, which would destroy my plan for the morning.

Looking over my shoulder, I realized it was already shredded.

He was still stretched out, with his legs crossed at the ankles, his hands folded on his stomach, and his head propped up by the saddlebags.

For a moment, we just looked at each other.

It was like waking up even though I hadn't fallen asleep the night before.

Every time I woke since Brix, I had that short second where it had never happened.

Now, looking at Tristan, the world slowed and stopped for a moment, and I had that second. Like a gift from the universe, I had a moment when I got to look into his eyes and see the version of myself that I wanted to be reflected there instead of the truth.

But he looked away, shoving himself up from the ground, and the spell was lost.

He made his way across the little clearing to my side and whispered, "What are you doing?"

That whisper, the way his voice played across my skin, made my knees quake and want to buckle. Tears threatened the backs of my eyes. How I wanted that whisper to come again, this time saying the things it used to.

"I'm taking him to the nearest guard station, and dropping him off."

Tristan furrowed his brow, and looked more closely at me.

"My brother lied to him, and he's never had a choice," I said. "Not really. I won't kill him."

"Good," Tristan said, his voice a touch louder than before. He didn't seem to notice when I glanced at him, his eyes now on Farmer's sleeping form. "I'm going with you."

"You can't." I was too loud.

The second the words were out of my mouth, I looked to Farmer, who only moved his shoulders and groaned, his mouth in a frown.

"Fine," Tristan said, anger flooding into his voice like my too loud comment was because I was taking something out on him.

I rolled my eyes and sighed, bending over to pick up Farmer. If he weren't prone on the ground, it would have been easy. But hauling him up was about to make my leg muscles really not want to ride.

Before I grabbed for Farmer, Tristan crouched down on his other side, and looked up at me with a nod.

Okay. That was good. Maybe.

Staying silent, I mouthed the words, 'Three, two, one.'

Tristan and I took hold of Farmer and sat him on the horse, leaning him over the mane.

Even through that, he only whimpered and said, "Ow."

"How hard did you hit him?" Tristan asked, adjusting the rope and securing our load to the horse so he wouldn't fall off even if he woke up with a start.

"As hard as I needed to." Maybe it was a good thing that I didn't have to hit him again. I might have killed him.

"I'll follow you west to the nearest guard station, and then head to an inn or tavern nearby," Tristan said, and I swallowed. "Find me when you're done."

My mouth was dry, and I couldn't talk around the lump that formed in my throat. All I could do was nod.

West. We were heading toward Lehar.

He didn't explain if we were going to Lehar, Thirteen Rivers Valley, the rest of Tavis—the duchy that included the Valley—or going beyond Lehar toward the other coast.

But he would have to tell me if we passed our goal, or needed to turn north or south from the road.

Tristan climbed onto his horse as I did mine, but I kept looking at him as I went about my tasks. Not once did he look back.

So, maybe he decided I wasn't going to kill him until we got the kids, or until he learned more about Ash's plans.

We had a long way to go.

CHAPTER 10

DIVIDED

Tristan

I kept looking toward Cinder while I got my horse ready, and she never looked back. Not even after she was mounted, holding the lead to Farmer's horse, and heading through the trees toward the road.

The half of me still screaming that she was a killer, ran the words of that asshole in the cells of Sandstone Castle through my head again and again.

The other half...

All it could think about was the broken way she sat by the fire as the revelations about her brother poured out of Farmer, and what she said about her scars.

Maybe if I didn't know, maybe if I had not seen myself, maybe if I couldn't picture, even now, the scars along her back shining in the morning light, I wouldn't be stuck here wondering if and how her brother caused them.

She told me they happened from the last war.

Was that another lie?

I swallowed as we emerged onto the road and picked up speed.

Only as she sped up did she look back, but it wasn't at me. She checked on Farmer as he groaned and shifted in the saddle as much as the ropes allowed.

But once we were moving fast enough, the uncomfortable jostling was past, and Farmer settled down for the ride.

There was no way to tell from back here if he was awake or still unconscious.

All I could hope for was that it wasn't more than a day's ride to the nearest guard station for Cinder to drop him off.

We couldn't keep hauling him with us, and there would be no way to go after the kids properly with him around. And we couldn't let him go no matter how much I wanted to.

Life was cruel.

Farmer's crimes were because of Ash, because he was lied to. Maybe we could convince him of the truth. Maybe we could save him from just another form of imprisonment.

After what he went through, I didn't want to lock him away.

One stop was all Cinder allowed. She rode hard all day with one stop at a stream near some farms for the horses to drink and eat some grass, for all of us to take a break and eat, and for poor Farmer to be retied so he was more comfortable.

Even that seemed to piss Cinder off. She paced the entire time, and glanced down the road in the direction we were heading repeatedly.

In another life, I would have asked her what she was thinking. In another life, I was allowed to care.

Now, I wasn't supposed to. Now, I tried to avoid thinking about her, and failed every minute of every day. Especially as I rode along behind her.

With the evening coming upon us, I began to really take stock of our surroundings. She had led us all the way through the duchy of Mariposa and into Tavis, to a small town at the crossroad leading to the Duke of Tavis' home. Thirteen Rivers Valley was inside Tavis. There the Lady Solaria was a vassal of the Duke of Tavis. We would probably arrive in the Valley tomorrow to start looking for the kids.

"This is a good place," Cinder said. "There's an inn in town."

"I'll meet you there, then." I didn't wait for her reply, just spurred the horse on to pass Cinder on the road, and went to find the Inn.

Not that it made any sense, but I wanted to say something to her. It felt unnatural to just leave. And I wanted to say something to Farmer.

But he wouldn't welcome anything from me. He didn't even know who I was.

And Cinder…

What did I have to say to her? Please don't find me? Just go to Augustina and Jacquetta, and let me handle this?

She would never do that. The Shield House kids mattered to her, even if I didn't. At least that much I believed to be truth.

The Inn, a larger building than I expected way out here with the modest size of the town, sat in the very center of the town on the corner of the two main roads that passed through here.

Like many inns, this one had a barn with an attendant sitting on a stool at the door, looking regularly at the sky, waiting for patrons.

I stopped in front of her, climbing down from the horse, my ass complaining about the long days of riding.

Groaning as I stretched, I waved to the attendant who gave me half a grin as she stood up.

"Hello, Sir. I'll take your horse, but the barn is full up. So, after I take care of her, this lady will have to stay in the yard tonight." The attendant spoke more to the horse than to me, petting her nose, and looking at her with soft, loving eyes.

Smiling, I took off my saddlebags.

"That's no problem," I said, handing the attendant some coins. "I trust she'll be well taken care of. And I have a… someone coming along soon. She's this tall." I tried to hide my stumble on what to call Cinder, and held my hand up to her height. "Brown hair that's travel messed, and wears weapons on her thighs."

At mention of the weapons on her thighs, the attendant raised her brows. I wasn't sure how to reassure her that Cinder was harmless when that wasn't true at all. But I didn't think Cinder posed any risk to the attendant.

Just to me.

I gave the attendant an awkward smile, more a twitching of my face that I couldn't hold, and headed to the Inn itself.

Walking through the door, it took a moment for what I saw to register fully in my mind.

Not only was the Inn full up, but they were having a wedding here.

Letting out a long breath, I debated staying another night in the woods.

But not sleeping the night before, watching Cinder stay awake all night long, and keeping an eye on the dark night sky, I wouldn't last another night like that.

How she went non-stop for three days when she rescued Augustina, I would never understand.

Rubbing a hand across my face under the shadow of my hood, I tucked my head in further, avoided the eyes of every guest, and made my way to the counter of the bar in the main dining room.

Bustling about with too many drinks and too many plates, even with the extra hands of the servers there to help, the Innkeeper looked over his shoulder and still managed to register my presence with a nod.

I nodded back. Even though I could imagine few rooms I wanted to be in less than one full of wedding merriment, I would wait until he had a second. But it didn't take him long to turn around and lean across the counter to me.

"Can I help you?" The Innkeeper asked. He was a large man with a round, amiable face and a bald pate shining in the hellfire lamps of the room.

"You're busy," I said, prepared to wave him away.

"Not at this second, but I will be again right quick."

Subtle.

My smile was more real.

"Okay, do you have two rooms available?" I asked, waiting for the rebuff, and bracing myself for how I would find any sleep in the woods again.

"We have one for you. Don't worry. Most of these people are local." He slapped the counter, snagged the sleeve of a server running by, and said something in their ear. "Just follow Ruthie, here."

Another grin my way, and the Innkeeper turned back to the steady stream of work he was doing.

Ruthie dipped her head without her eyes meeting mine, and led me toward the back of the building.

Making our way through the crowd, I kept my eyes averted, and tried not to run into anyone with my saddlebags.

It was probably a good thing I was so tired. The noise was oppressive.

A peal of laughter rang out above the din, and I cringed.

Something that was a joy to me not more than a week ago—a party full of people entertaining themselves and escaping from the weight of the war over the country—now made me want to be as far from it as possible.

Two floors up, we neared the back corner of the building, which started to feel like a maze now that I was inside.

At the door to the room, she handed me a key, and I handed her what I thought two rooms would cost. But she pinched her lips tight, and handed back half of the money in her hands.

"I have someone coming along behind me for a room. You can't miss her. She has unique weapons on her thighs." Why I didn't want to describe Cinder by any other feature, I didn't want to think too much about. People would notice her spikes anyway.

"You gave me too much. I'll take care of your companion, and bring up dinner soon." She dipped her head, and stepped past me toward the stairs.

"Thank you," I said, managing to get out words that weren't just arguing against calling Cinder my companion, and more than a little surprised that the prices were so much less expensive this far from Bridgeton.

Opening the door, juggling my saddlebags and the bow slung across my chest, I found a decent sized, clean room, complete with bathroom fixtures in the corner.

A bath. My whole body ached for the bath, and I was more tired already.

But first, I pulled the roll of fishing line out of my saddlebag, and put down my overload of supplies.

Placing the fishing line on the bed made sure I wouldn't forget to block the window before I went to sleep.

When I left Breakwater with the roll in my saddlebag, I thought the fishing line would protect me from Corvids. Instead, I needed it to protect me from the woman I couldn't get away from, even when she wasn't with me.

CHAPTER 11

IN THE LIGHT

Cinder

"Fighter, are you sure he doesn't need to see a doctor?" the guard asked for the third time as I climbed back onto my horse outside the guard station. "He's still talking nonsense. He doesn't even know who the King is."

"It's all some ploy to get him out of trouble," I said, maintaining the cover story I created. "As soon as he gets to the palace, General Pace and Rathmoreland will know what to do with him. Don't worry too much about his yammering."

"Of course. It was nice to finally meet you, Fighter Cinder." His smile was broad, and at my ill-begotten title he stood up straighter, and gave me the salute.

"You, too," I said, my heart in my throat as I rode away toward the inn at the center of town.

The last time I was here, I stayed at this same Inn. With one less scar on my face, and lot fewer in my soul. It was the last time I met someone and took them to bed while drinking.

Going to meet up with Tristan again, although he wanted me dead now, made me feel like I needed to warn him about my history with this place for some reason. That this inn wasn't a place for us. This was just a place.

But he didn't care about any of that.

All the places that were ours—Obsidian Palace, Sandstone Castle, the training grounds, even Shield House—would make the ache in my chest worse just thinking about them unless they became ours again.

One day I might have to step foot back inside one of our places without him.

Every muscle in my body tensed even thinking about it.

Seconds later, I finally arrived at the Inn.

The sky overhead was fully dark.

Light poured from the windows of the Inn, illuminating the grounds.

An attendant peeked out of the barn door as they opened it just a crack.

"Hello," I said, trying for friendly and probably ending up closer to indifferent as I dismounted.

Swinging the door open a little further and checking the sky, the attendant stared at my spikes strapped to my thighs.

"Your associate is inside, and already paid. I'm sorry, but your horse will have to stay outside tonight."

"Fine. That's fine," I stammered, unsure what to do about the fact that Tristan paid for my horse. "Um, thank you."

I led the horse closer to the barn door, and the attendant stuck out only their arm to take him inside to be groomed, fed, watered and prepare for the night.

Before I could turn around and head to my own bed, the attendant shut the barn door.

At least she was careful.

Looking to the sky myself, wondering if there had been any issues with Corvids way out here, I hurried to get inside.

Opening the door to the Inn, it was transformed.

Not just light streamed from inside, the elated noises of a wedding party did, too.

Closing the door behind me, part of me wanted to sleep in the yard with the horses, and not take a single step further into their merriment.

It had to be a wedding.

The happy couple was easy to spot in the center of the room, gold ribbons on their wrists, in their best attire, and kissing passionately for all the world to see.

Some other day, some other time, I would raise a glass to them along with all their guests.

Right now, all I could think about was the ruin I made of my own wedding plans, and Gus and Jacquetta's plans, too.

Closing my eyes, I took a second to breathe.

When I opened them, I realized who the groom was, and I almost laughed.

The man holding his bride close to his side and raising a tankard in the air was the same one I met here when I came through before.

At least one of us was luckier in love than we were the night we met, and didn't bother to learn each other's names. Although he did cry to me afterward about how upset he was about a Willa.

Maybe she was Willa.

I tried to tell myself that she was, that one of us got the happy ending we wanted as I made my way to the bar, and the man who was clearly in charge there.

People who worked at the Inn all focused their energy around one person who seemed to enjoy the activity.

Leaning against the bar, I didn't bother to interrupt. Instead, I allowed their practiced sort of chaos to seep into my bones, and finally give me something outside myself that wasn't my own physical exertion to relax me.

Watching people who were good at what they did was always interesting.

A few minutes later, a young woman who didn't look me in the eye tapped me on the shoulder.

"Hello," I said, impressed she was so shy but still brave enough to engage with someone who had blood under their fingernails and dirt caked all over.

"Your companion arranged for everything," she said, her voice steady in the loud room. "I can take you to your room."

"Oh, thank you very much." Tristan paid for my room, too?

Following along behind her, we went up to the top story of the large building. The noise of the party below us in the main room faded with every step until it became just a hum in the background.

At the door to the room, she stopped and handed me a little, metal key.

"Dinner is already inside. Let me know if there is anything else you need. I'm Ruthie."

"Thank you, Ruthie. This is great." I just wanted to try and get some sleep. Even with all my training, this stretch of days where the sleep I got either wasn't restful or complete, left me weary to ends of my hair.

Inside the room, there was a tray by the door with a few plates covered in copper cloches. Only one hellfire light was on, turned down low, in the area of the bathtub.

Picking up one of the cloches, I found some chicken, roast vegetables, and two rolls.

One of the others was probably a salad, and another was probably dessert. But this was what I wanted.

Taking it with me, I went to the corner with the clawfoot tub, and set my food down on a little chair while I undressed.

Maybe traveling with Tristan had some perks. I got to bathe and eat a full meal more often than usual, and I didn't get to at all when I went after Gus and Angeline.

Leaning over the bathtub, I turned on the faucet, the squeak of the fixture breaking through the general hum of downstairs, and the low light glow that made the whole room feel cozy.

"What the fuck?" Tristan yelled behind me.

I jumped and looked over my shoulder at the dark corner with the bed, where he sat up from laying under the covers.

"Cinder," he said, his voice like a lament.

Swallowing, I stood up, the only light in the room behind me as I faced him with my clothes in a pile at my feet.

Why was Tristan in here?

Did he see that I was naked over here? Could he tell in the mostly dark? Did he know I wasn't a threat to him?

He fumbled around at the edge of the bed until a hellfire lamp blazed to full light.

So much for the dark.

Then he froze and stared at me, his mouth part way open.

In the time I was at the guard, he bathed. His hair still damp, it stuck up from his head in a wild disarray that made me want to run my hands through it so much that they itched at my sides.

Part of me didn't believe he would ever look at me like this again. The way his eyes took me in. The way my body reacted and ached for him to touch me.

Seconds that felt like hours went by as the water continued to pour into the tub. My need to go to him increased, and he fumbled with his blankets, bringing his knees to his chest, putting his back against the wall behind him, and only leaving his face showing out of the cocoon of blankets.

All I wanted was a bath, a bed, and sleep.

But instead, I got this. I got torture.

"Ruthie said this was my room," I said, trying not to let the shaking in my hands show, and hoping he couldn't tell I had gooseflesh break out all over my body.

CHAPTER 12

THE LIE

Tristan

She stood there, coated in road and battle dirt, blood staining her fingernails, bruised, shaking, and so beautiful that it was devastating to look at her.

My chest ached. That place in my heart with her name stamped on it screamed for her. For me to go to her, to touch her.

Was she going to kill me while she was naked? Wash off my blood in the bath afterward?

Retreating even further into my blankets, I couldn't tear my eyes from her, couldn't make myself reach for a weapon even to protect myself. All I could do was breathe.

"I asked for two rooms," I said, my voice low and hoarse.

"There's a..." She started to say the word 'wedding,' her mouth forming the w, but no sound came out. "Party. They must not have the rooms."

Did that mean…she was supposed to stay in here? With me? Is that what she meant when Ruthie said this was her room?

"What are you doing?" I asked, mostly to myself, but it sounded like an attack on her.

Cinder took in a deep breath, her chest filling, lifting her perfect breasts, her nipples pointing directly at me, and she turned around to stick her hand under the tap, the hard muscles of her ass flexing as she bent to test the water.

"Don't worry, Tristan. I'll leave you alone as soon as I take a bath." There was barely-contained fury in her voice, and her body changed, curled in, even as she climbed into the tub.

Just as she picked up her last foot and placed it into the filling water, the way the light behind her caressed her back showed one of the shining lines of the scars that encircled her ribs.

The illumination had to be just right to show them at all, but of course in this moment, when it would only make this so much worse, was when the light did just that.

Fire poured through my veins, and I gripped the blanket in tight fists.

Even now, knowing what I did about who she really was, the thought of those scars, of what could have caused them and who might have been behind them, made me want to stab someone.

"Cinder," I said, my voice barely audible over the pouring water even to my own ears.

"You've seen it all before, Tristan." She turned to me, her shoulders folded over so I didn't actually see anything over the lip of the tub. "Are you really going to tell me I can't clean up?"

"No, that's not what I'm saying." I shook my head and bit my lip, not sure how to ask the question. It wasn't an answer she wanted to give me when she didn't openly hate me. When I didn't know the truth. Why would she give me the information now?

But, all night last night, while I watched her in the dark, my mind kept returning to it, rubbing up against it like a thorn stuck in my hand that I couldn't remove and couldn't ignore.

She stared at me, her eyes searching mine.

For what, I didn't know, but she raised her hands from the water and gripped the sides of the tub as she kept eye contact.

My chest ached, and I rubbed my hand against it while my fingers remained fisted in the blanket.

A few minutes later, as steam built up around her in the tub, she sagged, turned away from me, stopped the water, leaned back against the tub, and sunk below the surface.

When she went into the sea during the last battle in Breakwater, knocked out by the blast and sinking, I panicked, grabbed her, and pulled her out of the water onto the broken section of the still-floating boat that I was lucky enough to land on.

Even though she could swim—she swam across the river to Bridgeton and the palace—the same panic that made me reach out then had me leaning away from the wall and sitting up straighter as she stayed below the water now.

This wasn't a river. This wasn't the sea. This was just a bathtub.

I reminded myself that the fear coursing through me was ridiculous, but it didn't lessen the scalding heat in my blood as the image of her drowned ran through my head.

Finally, her head emerged, soaked and dripping. She took a breath, leaned her head against the back of the tub, and I sucked down air like I was the one holding my breath.

Maybe I was.

"Cinder," I said, trying again, this time my voice came out too stern.

Shit.

"What, Tristan?" she asked, her eyes still closed and head still laying on the edge of the bath with her face pointed at the ceiling.

"The scars on your back..." I choked on the words. How could I ask this of her? Why did it matter so much?

Her eyes popped open, her grip on the sides of the tub tightened, and she turned her head toward me, slowly, keeping it resting back against the tub.

Raising a brow at me, she seemed to be asking me to go on.

But I stumbled over the words.

"Do they disgust you now?" she asked, her voice flat and her face impassive.

She couldn't say that and believe it.

"Now who's being stupid?" I asked, words finally escaping from my closed-up throat, although I wanted to say far more than the word 'stupid.'

Aside from her mouth pressing into a line and the way she looked down and away from me, there was no answer to that from her.

I tried again, opening my mouth, losing my hold on the words, and closing my mouth again.

A minute later, she relaxed back into the tub, her hands moving back into the water, and I looked to the floor, away from her, to find the ability to speak.

"Who did that to you?" I asked, finally, and snapped my gaze back up to her face.

She squeezed her eyes shut, her mouth quivering as if she held back tears.

"You can't ask me that."

Gone was the calm, flat tone of her voice. Now it was raw and sharp.

"I need to know." For so many reasons, that was true. It didn't make sense. I shouldn't have cared. And I had no right. But I did have a need. It flared inside me, made my blood as hot as it had ever been, and forced me to loosen my hold on the blanket, stick my head further out to get some air.

"There are many ways to teach someone lessons," she said, and I shook my head, although she wasn't watching.

What did lessons have to do with anything?

"My brother chose pain. Those are from his first lessons after the war when I didn't try hard enough in training or questioned him."

Ash did that? To his own sister? Who was only fifteen?

I was wrong. I did have a right. Just so I would know when I killed him.

Shoving the blanket away from my head and neck, I sucked down air, and reminded myself that he wasn't here.

He and I would meet soon enough. Duke Ash ensured that with his treachery. And I would make him pay for that along with everything else.

But he wasn't here now. And regardless, I needed to know more now. All of it.

"Cinder, how did he do that?" My voice was rough and harsh, like a growl, and I hated it. It made me feel like I was out of control, and would attack something like an animal. But right now, I would have let myself turn into a monster, and reveled in my capacity to rend the world apart if Ash were here.

Ducking her chin, she opened her eyes, staring down at the water in front of her.

"Knives."

I sucked in a breath that hissed through my teeth and was cool enough to singe my mouth as my blood boiled.

"Later, his fists didn't leave scars on his investment. My brother always told me he proved he loved me by making investments in me. That I was his great investment." She let out a humorless laugh that made my blood run hotter. "It was a twisted version of my mother and father telling me how valuable it was for me to make an investment of time in my education. It started small, but by the time I was seventeen, the beatings were so common I didn't think them odd anymore."

Now that she started talking, it was like she couldn't stop.

Horror after horror, abuse after abuse, detail after detail poured out of her, every word of it stabbing me in my already aching heart.

All that time that I said I knew her, I thought I did, and when I learned what her bother sent her to do, I believed everything had been a lie.

But the lie was worse than anything I could have imagined.

Her brother didn't send his sister to kill me.

Duke Ash sent the shell of his little sister to do his bidding. Or die trying.

The lie was Cinder herself.

CHAPTER 13

CHOICES

Cinder

I couldn't look at him.

Not while I told him all the ways that Ash taught me. And not once I was done. I stared down at the bubbles in the water, and the way the dirt and blood were finally lifting off my skin.

"What about your injuries when you went home?" Tristan asked, his voice a raw, strained sound that made all the open wounds I was picking at bleed anew.

Rubbing a stubborn blood stain that ran along a cut on my hand that I didn't even notice was there before, I thought about that.

How would I explain that one and have him believe me?

So far, I wasn't sure whether he believed anything I told him, and I didn't have the strength to look at him to check, not while I talked about this. If I told him about going home, about the lesson I was taught because I loved him, would he ever believe that?

"After you sent us all home…" I said, replaying that moment in the courtyard of the palace over again in my head and trying to tell if that was the time. But again, it probably wasn't. I already didn't want to go home for the first time in my life. I already fought alongside him. For him. "Ash greeted me with blades, wielded by my own people, and his fists."

Tristan made another growling noise, low in his throat.

"But the face?" I touched along my eye where it was swollen shut for a while. "That was his boot."

Shuffling came from the bed, but I still didn't have it in me to look.

"You know," I went on, unable to stop now, "at the time, I convinced myself that he didn't mean it. That he wouldn't have actually killed me if General Pace had not arrived in the middle of it. Stupid, huh?"

I shook my head and laughed, a lifeless burst of air closer to the sound of the last gasp of the dying than real mirth.

Settling back against the side of the tub, I looked at the tin tiled ceiling, tracing the swirls of the patterns up there with my eyes.

"My own brother, sword raised high, was swinging at my head as I told him we needed to stand with you."

Of all the stupid moments in my life, of all the times I believed in an Ash that didn't exist, that one was probably the worst. The reality was more than directly in front of my face. The reality literally kicked me in the face, and even that wasn't enough for me to admit it to myself.

"Even then, I thought there was good in him. And I would have defended him, told anyone who would listen that he would never buy people from Amethyst or Corvid. He would never go against everything we were taught, everything our parents died for."

Yes, Ash had hurt me for years. But to go so far against everything our parents stood for, I would never understand it. My own brother made me kill so he could buy people. He made our people suffer and struggle in abject poverty, even in the face of the ashes falling and the inability to grow food forcing them to spend all their money just to survive, all so he could form his army.

I laughed again, that short exhale of whatever the opposite of humor was.

"Maybe stupid is a disease," one I wish I never caught, "and every time you've done stupid things, you caught it from me."

I stopped talking, and he fell silent. No movement, no growling, not even breathing came from the other side of the room.

So I sunk beneath the water again, my eyes open, watching the way blood and grime swirled in the bath above my face.

When I surfaced, I managed to look his way.

Tristan was still in his blanket, but now it had fallen, hanging about his waist, his eyes squeezed tightly shut, his hands fisting the blanket and pulling it taught between them like he was going to string a bow with the fabric.

Once, I thought of him as an archer king.

But I was wrong.

He was an archer god, bending the string of my fate in his hands.

With shaking fingers, I used the soap and shampoo sitting next to the tub to wash myself, ate as fast as I could, using the same water to rinse my hands when I was done, and climbed out.

Through it all, I didn't look at Tristan again.

Maybe his decision on my fate would be good for me, or maybe it would spell a disastrous end. But, tonight, I couldn't be here to watch while he made that decision.

Whether it was my parents when I was a child, Ash when I

was older, or Tristan now. Somehow, I was never in charge of my own future. Not really.

Once, only one time had I ever made a conscious decision for myself that wasn't based on what was best for everyone else and was only what I wanted.

I wrapped my hand tight around the ring hanging from my neck, and pulled the drain on the tub.

As the water emptied, taking the last of my lies and those of my brother with it, I redressed in the dirty and worn outfit that Madam had crafted for me.

The first time I put it on, it was a beautiful representation of Fighter Cinder, the soon-to-be Queen of Onyx.

Now, with blood deep in the grooves of the leather, the metal dirt-stained, it looked more like who I really was.

When I was dressed and ready, I opened the door to the room, the hum of the party still coming up the stairs, and I shivered.

"You're leaving?" Tristan asked, his voice hoarse and low with an otherworldly quality to it I had never heard before.

"Both of us need to sleep, and there's only one bed." I stepped into the hall, and shut the door, leaning back against it for a moment to let my legs stop shaking before I almost ran down the stairs.

Darting through the main room, avoiding making eye contact with anyone, I finally made it outside. I ran through the chill of the night to the yard where my horse nestled under an eave of the barn, head down.

When I got to him, I finally took a whole breath, allowing the ice in the air of the winter night to enter my lungs, and bring me closer to the cold place in my mind that seemed so far away from me now.

I placed a hand on the horse's long face, and he pushed his soft hair against my palm.

But a minute later, the door to the Inn opened and I tensed, stepping further into the shadow of the barn and the horse, praying to Mom and Dad—who I was afraid to ask anything of lest they find out about Ash—that the person wouldn't see me.

That prayer wasn't answered.

All it took was a few of their steps for me to realize who was out here with me.

I felt him.

Even now.

"Cinder," Tristan said, his voice back to something closer to his own, "come to bed."

"You won't sleep well if I'm in there," I said, shaking my head.

"Please."

Simple, unadorned, with no hint of the King hidden in it, that one word undid me. Like the first time we kissed, the first time he told me he loved me, the ground disappeared, and I tumbled through the world, unmoored from anything but him.

With a deep, shuddering breath, I turned around and faced him.

He reached out a shaking hand and then turned it so it was an invitation to go ahead of him.

I nodded, not sure what I was agreeing to, and did as he asked.

No matter what, we were beyond the King and the Fighter who was an assassin. As a man and a woman, I was still his. Of all the decisions I needed to make for myself, this one I was most sure of. I needed to make him mine again the way he used to be.

CHAPTER 14

PRETEND

Tristan

What was I doing?

Following Cinder back into the Inn, my bare feet went from melting the frost coating the grass to warm on the worn-smooth, wood floor of the main room where the wedding party remained deep in their joy of the day.

The heat raging in my blood kept me from being cold in the chilled night air, but thinking became difficult.

How could he do that to her?

And why didn't she tell me?

In the cells of Breakwater, she didn't say a word. Not once did I suspect her own brother would...

Did she have so little trust in me?

Cinder walked up the stairs with that damn curl to her shoulders, and as much as I hated it before, that was nothing compared to the way it made me want to hunt down her brother right this second, and fillet him for causing it.

Because it made sense now.

The way she held herself as if she expected a blow, and would only allow her body that fraction to protect herself…it all made horrible sense.

When she reached the room, she stopped.

She didn't open the door. She didn't even move her hand to turn the latch. She stood still, pointed like she would go inside the room, but she just looked at the floor.

"Go ahead. You can take the bed tonight."

"No." Lifting her head, she stared at the door in front of her, but remained unmoving. "Don't feel sorry for me."

How could I not? She was abused. For years. By the person who was supposed to take care of her. By the only family she had left after the last war. And right after she lost her parents and Lehar was blasted apart.

"Fine." My voice was thin, and I couldn't be sure she didn't hear the lie in it. But she needed to get inside and get some sleep.

The day seemed heavy on her, and it was on me. There was only one way I was going to be able to sleep now. And that was if she was safe in the room with me.

Even if she still wanted me dead. I had no choice but to keep her close. At least for tonight. Tomorrow, in the light, maybe I could think around the inferno burning through my veins.

She looked back at me, her eyes searching mine for something I couldn't begin to guess at.

But she must have found it. She reached out and opened the door, leaving it hanging open for me to follow her.

As I shut the door, she froze in the middle of the room, staring at the bed.

"Take it, Tristan," she said, her voice low and even. Though it was my name, what I heard was her giving up.

"No. I want you to take it."

Cinder shook her head, her still-wet hair dripping along her back.

"I can't do that."

Part of me wanted to grab her and shake her. Part of me, a part that didn't seem to want to stop no matter how much I tried to silence it, wanted to drop to my knees and beg her to love me the way I thought she did before the cells.

Neither of those were real options. Not now. And I didn't think they would ever be.

Letting out a long breath with my cheeks puffed out, I curled my hands into fists, and squeezed my eyes shut.

"Fine," I said, opening my eyes and watching as her curled shoulders relaxed, which only made me feel worse, "we'll share the bed."

She whirled around, her mouth hanging open and her eyes wide while we stared at each other for a minute. It didn't take long for her to start shaking her head, but it was slow and awkward when no movement she ever made was awkward.

"Come on, Cinder. I'll stay on one side. You stay on the other."

Did she hear it? That tone in my voice that I tried and failed to force away? The one that admitted part of me wanted this sharing of a bed to be the way it used to be.

It took a minute more, while the heat raging through my veins called out to her, desperate for this to be different, for her to finally nod.

Turning to the bed, she began to disarm. First was the sword across her back. Then the daggers at her sides. Next came the throwing knives she had in her cuffs. Only after all those blades were piled next to the bed on the floor, did she lean over and unstrap her spikes, one after the other.

When all her weapons were set aside, she didn't take off any of her layers except her cloak and her boots before she climbed into the bed and hugged herself against the wall so tightly that I wondered if the mattress would move and leave her on the floor.

Dropping my cloak next to hers, I debated putting on a shirt, but I needed to lay down before she decided to argue with me more.

Climbing in, I kept myself to the edge of the bed, facing into the room, balanced precariously close to falling face first on the floor.

She was behind me, the mattress pressed and stretched because of her presence.

For the first time since I left Breakwater, it wasn't just sleep that clawed at me as I lay there in the dark while thoughts of her, the war, and the danger the kids were in tangled up and ran in circles in my head.

Now my body fought the insistent urge to relax.

It didn't matter what my brain said. My body responded to her as it always had.

With no other choice, as soon as her breathing settled, my eyes slipped shut and sleep claimed me.

My dreams, just like my waking life, were full of her.

By the time I woke up, as the sky outside showed the first signs of lightening, I wasn't surprised to find that we both moved in the night.

The length of Cinder's body pressed against my side, one of her hands gripping my arm like she might still fall between the mattress and the wall, and needed to hang on to me to stop herself.

One of her legs was flung across my middle, and the hand of the arm she clung to was wrapped around the side of her thigh.

It was morning, but even that didn't explain how hard my cock was while it ached beneath her leg.

Pictures of her the night before, naked in the tub, plagued me. My heart raced, and my breath sped up.

Someday I wouldn't want her. Someday this aching need to

feel her body on mine would disappear. It had to. Because every second of every day I spent near her knowing I couldn't be with her made my memories of her more vivid.

With deliberate, slow movements, I peeled my fingers from her thigh.

Cinder made a small sound, her grip on my arm tightening to the point of pain as she pressed her body even more firmly against my side.

Gods and Goddesses, she needed to stop.

Maybe if I knew what she was before we had a chance to be together then this wouldn't be so hard.

But thinking back, I tried to find a moment when it would have been easier to know what really brought her to the palace.

I couldn't find it.

Long before I proposed, I dreamt of her standing beside me with a crown. Long before she ever let me kiss her. Even before we fell asleep together the first time in her room.

When was it?

Part of me wanted to wake her and ask. Did she know when it was that I fell in love with her?

She must have known. She must have seen it. She must have been well-versed in the way people were in certain situations before she came to kill me. Her brother must have trained her to prepare for this.

But I couldn't find that point in my own head. Now, she was so much a part of me, my heart hurt thinking of her even as she pressed against me. My body throbbed for her to be closer.

Going back to the first time I met her, those memories were shaded with my need for her, my love of her, and wondering if anything she told me of her feelings were true.

At that second, what I needed was to get away from her, to put space between us.

Instead, I rolled over, allowing her leg to wrap around to my back, and folded her into my arms.

The noise she made then, as her hands relaxed where they lay flat on my chest and the rest of her body followed suit, was more a sigh of my name than anything else.

Knowing the truth, more of it than I ever thought there was to know, didn't make anything clearer. It didn't make it any easier to let go of her.

Especially when holding her in my arms was like going home.

Burying my face in her neck, breathing in the scent of her skin, allowing the heat of her body to seep into my own, fueling the boiling in my blood to an inferno, I pretended to fall back asleep.

CHAPTER 15

DREAM

Cinder

He was with me in the baths at home.

In my dream, he held me tight to him in the water, the heat of him and the room on top of the hellfire source surrounding me in an embrace I didn't want to end.

At least in this dream I was relaxed, at least I didn't have to hold on to him as tight.

Most of my dreams and nightmares lately were moments when I had to hold on to him so tight my hands ached in the morning.

Holding him as he teetered on the edge of a cliff.

Keeping my hand latched around his arm as we tumbled through the air after the last battle in Breakwater so he wouldn't drown.

So many nightmares and dreams that morphed into nightmares to plague me.

In this dream, though, deep in the baths under my home, in the shining white tile and billowing steam, we wrapped around each other and melded together.

Tristan was mine, and I was his, and we found home in each other again.

But it was just a dream.

Even as it happened, even as I held on tight and begged for it to be real, for him to love me and look at me the way he used to, I knew it was only in my head.

The nightmare of my reality remained with me, heavy and cold within me.

Images of Ash, my brother, traitor, stealer of lives and buyer of souls, broke in. Behind those flashes of pain-filled truths, the unknown fate of the Shield House kids pressed in on my mind, and screamed for me to wake up. To move. To find them.

Now.

Opening my eyes, holding on too tightly to that moment when my dreams might still be real made me hallucinate.

My vision swam as I looked on Tristan's skin, my head tucked against the heat of his chest and my eyes running over him, drinking him in, fantasizing about kissing his body, every inch of it.

A second later and the crushing reality of losing him didn't yank the vision away from me.

I opened my eyes wider and watched the way his chest rose and fell with his breaths, felt his hands on my back, my leg wrapped around him, pressing my sex against the hard length of his cock as it greeted the morning. I throbbed with need of him.

But I didn't have him back.

Not really.

Any second he was bound to wake up and recoil from me.

This was an accident.

He didn't want me. He was just kind to me last night, and we folded into each other in our sleep.

If I ventured to do what I wanted, if I pressed my lips against his chest or rubbed against him, it wasn't something he would welcome. I would be taking advantage.

Gods and Goddesses, I prayed, give me the strength to let him go so he doesn't wake up to me this way.

Staying pressed against him, if he woke up to find me, he would be horrified, and I would crack.

And if I moved, I risked waking him up, scaring him, making him think I was still going to kill him, and might be reaching for a weapon.

My mind raced through the possibilities of what I could do, and came up with no good options.

He moved.

One of his arms unwrapped from around me, and I pulled my leg back from him.

Without a word, we both moved away from each other and ended up on our backs, side by side.

"Interesting way to wake up," he said, clearing his throat.

"Uh, huh." I couldn't look at him. I didn't want to see his reaction.

"The kids are waiting for us to find them and get them out." His voice was heavy and rough, and I tried not to think it was because he was upset by how we slept.

"Yes. Let's go." I sat up and threw off the blanket, climbing to the foot of the bed to get out instead of going over him.

"I'm going to use the bathroom down in the main room, and grab food after I get my weapons on." I was rambling. I needed to stop. My mouth still wanted to keep talking about nothing, about everything, just so I could fill the air with something other than this damn heavy silence waiting for him to respond.

Gathering my weapons, I attached them to myself in swift, practiced movements, and still didn't look at him.

"Cinder," Tristan said, sitting up in the bed and swinging his legs down to the floor right by me, which froze me in place a moment and made my hands want to shake, "Maybe we should, um, talk about last night."

"We don't have time." I raced through tucking the throwing knives into my cuffs, and just scooped up the straps with my spikes attached in their sheaths. "I'll meet you down there."

Making my way out the door, Tristan swore under his breath behind me, and I cringed.

It was exactly why I didn't want to talk. I didn't want him to tell me again all the ways in which I was his nightmare even as he was my dream.

Getting down the stairs, every step felt like my knees might buckle and send me tumbling down.

Once I got to the main room, I waved to the Innkeeper behind the counter and sat at one of the tables to strap on my spikes.

On solid ground again, I took deep breaths until a server came to check on me.

"Morning. Can I get you breakfast?" he asked, far too chipper for this early. People who woke up that prepared for the day were terrifying.

"Just some traveling rations, please. Thanks." I was not about to sit here through an entire meal. But I smiled, and the server returned the gesture before nodding and heading to the counter.

Tristan paying for the room and my horse at least meant I had enough to get some food and still have a couple coins left.

Leaning back in the seat, I allowed myself a minute to close my eyes and breathe, trying to find a place in my mind where Tristan's body against mine didn't leave me frustrated and distracted.

But the only place that was really true was in memories of being with him, and those didn't help me now.

"Excuse me," someone said, and I popped open my eyes, realizing I wasn't wearing my cloak at all, let alone my hood to protect my identity.

Standing in front of me, his face breaking into a broad grin, was the groom from the wedding last night, and the man who I had sex with the last time I was here.

"I thought that was you," he said, taking a seat at the table with me and taking my hand in his, making me stiffen. "How are you?"

"Fine. Um, congratulations. I saw the party last night." What was he doing? He should have been in bed with his bride, not talking to me.

"Yes. Willa and I owe this to you, actually. I want to say thank you."

He…was serious.

"No thanks needed." If he was about to tell me that I was so bad in bed or so gross he knew he needed to run back to her, new groom or not, I might punch him in the face. With a sword.

"That night, I wanted to go back to her, but my pride wouldn't let me. Then I saw you, and you were beautiful, fierce, and even stronger than me when you picked up that rowdy man, and tossed him outside. I thought that if I couldn't fall for you, then I was truly in love."

Oh, good. I was an experiment. That wasn't better at all.

Curling my free hand into a fist in my lap, I tried to smile and not hit him.

"You see, I figured out where I belonged."

My fist opened and I nodded. I understood what that meant.

CHAPTER 16

THIS IS FINE

Tristan

Holding her cloak in my hand, it was hard to not run imagined conversations with her through my head as I made my way down the stairs.

Somehow, I got too fucked up.

I thought I knew what the rules between us would be during our mission to save the kids. I thought I knew where Cinder and I stood, and what she really was. I deluded myself into thinking I finally knew the truth.

But I saw her face. I watched her reaction to me when she wasn't quite awake, and, when she did wake up, the fumbling, the rush.

Even after learning what I did from her, even after being with her for that short time we had, I still stumbled down the stairs as the realization hit that I might not have known her at all, that maybe I only knew what she thought I wanted her to be.

What I didn't understand, what made my mind snag every

86

time I tried to think it through, was why she kept up any act for me.

That didn't make sense. Not now.

Reaching the bottom of the two flights of stairs, I took a deep breath and shook my head, trying to focus on what I needed to, not what distracted me.

Cinder managed to be a distraction since the night I met her. Everything else may have been different, but that didn't change.

I turned to head into the main room, and stopped dead.

She stood near the front door of the Inn, in an embrace with a man who smiled the kind of grin only someone lost in love would.

Looking away from them as fast as possible, before I saw anything else on his face, or found something that would tear me apart all over again in Cinder's, I tucked myself back into the stairwell and waited.

Maybe he was an old friend of hers and…Cinder didn't have any friends. Other than Augustina and Jacquetta, and they were new in her life.

Slamming my head against the wall behind me, I ground my teeth together.

Every time. Every single damn time I thought….

"Fuck," I muttered.

There was no point in this. In torturing myself.

She wanted to kill me when she first got to the palace. She planned on it. Even though her brother made that real, it was true.

And even though she might have changed her mind about killing me, it wasn't because she loved me. I was right about that.

My blood turned to ice, and I shivered. But I would put up with being cold for the rest of my life if it meant that she would get out of my head, and that maybe I could stop the ache in my chest.

I rubbed at that ache, and made my way out from the stair-well again. They were both gone.

Where the man went, I didn't know. But there was only one place for me to look for Cinder.

Fine.

Running my hand through my hair and adjusting the hood of my cloak, my other hand strangling her cloak instead of throwing it like I wanted to, I made my way outside to where Cinder was putting the saddle on her horse.

She moved in that practiced, swift, sure way she always did, her body an art she performed in even the smallest of actions.

And I couldn't watch her.

That damn heat was back. Not like a warm bath, not like a campfire, but like an out-of-control inferno that might light the world on fire.

I tossed her cloak over her saddle, and turned to ready my own mount for the day.

"Oh, Tristan, thank you," Cinder said as I walked away. "I forgot it this morning."

What did she expect me to say?

Don't worry, Cinder, I grabbed it for you.

No. I didn't intend to speak to her unless I had to. One too many times, just listening to her undid me.

And every time, I should have known better.

She kept looking at me as we prepared our horses. But I kept my eyes from meeting hers, and focused on what I needed to do.

The faster we got the kids from these assholes, the faster I could go back to the palace, meet with Rath and General Pace, and head to the front to end this damn war before Ash could make any of his moves.

Cinder didn't need to follow me.

I took a second to close my eyes and hope she would.

She could help get the kids back, but I didn't want to explain to her all over again the reasons she couldn't be at the palace, the reasons this needed to end.

Finally, my horse was ready.

Without bothering to check where Cinder was in the process, I jumped on my horse and urged it to gain speed.

Once again, I rode without bothering to have one eye to the skies.

As far as I knew, the Corvids had yet to be a problem here the way they were in Breakwater and Bridgeton. But it had been days since I was at Sandstone Castle and received an update. It likely could have become a problem in that time. War moved fast.

But even acknowledging that to myself didn't make me pay any more attention to the risks of riding in the area.

"Get there. Find them. As fast as I can. Go back to the other things that matter." I repeated the words over and over again to myself, like I was trying to cast a spell to get my damn mind, body, and soul to focus and do what they needed to.

This, whatever this was, didn't matter. It couldn't. Not anymore.

Looking behind me, Cinder was right with me, though.

Of course she was.

We rode hard the rest of the day, and I only stopped once to take a break. Cinder stopped with me.

She seemed contented to keep her own council.

Not that I was welcoming. I probably looked like a thundercloud. Everything in me felt like a lightning storm. Scorching chaos.

Finally, as the day began to turn toward night, we passed the last foothill of one of the outlying Protectorate Mountains where it sat separate from most of the mountain range.

Unable to help myself, I looked up the rocky slopes, wondering as I had all my life where and how the magic users of the mountains lived in their isolation and self-governance.

Even with the best education my parents could offer me, there was still little we knew of the enclave. And the priestess who came to be part of the bridal hunt didn't allow anyone to learn more.

What were they doing up in their mountains? Did they even know about the war? If they were forced to, would they pick a side?

I couldn't worry about them. They didn't answer to me, and, as far as I knew, they weren't helping Ash.

Thank the Gods and Goddesses they weren't. All I could do was hope it stayed that way.

Making our way into the edges of Thirteen Rivers Valley, the view laid out before us. I took a deep breath of the unique air, and tried to allow the cool wash of it to subdue the river of fury in my blood. The constantly moving fresh water of the rivers through the lush landscape of the small islands of the valley made the air here, even in this winter, smell as if hope were a tangible thing.

But as I closed my eyes and tried to allow it all to remake me as the land was remade every spring, Cinder pulled her horse up next to mine. Just the knowledge that she was there, next to me, was enough to set my blood boiling again.

"Are you ready?" Cinder asked.

I turned to look at her, and had no way to answer.

CHAPTER 17

THIS IS NOT FINE

Cinder

Tristan didn't answer me. He stared in that impassive, cold way I was never going to get used to.

I swallowed and looked away, down the lane toward the Inn on the edge of the valley.

"We...Um, taking horses through the valley can be a challenge. We can leave them at that inn." I pointed it out.

"But," I went on, knowing now I had to look back at Tristan, face those eyes so devoid of his warmth that they sent ice through my blood, "you should probably tell me why you led us here, and tell me if Solaria and her child are in danger. She's been through enough."

He took a deep breath, exhaling with a gruff sound that stiffened my curled shoulders, but he nodded.

"Not out here in the road." He took off toward the Inn, and I had no choice but to follow.

For all I knew, we needed to be at the other end of the valley, but Tristan and his damn inability to see that I was helping him in this made it impossible to make the right decisions about what to do.

The Inn at the edge of the valley was a place I stayed only once, but it was a common enough stop for the people of the valley on their way out. Or for travelers on their way in for provisions. Everyone knew about it.

I didn't think he would agree to do it my way—leave the horses to graze on the other side of the last Protectorate Mountain, make our way into the valley by night, steal through to wherever he thought the children were, kill all the people that took them, and bring them out with us.

No. Tristan would probably think that plan somehow lacked something.

Meanwhile, his plan was to take a nap every damn day, not tell me anything, and then what?

The fact that I had no idea what he planned to do now that we were here didn't bode well for our success at working together.

And it meant I already failed in at least part of my goals in following him here.

"So far," I whispered to remind myself as I brought my horse to a stop next to his in the small yard. I had only failed, so far.

Giving up now, after everything…No.

Bending over, I stretched my legs and my back after so long in the saddle.

The sheet of my hair hanging down gave me a chance to sneak a look at Tristan as he spoke to the barn attendant and handed over his reins.

We were a long way from the King right now, out here where none of the people he dealt with even knew he was King.

Once, I would have said it would be better for us if he wasn't King, or even nobility.

Whatever that version of myself saw happening in that

scenario, it was never that the man would want as little to do with me as the King.

I thought we might have managed to make some headway after last night and this morning. But yesterday he didn't curl and uncurl his fingers into fists every five minutes.

He didn't trust me. Maybe something I said triggered that mistrust all over again.

Damn it, he was going to drive me mad.

After bringing my horse over to the attendant and smiling as I handed him over, it took me a minute to figure out where Tristan was.

Somehow, I moved so slow, so distracted by thoughts of him running through my head on a loop, I missed when he went inside.

But there he was. Through the window I watched as he took a seat against a wall, resting his fists on the table in front of him.

We needed to move, to go. This inn after inn, sleep after sleep, only allowed the enemy more time to damage the kids.

Even if they survived this, even if they weren't physically injured, I knew more than most how unseen wounds could be even less likely to scab over and stop bleeding.

Swinging open the door to the main room of the Inn, the noise I expected didn't rush at me, nor did the press of too many eyes fall onto me.

The room was almost empty.

Besides Tristan, a server, and the innkeeper, there were only five other people in the whole place.

In the large room, the scant number of people were like a couple of pebbles rattling around in a jar.

For a minute, while Tristan chewed on the inside of his lip and stared at the table in front of him, obvious in his preoccupation and still giving me no hint at all what he actually thought about, I wondered if another table wouldn't be a good choice.

Only for a moment.

We had too much to do that was too important for me to get scared off now.

I marched across the room and sat right next to him with my back to the wall as well.

"Cin," he said, using that stupid fake name that was only marginally better than Cindy, "what are you doing?"

"Sitting in a better position for you to tell me what you know without anyone overhearing you." My voice was low, and I still didn't trust that no one here was close enough to hear me.

The problem with a small crowd was that every voice was louder.

"Fine. If I tell you, will you go to another table?"

I froze.

With my hood up and my head turned to take in the man near the fireplace who rubbed at a spot on his arm that looked oddly thick under his shirt, like he had a weapon or a bandage, I couldn't see Tristan. Maybe it was a gift not to be able to see his face when he said something like that. Maybe it was a curse because the disgust with which I painted his face in my mind made the words so much worse.

"You want me to go after them by myself?" I asked, not sure if he heard the screaming that I shoved down into my stomach that nauseated me.

"No. I want you to go home."

"Fuck you." Slamming my hands against the table, I shoved myself up to standing, and rounded on him, no longer capable of caring if the entire world watched.

"What?" His mouth fell open, and he had the audacity to look shocked.

"I said," I made my words as clear and distinct as possible, "fuck you."

"Oh," he pushed himself up and leaned so he was close enough to my face I felt his frantic breaths tease across my lips, "you made it clear you would rather fuck anyone other than me."

"There is something wrong with you." How could he pretend to be jealous? There was no reason back when I was happy, and there was less than no reason now that I was miserable.

"Yeah," he said, "there is something wrong with me. That I'm stuck with you. Go home."

Shifting to lean on my knuckles brought me so close to his mouth that I wondered if I would accidentally touch him. His eyes blazed bright green.

"I don't have a home."

He pulled back like I slapped him, his mouth slack instead of pinched and tight.

"What?"

"Right." I shoved off the table and stood up all the way, staring down at him as I shook my head. "Keep pretending like you don't know that I gave up that home for you."

Turning around, I took two steps before the sound of his chair scraping across the floor became the loudest thing in the room. I cringed, my shoulders curling in further.

"Cin," he said behind me.

I stopped in the middle of the room, rubbing that ache in my chest and not sure if I should turn around or not.

"Let me tell you what I know."

Fuck.

Shaking my head and pressing the ring hanging from the chain around my neck hard into that ache deep in my chest, I took a long breath and turned around.

"Fine."

His mouth twitched at one corner, a bitter mockery of a smile.

"That word has never come closer to sounding like a swear word."

"Good."

With a single nod of his head, he gestured me to the seat across the table from him.

Rolling my eyes, not caring if he thought it was childish since he was being an oblivious fucking asshole, I went back to the table and slumped down in the seat.

Staring at each other across the expanse of the table, it seemed like the space between us grew.

Just this morning, there was no space. Just this morning he held me to him, and I wrapped myself around him.

Now, sitting close enough to touch him, he was as far away as if we were on different continents.

The innkeeper arrived and put plates of dinner down in front of us, her face in pinched lines.

"You two will be kicked out of here if that turns worse. I don't like cursing," she said, pointing at each of us, one eyebrow lifted high.

"Sorry," I said.

"My apologies," Tristan said at the same time.

With a 'hmph' sound through her nose, she turned back toward the counter.

Looking down at the dinner in front of me, I wasn't sure if I should eat it.

He paid for it, but he wanted me to leave. He couldn't want me to sit here and eat with him.

But my stomach growled loudly enough to give me away.

"Eat," Tristan said.

I did, but it all tasted like need, hollow and unending.

TRAITOR

Tristan

Eating with Cinder, pretending not to notice how close she was to me as she crammed her food into her mouth so fast that she looked like a starving animal fed for the first time in a week, made other meals with her run through my head.

We were close to alone in here.

It was as near to sitting with her alone in her room at the palace or in my room on the ship to the Lighthouse as we had been since it all fell apart.

But this was so different from what those times were.

She was never hurried then.

Every bite of those meals she seemed to savor and enjoy, she even made little noises if she was really impressed with some dish.

Now, the food may as well not have had any flavor at all.

There was no way her tongue had the food on it long enough for the taste to register.

All those other times, no matter how informal the setting, she didn't hunch over her plate like she did now, as if she feared someone would pull it away from her.

There was so much I didn't know about her when I fell in love with her.

Why did I still—No.

I shook my head and went back to my meal, trying to speed up so we could get through this conversation. I did not need to talk to her anymore than I absolutely had to.

"Are you going to tell me?" she asked in between bites. "Or just sit there and take too damn long."

Part of me wanted to yell at her again, to lash out, to release some of the pressure building within me, to extinguish some of this damn fire burning inside my body. But we needed to get this finished. We needed to get away from each other.

"They're here in the valley somewhere. Rath thinks they're connected to the groups that took over farms on the outskirts." I shoved a large bite into my mouth, trying to catch up to her.

Cinder stopped, took the last bite of her meal, drank half her tankard down, and wiped her mouth before she leaned back in her seat and met my eyes.

"My brother's group has the kids, then." Her face was an impassive mask, but on the word 'brother' there was a bite in her tone even I couldn't second guess.

I stopped. With a half-chewed bite in my mouth, I couldn't think through her leap of logic fast enough.

She waited while I ran through it in my head.

"You're probably right," I said, finally, sagging and furious with myself for not seeing it when Farmer told me about Ash's army.

"When Amethyst invaded in the last war, they came through

one of the passes between the Protectorate Mountains, and attacked here before they got to Lehar."

I knew that. But it was a fact among a million about that war for me.

For her, the way Amethyst came to Lehar was probably at the front of her mind in a way I would never understand.

Rubbing my hands across my face and into my hair, I shoved more food in my mouth even though my appetite was gone, just so I could do something.

"Do you know anything else about where they may be?" She twisted the fingers of her hands together in front of her on the edge of the table, her eyes far away like the battle for the kids already raged in her mind.

"All I know is something about farms. Someone in Rath's network seems to think that farms are a focus of the groups coming into Onyx. Farms as isolated as possible."

She narrowed her eyes at a spot above my head.

"Do you know of any places that would fit that description?" I asked, shoving more food in my mouth as she kept wringing her fingers.

"I might." She paused and let out a long breath that seemed to shrink her before she looked back at me. "I need to tell you something."

There was more?

Not only was my food tasteless now, but my stomach wanted to reject it. I nodded for her to go on, to get it over with.

"You need to know I don't have proof of this." She leaned forward, chewing on her bottom lip, her hands stilled but pulled tight on each other.

She didn't continue. I waited, but finally realized that she was waiting for me to acknowledge her.

"Okay." My voice came out strangled.

"This war is my fault." The grip of hands eased, her whole

body slumped, but all the tension she held in it transferred to her eyes as they swam in unshed tears.

If she cried, I might lose my ability to keep her from diving deep into my soul again.

But what she said didn't make sense.

"None of this could be your fault. You weren't even there when the attack on the palace happened, and Princess Fiachra died. You were with me." I swallowed and had to guzzle down my own drink.

Cinder shook her head, a sad frown on her face.

"My brother attacked the palace."

Snapping my focus back to her, I almost spit out the drink in my mouth.

"What?"

"I can't prove it. But I know. I found a message from him in my room when I got back to it. He caused this. All of it. Because of me."

"Just because your brother is a traitor, doesn't mean you're at fault." I was too loud. The second the words were out of my mouth, I knew. Far too loud.

Everyone in the room turned to look at us, and Cinder blanched.

One of the men at another table lurched to his feet, stomped over to Cinder, and grabbed her by the shoulder.

I shoved up from my seat, but she beat me to it, spinning to a stand and shoving him back from her.

"You're a traitor lover?" The man spat, finger in her face and swaying where he stood. "My brother died in Bridgeton with the guard."

She didn't say a word. She just stood tall and took his presence. He was too close to her and too irate.

While she stared him down, I made my way around the table to be closer to them both if they needed me to step in. This man was drunk, and Cinder would kill him. He didn't stand a chance.

Around the room, the other people watched, looking too closely at us when we weren't supposed to attract any attention.

"Fuck, Cin…" I muttered, hoping she would hear me, and the innkeeper wouldn't.

With a tiny shake of her head, she dismissed me. But if any of these people figured out who I was, who she was, the kids might be lost for good.

"I work with the guard," she said through a tight jaw. "I am not a traitor. My brother is."

"Maybe you should get locked up with your brother. We can't be too sure." The man narrowed his eyes at her, his hands in fists.

Cinder's lip curled like she was prepared to bite him. I got a step closer, knowing this wouldn't end well.

"Don't," I hissed at her, "the kids."

"And maybe," she said, "you should know, because your brother was a hero, that sometimes siblings are opposites."

"You calling me a fucking coward? Fuck you," he screamed, and swung at her. At the same time, the innkeeper took a step out from behind the bar, and Cinder ducked.

Not knowing if I would get to Cinder in time, I dove for her, knocked her to the side, and held her back from the man.

"Out," the innkeeper yelled in the man's face, pointing to the door. "And no more from you." She pointed at Cinder, who struggled in my arms.

"Room, please," I said, fishing a coin out of my pocket, and throwing it on the table as I struggled with Cinder.

"That bitch is a traitor," the man yelled, earning him another shove toward the door.

"Let go of me," she snarled at me, "I don't want to hurt you."

"No." I bent down and grabbed her by the waist, throwing

her over my shoulder as she stopped holding back, kicking me in the thighs and pounding at my back with her sharp fists while I followed after the server down the hall. "Ow, Cin. Stop it."

"Put me down. I'm not a damn traitor." She punctuated every word with a new strike on my back, and if she didn't mean to hurt me, she failed. There would be bruises.

The server stopped to unlock the door and open it as fast as her hands could while I held on as tight as I could.

"Damn it." I gritted my teeth and tried not to grunt with every impact as she squirmed.

She was heavy, solid, and enraged.

"Let me go." One of her flailing knees caught me in the stomach, and I almost dropped her.

But I managed to get her in the room, to the bed, and throw her down on her back so she bounced.

"He called me a fucking traitor." She surged up from the bed, and tried to make it past me out to the main room. I grabbed her and threw her back down on the bed, pinning her with my entire body pressed against hers.

"Tristan, let me go. No one gets to call me that." Her face set in hard lines, her voice like a blade twisting in my side, she paused her struggles, taking in deep breaths.

I called her that. In the cells, and even more recently. I did that to her. But she didn't do this to me, didn't go after me like she did that man.

Looking down at her, into those eyes that seemed deeper than the sea past the coast. I wanted to take it back.

She didn't struggle against my hold on her, but her breathing grew even more ragged, matching mine, her body turning soft and welcoming beneath me, making the sensation of her hips pressing against mine harder to ignore.

"Cinder," I said, my voice low and quiet with no idea what else I meant to say.

Her mouth opened a fraction as if she would say something.

Instead, she touched her tongue to the inside edge of her bottom lip.

My breathing frantic, my need of her grew ravenous along with the beat of my heart as I stared into her eyes and felt the hitch of her breath against my entire body. Her breasts pushed against my chest. I tried hard not to think about her pussy, but it pressed against me. My cock rose no matter how hard I willed it not to.

"I…" Believed her? No. I couldn't. Could I? She lied about everything. I didn't really know her at all. How could I trust her when the last time I did was a mistake?

But I couldn't stay like this. I couldn't give in. And every second spent so close to her made it more likely I wouldn't be able to give her up either.

Shoving myself up and away from her, I stood over where she laid in the bed. But she remained in the same position, and in my head, I heard her say "please" like that first night we were together.

CHAPTER 19

BURNT

Cinder

Tristan stumbled back from the edge of the bed, moving to the other end of the room to lean against the back of the door like he was a piece of driftwood washing up on the shores of Breakwater.

I sat up on the bed, staring after him, and it was everything I could do not to beg.

Please, Tristan, forgive me, kiss me, love me.

My breath came in gasps and gulps, and my heart didn't want to slow down. It hammered away in my chest, ripping me apart from inside, and leaving pain in the wake of every beat.

Swallowing, I opened my mouth, but Tristan held up a hand, palm out.

"What's the plan, then?" he asked, leaving me to tilt my head, and run through every word we spoke to each other since the argument in the main room started.

All I could do was shake my head, with no idea what he was talking about.

He coughed, gulped down air, and stood up straight, his hands in fists at his sides.

"Do you have any areas of the valley you think we should search first for the kids? You must know this area better than I do."

"I…" What? My heart stopped beating too fast, skidding to a halt. When it picked up again, it came along with a straightening of my spine and hardening of my face. "Most of the areas that have enough land for real farms, and are remote enough for people to take over without immediately raising suspicions, are on the other side of the valley, next to the mountains."

"Can we get there before nightfall?" he asked, with a deep breath. His shoulders relaxed, and that made me want to punch him.

"You can't." Which felt good to say, but was also true.

Tristan wouldn't be able to follow me going about it my way. And my way was the only way I knew to travel through the valley at night and not have to explain ourselves to every person we passed. Most people traveled the main path to the Lord's house, or kept to the edges. But the last thing we needed was to alert Solaria to our presence. She would involve the guard, and I remained terrified of scaring whatever monster Ash put in charge of the kids into killing them if they thought we were on to them.

"Okay, so we stay here for tonight," Tristan reached behind himself and opened the door, "I'll get you another room."

"No," I said, standing up.

He stilled halfway through the door, and turned a tiny bit at a time back toward me until he made eye contact with me and swallowed hard, his eyes wide. But a second later he looked down at my mouth.

"I can make it there tonight if I go alone."

"Are you out of your damn mind?" he yelled, slamming the door closed and stalking across the room to me. He reached his hands toward me and dropped them back to his sides where they shook.

"Explain to me," I said, "how you're going to climb across rooftops, through the trees, and use all the boats, bridges, and nets to hide as you make your way across the valley floor." I planted my hands on my hips, and leaned forward, one eyebrow raised.

"That can't be the only way to get there." He threw his hands up and let them slap back against his thighs.

"Oh, sure, because you've crossed the valley in the middle of the night without anyone knowing, huh?"

"Wait." He took a step back, and studied my face as I realized I said too much. I crossed my arms over my chest. "You killed someone here. For your brother."

"No." He relaxed, but I had to tell him the truth. And this time I was proud of it. "I killed a man who beat my very pregnant cousin until she went into labor early."

Tristan's mouth, like it was on faulty hinges, slowly dropped open.

"I didn't do it for Ash." Some people just needed to die.

"Lord Fall was…" He turned his head and looked off at the wall, something playing across his face until his eyes hardened. "Bastard."

He looked back at me and nodded. I could breathe.

For some reason, of all my revelations to him, his reaction to this kill meant more to me than other things.

"But your usual way isn't going to work this time," he said, his voice missing that edge it had before.

"Why not?" I tried not to yell at him, but it was close.

"You have no idea what you're walking into, and you will need more than just you to get the kids out of there if you find them."

"I'll just kill every single person that's around them, and then wait to lead the kids out until morning when I can alert the guard at the first house we come to."

"Fuck, Cinder. Really? That's your plan? Kill everyone?" he yelled.

"Yes. If it gets the kids back, then yes." I yelled back.

"And what if it gets you killed instead?" He grabbed my upper arms then, not dropping his hands back to his sides.

"Who cares?" I shoved at his chest, breaking his hold on me.

"Stop it. Your friends would fucking care."

"My friends just lost Madam Valentin because I chose to stay and protect you instead of going to help Bridgeton. They lost their wedding, their lands, their titles, all the things they had planned. My friends are busy caring about other things they lost. They won't care about me."

All the anger was gone from his face by the time I finished yelling at him. Instead, he just looked at me, his mouth turned down at the edges, and shook his head.

"You really think that, don't you?" His voice, so different than a few seconds ago, was soft and somber.

"Everyone thinks that." My voice was strained as my throat closed, and I looked down at the floor.

We stood in silence for what felt like hours, but was probably only seconds.

Finally, he said, "If you go after the kids, and they catch you or kill you, they could murder the kids, too, thinking more people will be after them."

I snapped my head up and bit my lip, trying to think my way around the problem.

"Cinder," he said, his voice a sigh that sent a thrill through my body no matter how much I didn't want it to, or how inappropriate it was at the moment, "you shouldn't do this alone."

He didn't say I couldn't. He didn't dismiss me, or my efforts, or tell me it was too dangerous, or say he needed to protect me. He said I shouldn't. And with the kids at risk…

"Maybe you're right," I said, my voice hollow as my breath left me empty.

Tristan raised a skeptical brow at me, and I didn't have it in me to argue with his mistrust. I earned it.

Staring into his eyes, the flaming green in them again, I couldn't help leaning forward, toward him. I leaned until I felt it fall over me. His heat.

Not as blazing warm as before, and nothing compared to when I woke up to him this morning. But it still existed. He was still my Tristan.

After another minute, as I drifted closer to him, and the silence grew so large that I wasn't sure how to break it anymore, he asked in a low voice, "Do you have a plan to get us there tomorrow?"

I nodded, stepped back, and coughed into my hand, trying to force my heart back into the barbed cage of my ribs.

"Care to share it with me then?" The distance between us grew with the bitter edge in his words.

"We'll skirt along the edge of the valley like most visitors would."

"But we can't take the usual roads."

"No. There isn't really a road. It's just a direction."

He narrowed his eyes for a second and shook his head.

"Then how do you propose we find out which place they'll be? Go house to house?"

Did I really want to tell him? If I let him in on this, my own knowledge of the area, there might be more I would have to explain.

I rubbed my face with my hands, and flopped down to sit on the edge of the bed, staring at my fingers.

"On the other side of the valley, close to Lehar, is a small town around a square. That's where all the larger farms along the edge go to trade with Lehar. We're their biggest buyer since we can't grow much. It's one of the only places in the entire valley set up similarly to the towns and cities in the rest of Onyx."

Even though I tried to hide it, he heard it. I saw it in the way he ran his hand through his hair, tightened his mouth, and softened his eyes. But he wouldn't look at me. He heard the sound in my voice that meant there was more hiding in the spaces between my words.

"They don't go into Lehar to drop off the food?"

I laughed a short huff through my nose, and looked up at him.

"No one goes into Lehar if they can help it. The air, the ash, makes people sick if they breathe it for too long. But that's not all they trade in."

With a slow nod, he took a step back and finally looked at me.

Maybe, one day, every secret in me—stored deep and carved into my soul—might be forced to see the light of day. Even the ones I didn't want to look at. And I couldn't tell him all of them right now. I didn't have the words. But I had to hand him this one.

"Rath has his ports and his fellow sailors as a supply of information. People living inland have the Burnt Market. Food… other things. Everything is for sale there. But their most profitable trade is in rumors and secrets."

Tristan's brow furrowed, and he turned his head to the side, his eyes darting back and forth as if he were reading a text written in code, before he turned back to me.

"Burnt Market?"

"After the most dangerous secrets are passed, the paper they're written on is burned. Those most commonly buying all the physical goods to take them back to our people are covered in ashes. And the physick in that town is where many victims of the blast at the end of the last war were brought to heal. It took a long time for some of the people hit with the explosion to die. One of the buildings in the town still smells like fire and burnt flesh because of it. No one goes inside."

None of those facts were among my secrets involved in that place. But they were something I could give him, something that wouldn't make the shattered monster thundering inside my chest break me open any more than I already was.

"Fuck," Tristan muttered and threaded his fingers together behind his head as he looked up at the ceiling.

I waited for him to say something else, to come to terms with the sad, recent history of my home and the way it reached its broken, soot-coated fingers of despair into the rest of Onyx.

But he didn't say a word as he turned around and walked out the door.

CHAPTER 20

THROUGH IT

Tristan

It only took a minute.

Just one minute wasn't enough time for Cinder to run off and try to save the kids on her own.

Still, I ran back to the room once I was done, my heart afraid to beat lest I was too slow, and she was already gone.

But when I swung open the door, she remained sitting on the bed, her face in her hands.

Her head snapped up as I walked in, her eyes red, and tracks of wet traced down each of her cheeks.

Cinder shuddered and turned her face away from me, pawing at her cheeks.

My body screamed, my blood like fire.

No matter how stupid I knew it was in my head, no matter how much my brain told me I couldn't trust her, that there was no love without trust, that I refused to have a future without love, my fool heart ached.

"I…" I shuffled in place, unsure what I intended to say, and with no idea how to make this stop.

"What, Tristan?" she asked, but the words hit me like staring at a puzzle, with layers of meaning I couldn't see down through to the bottom of.

"Um…" Fuck, I needed to find the words, something, anything to say to her, but this was too hard.

My chest tightened and ached too much, and my brain was an asshole who wanted to rage and scream and tell us both to be smart, to stop talking about anything other than the kids and the goal.

The seconds ticked by, then the minutes. Still, I said nothing as a follow up, nothing to get us back on track. Because I couldn't find what I *needed* to say through the maze of things I *wanted* to say.

After everything, there was too much in my mind that circled and flowed around the place with her name in it. All the while the entirety of my heart ached for her, and beat in time to her name.

"First light." Her voice was thin, and she kept her face away. But she dropped her hand back to her lap. "We should leave at first light."

"Of course." Shit. I sounded cold, and it still wasn't the right thing to say. I still couldn't find the words. I sounded like the practiced king diplomat again, say nothing by voice or by word until sure of what to say.

At least I didn't stammer or mumble this time.

"You should get your room, get some sleep."

I took a deep breath to explain, but a knock on the door at my back interrupted.

Opening it, I found myself grateful for the chance to avoid trying to make sense out of myself enough to talk to Cinder for a minute.

The innkeeper waved in two young men who filed in the room, leaned it against the wall, and walked out again.

"You're lucky we have one," the Innkeeper said, narrowing her eyes at us. "Few places do, and if we were busier, you wouldn't get it. But I don't want any more outbursts."

She pointed her finger at us both and walked out.

"Thank you," I said before I shut the door and turned around to where Cinder stood next to the bed, her hand on her spike and her body in that loose, ready stance she had that I knew as a marker of her lethality.

"What are you doing?" she asked, her voice low even as she held too still for anyone other than her.

Between her stance and her voice, I should have been afraid. An assassin stood before me. Not the Lady of Lehar, not the woman, the killer. But fear didn't flood through me. Something closer to pride and awe rode the flaring heat in my veins.

I shoved it away like an artifact that I neither had the time to look at, nor the brain capacity to think about. As my chest hurt worse in response to both, I took a breath and focused on getting through the night.

"If you have your own room, what is the likelihood I would wake to find that you thought better of this plan, and went off on your own?" I grabbed the small, padded cot they left, and placed it in front of the door.

"Tristan," she sighed and collapsed on the bed, shaking her head at me. All the killer in her gone in a second, and replaced by the same version of her that she was when I walked in, minus the tears.

"Don't worry, Cinder." I unfolded the carefully tucked blanket from the little bed, and took off my cloak, setting it aside along with all my weapons before steeling myself and walking toward her spot on the bed.

The heat and the ache grew with every step closer to her. Her eyes tracked my progress.

Her gaze was physical. It wasn't the cold calculation I knew from the battles we fought side by side. It wasn't the hungry devouring I knew from moments we shared in bed.

The way she looked at me now felt like the farewell caress of the future I thought we had waiting for us—heavy with the weight of broken promise, and sharp with shards of shattered hope.

Reaching down next to her, she swayed toward my hand for a second before she froze, holding her breath.

I grabbed one of the extra pillows on the bed, and hugged it to my chest like it would be a barrier from her ability to make me feel what I didn't want to.

But I couldn't turn right back around and go to the little bed. I couldn't move at all.

All I could do was stare at her, take in how soft her eyes were as she gazed back at me, even as the scar on her cheek suggested little was soft about her, and the strong line of her jaw made those full lips stand out even more.

Cinder was a study in contrasts and opposites that fascinated me, but I wasn't allowed to keep looking. Even though she made it impossible to get enough.

Finally, I broke away and walked across the room on shaking legs.

Gods and Goddesses, I loved her. Still. No matter how hard I tried not to and told myself I was wrong, that I couldn't possibly since I didn't know her. It was all a lie.

I set my pillow down on the little bed, and looked over my shoulder to where she remained in the same spot, with the same look on her face, the same unknowns about her past and her future that made everything I felt make zero sense.

"You could still go," I said, laying down on the little bed that didn't really fit me. It forced me to bend my knees, and lay on my side to avoid hanging off the end.

"What do you mean?" she asked, beginning to take off her own weapons.

"This bed blocks the door, but this is for my own peace of mind. I have to feel like I am doing something to make this work, to make this successful."

She paused, nodded, and continued to take off her large collection of blades.

"But there's always the window, and we both know you're at war with walls."

Cinder actually laughed.

It was small and short, but sounded real, soaring through me in a way that eased the ache in my heart for a second before it crashed down on me anew. She looked to the window, and I held my breath, waiting for her to decide.

After a moment, she let out a long breath, climbed into the big bed, looked back at me, and turned off the hellfire powered light next to the bed.

Eyes wide open, I stared into the dark long after the sound of her breathing evened out, and I tried to find my ability to sleep.

But my mind kept running through it. Through the moment I realized that no matter how hard I tried not to, and no matter how nonsensical it was, I remained in love with a woman who wanted to kill me.

CHAPTER 21

PURPLE

Cinder

He finally fell asleep.

Exactly what it was that made me sure, I didn't know. But Tristan awake and Tristan asleep made the entire world feel different.

I wondered what the world felt like before he was in it. He was born before me, so all my life he existed, changing the world around him. And I never wanted to find out what it would feel like after he left it.

Just having the thought float through my mind, unwanted, unasked for, as I stared into the dark, made my hands shake under the covers, and chills run through me that left me shivering.

And it answered my question. That's what the world would feel like if he wasn't in it.

Cold.

Flinging the blanket off me, heedless of the relative stupidity of the move, I lurched out of bed and stumbled my way to his small one.

Tristan blinked open his eyes and jumped, but settled back before he said, "Do it, Cinder."

"What?" I whispered, moving the blanket where it lay over top of him.

"If you're going to kill me," he said, his voice a hushed sigh in the dark as I sucked in a breath, "just make it fast."

Squeezing my eyes shut, I fought the urge to vomit.

How would I ever convince him I wasn't a threat to him?

"Move over," I said instead of any of the other possible things running through my head.

"What?"

"I said, move over." I pushed against his shoulder.

Cold at first, his unique heat flared up to meet my touch, and the shivering in my body finally stopped.

He scooted over on the too-small bed, and I curled into place with my back to his chest, pulling the blanket back over us both.

"I was cold." My explanation was weak, and it couldn't have made much sense to him. But sleep already clawed at me, and I didn't care. I belonged here.

Before the first light of dawn crept in through the window, I opened my eyes as I meant to, the mission already playing in my mind, but found focus hard when encompassed in his warmth.

Even more than the night before, the heat of him was everywhere, the call of it seducing me back toward sleep.

Fighting off the urge to let it win, I realized he wasn't just pressed against my back. His legs tangled with mine, and his arms wrapped around me, hugging me to him.

Slipping out of his arms and to my feet was an act of will that required running images of the kids through my head.

Once I stood next to the little bed, I looked down at him and found his eyes on me.

Not sure what to say, I nodded and went to the larger bed and the pile of weapons waiting for me.

We got ready for the day in silence, and no words passed between us as we moved his temporary bed and made our way outside to the horses.

Going through the bottom of the valley, over all the winding knots where the rivers met in the middle, and moving from little island to little island would make the horses useless. But going this way along the edges meant we could hang on to them a little while longer.

Something about the view down below looked…changed. But I couldn't quite place it. Everything seemed similar, the people focused down at the water of the rivers, or their little garden plots, green and brown everywhere, the river spotted with the low-bottomed boats everyone used here.

"The air here is so clear," Tristan said.

"Always is." Too clear.

Right through a pass, Lehar languished under constant ash fall. But here they managed to avoid it so completely that they had the clearest skies in all of Onyx.

Maybe the Protectorate Mountains were magic all by themselves.

"What do they have hanging over their boats? Is that some kind of canopy?" Tristan asked from behind me.

Looking closer, that was it. The thing that was different from the last time I was here.

"Those are their nets." I pointed to one a little closer along our path where a bridge stretched over one of the rivers as it came into the valley. "Vine woven together. They work in the rivers to catch fish, but they're everywhere now."

Adding another layer to the tapestry of green, brown, and blue that was the rich valley spread out before us, the nets must have made it more difficult for the Corvids to see from the sky where people were. Even if I weren't sure they would hold against an onslaught.

"Everything is changed," he said, his voice low and a chasm of sadness echoing out of it.

I wanted to tell him it wasn't. I wanted to make that sound leave his voice with some well-chosen words. But I didn't have them. Because I was done lying to him.

Stealing a glance at him from under my hair, instead of being able to watch him as the scenery passed, I stared into his eyes as he looked at me.

He wasn't talking about the valley.

Finally, the truest words came to me.

"Not everything changes." My voice started hushed, my hands shaking as they tightened on the reins, unsure how he would respond, but it grew in strength as the truth rang out. "At least one thing will never change."

Tristan squeezed his eyes shut and his jaw tightened.

I turned away and focused ahead of me. The shaking in my hands disappearing.

When I told myself all I needed to do was remind him that this was real, and keep reminding him, I didn't know that it would tear open another wound every time I did so.

Maybe if I had known…no.

Smiling to myself, I shook my head.

It didn't matter how much blood this sacrifice required. I would bleed out on the altar of this truth before I stopped. What was a little more blood when I had already spilled so much of my own and of those around me?

At least this was a worthy sacrifice—to be back where we belonged.

"Cinder," he said, his voice so low I wasn't sure if I imagined it.

But turning around, he wasn't looking at me.

Following his gaze, I saw what he did.

Purple pennon flags waved from poles carried by people on horseback as they entered the pass most of the way around the edge of the valley from us.

The group was too far away to make out much in the way of details. I wasn't sure exactly how many there were, what they were doing, why they were flying purple pennon flags, if the flags had sigils, or even if the group actually included who I suspected it did.

"Is that the pass that leads to Lehar?" he asked, louder now.

"Yes. And they're turning the corner into Burnt Market." Did they include my brother?

My brother could be there. My brother who I wasn't sure I was strong enough to face. Not now. Not yet. Maybe I never would be. But the kids needed me, and my brother could be in the way of getting them back. What would I do? What could I do? How could I save them? Could I do it without confronting Ash?

Tightening my hands on the reins, I tried to keep them from shaking. No matter how many ways I broke from my brother, here he was. No matter how far I ran, he haunted every step, attacked everything I loved, destroyed it.

And Tristan.

More than anyone or anything, I needed to protect him. And here we were, heading toward the person most likely to want him dead, to hurt me.

How could I protect Tristan now? Could I get him to trust me enough to let me? And how would I prove to him that this was real if I couldn't face my brother? Would I have to kill Ash? What if I couldn't kill my own brother?

Would any amount of reminding Tristan that I was his and he was mine work if he thought I betrayed him again?

Looking back at Tristan, my heart pounding so hard he had to be able to hear it over the sound of the horses' hooves on the ground, I couldn't breathe waiting for him to refocus on me. Tears threatened at the backs of my eyes.

Finally turning my way, Tristan's eyes blazed green, every part of him taught like a bow about to be fired.

"That fucker will never touch you again," he said, "I'll kill him first."

CHAPTER 22

WATCH

Tristan

Cinder's hands still shook on her reins, her mouth still moved down at the corners, and her eyes still swam in unshed tears from time to time long into the day and after stopping multiple times to talk with the locals.

Every time it happened, I wanted to rip Ash's head from his shoulders with my bare hands.

Knives.

He slashed her with knives when she was a child because she displeased him in training.

Not only was he a fucking traitor, but he had also hurt her.

Over and over again. For years. He brutalized her, tore her apart, left her bleeding and wounded, and did nothing to help her or heal her or protect her like he should have.

If Ash was there when we got there, it didn't matter how many people he had with him, I would kill him.

Cinder struggled to tell me the truth so many times.

The way she broke apart as she finally did, the way her eyes looked now, as if the ghosts haunting her were on display for the world to see instead of shoved deep within her, well...I didn't lie to her when I told her that I would kill her brother. And he was never, ever going to be able to lay a hand on her again.

"We should get off the horses here," Cinder said as the sun still shone overhead, at least three hours until the lowest rays of the sun would tuck themselves below the edge of the Protectorate Mountains.

"But this isn't really anywhere," I said, looking around us at the small, flat spot covered in the thick, loamy green of the valley.

"The horses won't go far," Cinder said, "should we need them. But riding them straight into the Burnt Market might attract attention if not many people have come on horseback today."

"People came under a banner. Won't we be easily forgotten?"

"Since when are you easily forgotten?"

I almost laughed and made a joke about her being the one that no one could forget, but it was a reflex of the words. I held my tongue because her tone made it clear she wasn't joking.

We left the horses, both of us with a few too many weapons on to remain completely inconspicuous, even with our cloaks.

Cinder adjusted her hood so it fell to obscure her face further, and I followed suit.

Everything in me screamed to reach out to her, to tell her, to change this before we walked in there and faced whatever was about to come at us, but she put her carefully crafted assassin face back on.

Her whole body morphed before my eyes into a creature who brought the night with her wherever she went. Her movements were so fluid that I questioned if she had moved, or if I misremembered where she was standing every time I looked away from her.

She became that deadly, blindfolded wraith she was in the training grounds when we practiced flying with the rope.

Part of me wanted to laugh because I didn't see it then. It was so obvious.

But I was too in awe of her right now to say a word, and I was even worse on the training grounds.

I shook my head, and tried to focus on what we planned to do.

"Are you sure this will work?" I asked as I fell into step beside her, moving toward the little town and the Burnt Market.

"We're going to find the kids." She didn't sound sure so much as she sounded like she was making a promise. A vow.

My feet stumbled over nothing. The sound of her voice like that made too many moments run through my head, none of which I had the time or the ability to look at right now.

Cinder was right about the little place.

It couldn't have been more than twenty-five buildings all set up around a little square with stalls and people wandering through. Some of the people were dusted in the ashes of Lehar, their hair and clothes washed out grays, and their skin coated in it.

Next to me, Cinder went stiff for a moment, turned carefully to avoid their eyes, and returned to stalking through the place.

After a thorough circuit, Cinder settled into a pattern of listening as she pretended to look closer at some things, and talked to some of the vendors.

Keeping my own voice silent, I paid attention to everything and everyone.

So far, there were no signs of any Amethysts, no one who had the mark on their hand like Farmer did, and no sign of Ash.

From where we were I couldn't tell exactly how many he had

with him. Maybe he went to some other place in the valley or along the edge, but I just knew he was with the people that flew the purple banner.

But...where did he and his retinue go? And if he wasn't with them, then what were his people doing here, and where were they?

After Cinder made her circle of the open market, she tipped her head in a gesture to follow her, and led me to one of the smaller buildings lining the square.

She stepped inside first, and I followed, watching her more than the surroundings no matter how much I knew what I should have been doing.

We went to a spot in the corner, but she threw up another gesture toward the bar before I turned around to face the room.

"Ordering something?" I asked, my voice low. I tried to remember how she moved her hand. Maybe I could order the same way.

"How long do you think it would take for someone to get suspicious if we just sat here in the corner and didn't order anything?"

By some unspoken agreement we were both careful in our placements at the table, leaving neither of us with our backs to the room, not exactly sitting next to each other, and not exactly across from each other either. It left us both with the job of watching the other's blind spots.

A few seconds later one of the servers put two tankards of ale on the table, and Cinder handed him a coin, leaning to whisper in his ear.

He grinned, cut his eyes my direction, and whispered back to her.

She nodded, gave him the flirtiest smile I had ever seen, and ran her hand along his arm as he pulled away.

Once, those kinds of looks were pointed my way, although the ones she gave me were different, *more* somehow. It made me want to scream, watching her look at someone else that way.

"Friend of yours?" I asked, my hand in a fist below the table, holding the emotions raging through my body in a tight grip.

"If we find someone we need to question, now I know where to take them, how to get them there, and the owner will think it's just sex."

"We? How am I supposed to be part of your questions in that scenario?"

Cinder turned from her perusal of the room, setting those eyes on me. She picked up her tankard and took a long, languid drink, staring at me over the rim, hunger in her eyes that made the heat rising in my blood center in my cock.

Pulling the tankard away from her mouth, she licked the ale from her lips in slow movements that had me tightening my grip on my own drink.

She leaned in, lifting her ass off her seat, almost crawling across the table to me, her face a breath from mine. Her eyes scanned my face, she bit her lip when she looked at my mouth.

My breath grew ragged, and I couldn't stop leaning closer to her, until our lips almost touched.

"I told him," she said, voice low and rich with promise, "you like to watch, and then fuck me until I scream louder for you than anyone else."

No one else was going to touch her. She was mine.

Yes, I wanted her to scream for me.

Right now.

"Damn," I muttered, and she grinned before she crawled back to sit in her seat.

"Now that the server knows, word will spread that's what we want. Maybe we can find the right person to talk to."

"Was there a reason you never flirted like that at the palace? To my eternal shame, you probably would have had a better chance at killing me." I tried to make a joke to escape the desire racing through me, but my throat was too tight. And my voice had too much accusation in it.

Her brow furrowed. She opened her mouth a second, closed it again, and finally whispered, "That wasn't flirting. That was manipulating the people watching and letting them see my ass."

Whatever else that was, it was fucking flirting.

She took another drink of her ale, this time her eyes cut to the side, and the flash of sadness in them made everything else stop.

I put my hands on the table, ready to get her as far from here as I could. There had to be another way to get the information. This way, using sex as subterfuge for violence, hurt her too much.

But one of the men in the room put his hand down on the table between us before I stood up. It had a crow-shaped burn on the back.

With one look, I knew she saw it.

That was fast. So fast it made my stomach want to return its meager contents to the air and strangle him at the same time.

He made innuendoed small talk with Cinder while I gripped the side of the chair. My fingers screamed what I couldn't say out loud.

Finally, she slipped her hand in his, and he pulled her to her feet.

Leaning down, he tried to go for a kiss, and I shoved myself up to standing as she deftly avoided his lips.

A twitch of her eyebrow when she looked at me had me following them from the room down a dark hallway and into a small basement, crammed with crates and barrels.

The second we were down the stairs, she twisted and held tight to his throat while my blood heated until sweat poured down my back.

He made a strangled laughing sound.

"Not really what I'm into, baby," he said through his constricted throat as he grabbed her ass and pulled her closer.

She took one of his hands off her, bending it unnaturally until he cried out. I peeled the fingers of his other hand off her ass, slamming his arm against a barrel as she snarled in his face.

"Baby," her voice a caustic mockery of his, "what I'm into is hearing about your King."

"What?" He looked back and forth between us, me standing over her shoulder, as it sunk in that this wouldn't go the way he thought.

"Tell us where he is, and what he's done with the kids."

It was a damn good thing she asked the questions, because if I opened my mouth, I was likely just to growl with incomprehensible rage as I tore him apart.

CHAPTER 23

AGAIN

Cinder

I slammed the man's head back against the wall, turning him into a sack of humanity as he sunk to the floor, out cold.

"Cinder," Tristan said, his first words since we came down here, his voice as sharp as my spike, "you can't do that again."

"Just because he didn't know anything about the kids or Ash doesn't mean this plan won't work." The man admitted plenty of what we already knew, and even added more to our knowledge of their overall plot.

More of Ash's troops moved through the passes from Amethyst every day, gathering here before they went on their way to Mariposa north of Bridgeton where they would gather before attacking the palace.

He grabbed my shoulder and turned me around to face him, his eyes that raging fire of green they had been since I told him what the plan here was.

"No. We'll find another way to do this. You can't."

"Can't?" I tossed his hand away and shook my head. "You can't stop me. You don't get to tell me what to do. You gave up any say."

Tristan squeezed his eyes shut, his mouth twisting into a grimace as he yanked at his hair.

I darted up the stairs and out of the basement, not giving a shit about his reasons for telling me not to do things.

He couldn't keep pretending that trying to keep me out of things was to protect me. Not when he made it clear he didn't care.

"Damn him," I muttered, making my way back to the main room, and heading to the bar instead of back to a table.

The bartender raised an eyebrow at me, but did as I gestured, giving me another tankard of ale.

Instead of sipping at this one, I threw it back and drank it down until the last of it poured down my throat. I gasped as I wiped my mouth.

Dropping my hand from my face, I watched Tristan talking to a tiny slip of a woman.

She was pretty, with golden skin and dark hair, tiny features, and a fitted little dress that made her small curves look like more.

He allowed her to take him by the hand, and lead him from the tavern without looking back at me once.

The bartender bit his lip on a grin at my expense, and I slammed the coin for the ale down on the counter as I went after them.

Following them through the market as night fell and the tradespeople carted off their unsold items while the people still wandering through turned to the kinds of pursuits best suited to night, the cold place returned to me in a rush without seeking it out.

Maybe I would have lashed out at someone without it.

Maybe I would have got us caught by the enemy or caused the kids' deaths by attacking, but it wasn't strategy and clear thinking that stopped me. It was the cold place in my mind finally returning. Just when I needed it.

One little house on the valley side of the market hung over the edge of the river where it ran by.

Tristan and the woman went in the front door.

Making my way toward the house, to find a way inside, I caught sight of a familiar head of hair disappearing between two other buildings. My heart stuttered in my chest.

Ash.

Running, not trying to hide myself at all or make any explanation for sprinting down the middle of the lane, I made it to the alley he walked into.

But it wasn't Ash I found waiting there.

The slave woman from the fight in the woods stood guard outside a door to the larger of the two buildings.

She sucked in a breath when she spotted me, darting looks around her.

I stopped in the open end of the alleyway, looking behind me into the street, and trying to see what she kept looking for at the other end of the alley.

Was I about to walk into a trap?

Putting my finger to my lips in the shush gesture, I stepped to the side to make my way around the building, and she ran for me with her hands in the air, palms out.

A swift crouch, turn, and pull, and I was in the shadowed corner of the house's front porch with my spike in my hands as she ran past me and into the street, looking behind herself at me as she ran toward the valley.

It didn't matter that I saw her run before, nothing this woman did made sense to me.

Sticking my head around the corner just enough to look down the alley again, it made a fraction more sense.

Other people, these bristling with weapons and loud in their very drunken chatter, stumbled from the house she was guarding.

"No. It's perfect," one of them said when another shoved at him.

"It won't work," the shover shook his head, and untied his pants to pee on the side of the house.

Looking up at the building I crouched next to, I wondered why so many men chose to pee on the side of a house or tree rather than use the bathroom this place must have had.

"Yes, it will. The King is brilliant. That's how they got this house. Tricked the man to going with them for sex, and got his house after they killed him."

I didn't bother to listen to what else they said, or wonder if Ash was inside, or think about anything as I made my way through the deepening shadows back up the street to the house Tristan went into.

He said I couldn't. Controlling asshole.

Tristan said I couldn't use sex to trick someone again to get information, and what did the idiot do?

Got caught by the same damn tactic.

A pretty, tiny woman was going to kill him because Ash always used sex as a weapon, like everything else. And I was too stupid to see it happening in front of my eyes.

What was Tristan thinking?

If he wanted to have a turn in bed that damn bad, he could have just asked last night when I climbed in next to him.

My hand slipped off the doorknob as I opened the door on the side porch of the little house when it hit me.

He didn't want me last night.

"Fuck that," I muttered, darting through the few rooms of the house on my toes, not making a sound, checking every room for anyone who might cause me a problem.

In one bedroom I found two men asleep in the beds, snoring loudly, and silenced them forever with quick jabs of my spike.

"Tell me where you're from. No fucking around this time," a woman's voice yelled from the bedroom next to me, her voice clear through the wall.

"Maybe you should tell me why you're doing this," Tristan said back, a soft thud following as he grunted.

"We ask the questions here," another woman's voice sneered, and I slipped a throwing knife into my free hand.

No. They didn't get to hit him, question him, do a damn thing to him.

I slammed open the door to the room, revealing Tristan sitting in a chair with his hands tied in front of him, his lip split and bleeding, one eye swollen, blood seeping out of a swiftly-blackening wound at the center of the swelling, and two women standing over him.

One of them was the tiny one I saw before, and the other towered over even me. Strong and imposing, she held a long sword, the hilt of it stained red.

"Fuck you. This prisoner is ours," the small one yelled, grabbing for a dagger next to her, but coming up short when my thrown knife stabbed into her eye, toppling her to the floor.

"No," Tristan yelled.

"He's mine," I said, my voice sharp.

The large one yelled a kind of war cry, hefting the long sword to the side like she was going to swing all the way around her body with it, which wasn't a smart move in the close quarters of the room.

I ducked as Tristan said, "Damn it, Cinder." The sword passed above me, and slammed into the wall. I surged up, inside her guard, and drove my spike between her ribs and through her heart.

Her eyes popped open wide, and she slumped down to the floor.

Yanking my spike out, I turned around to find Tristan standing in the middle of the room with the rope held in his hands instead of around his wrists.

"What are you doing here?" he asked, his voice the opposite of grateful. It was an accusation.

"Are you serious?" I gestured with my spike at the rope before I wiped it off on my pants and put it back in the sheath on my thigh. "You were able to get out the whole time?"

"Most people are shit at knots." He lifted the rope up like I should have known, but who would have guessed?

"Fine, next time you decide to let two people beat you, maybe let me know you think it's foreplay so I don't try and save your ass."

I turned and stomped into the hallway, but he grabbed me from behind, twisting me around and tangling my hands in the rope, all with one move of his body and swift flips of his hands.

"Damn it, Cinder. Why don't you ever listen?" he said, again, his voice that low growl that even now sent my body to a different place, one where we were different to each other.

"You said I can't do this kind of thing, but here you are." I clung to my anger as tightly as his small length of rope bound my wrists.

He backed me up against the wall of the hallway, lifting the rope so he pinned my hands above my head, his arms bracketing my face.

"Because it isn't fair, after everything, for you to have to do this. You deserve..." His voice faded away, his breath coming in harsh, frantic bursts as his eyes bored into me.

It wasn't fair.

Not after what Ash made me do.

That's what he meant.

I deserved...what?

My muscles turned to liquid as I realized how pressed his

body was to mine, and how his eyes turned hungry as he looked at me.

All along, I hoped for that look, longed for it, dreamt about it. That one, and the soft one that said he loved me, they were all I wanted.

Opening my mouth to say something, although I didn't know what, Tristan leaned in further, his breathing matching mine, uneven, heaving, and desperate.

Even as he pressed against me, I felt his cock harden and grow between us. Heat pooled within me as my need grew in response. As my want grew.

A sound, plaintive and small, eked out of my mouth, and he hummed in response, pressing his cock against me so I throbbed.

"Tell me what you want, Tristan," I whispered, and he claimed my mouth with his, uncontrolled, bruising, and tasting of the metallic tang of the blood from his split lip as his tongue punished mine.

I tugged on the rope, wanting to wrap my arms around him as I moaned into his mouth, and pulled him closer to me with one leg around his waist.

"Cinder," he growled, pressing his cock against my clit through my pants, almost sending me falling over the edge.

My body responded to his every touch with an overreaction of sensation that made me quiver.

A pleading sound poured out of me.

Using the rope around my wrists, he turned me around, moving me with one hand while the other slipped to my front and undid the laces of my pants.

With deft movements, never stopping the rubbing pressure of his cock on my sex from behind, he plunged his hand into my pants, and caressed his fingers against my clit.

"Tristan," I cried out, arching my back, and needing him

inside me as he drove me over the edge, my entire body trembling while I shattered.

Moving the hand that held the rope, he kept me in place while my legs shook. He didn't let up with the slow, perfect circles of his fingers that sent me on an unending wave of pleasure.

"Please," I moaned, he had to know what I wanted.

"Not yet. I'm not done. I'll show you foreplay." His fingers on me increased the pressure as he whispered in my ear, kissing and sucking on my earlobe.

I started to slide my tied hands down the wall, but Tristan grabbed the rope around my wrists and stretched them above my head again, maintaining the constant rubbing with the fingers of his other hand.

"No," he said, that growl in his voice that made me writhe. "Stay right there."

A whine that sounded like begging emanated from somewhere deeper than my mouth, my need made audible.

"Will you stay?" he asked, pressing his cock against me, so hard I felt him throb even with the leather between us.

"Yes, yes, yes," I would stay however he wanted me, for however long he wanted. Forever.

"Good girl." He rewarded me by pressing two fingers inside my wet, aching center, and I cried out, throbbing, before he rubbed his slick fingers against my clit again, and then let go of the rope.

Pulling my pants down just enough, still driving me through the dissolving of my body again and again, he finally pressed his cock against my wet, waiting, desperate sex, making me break apart further, my legs turning weak.

I yelled and he growled into my neck as he bent over me, rubbing himself against me.

"Now. Tristan. Please." My need grew along with the ever-increasing waves of my orgasms, like he drove me to higher and higher mountains only to push me down the other side and make it happen again.

He slipped his hand out of my pants, and ran it down my thigh instead. I moaned a desperate sound as he pushed on one thigh and then the other to make me open my legs wider.

"Tristan, I need you." My legs barely worked, they shook too hard, and opening me up just made me throb more.

"Do it, again," he said, his voice low and ravenous as he brought those fingers back to my clit. I moaned, and he held me in place with one hand on the rope, one on my clit, his chest along my back, his lips on my neck and my ear, and his cock rubbing against me. "Cum for me."

Breaking at his words, my legs giving out as they shook uncontrollably and he held me up, I screamed.

He moved then, so fast I didn't fall to the floor on my useless legs, he pulled away and slammed his cock into me which made the world come undone.

Nothing about the way he moved in me, or the way his hand held the rope around my wrist was sweet or tender.

Moving inside me, his fingers still rubbing against me, his other hand tugging the rope tighter until it bent my arms so he was even deeper, he bit my shoulder and sent me falling through stars, no longer tethered to the land at all.

Pounding into me with a force that rattled through my liquid bones, sending waves of pleasure and desire shaking through every part of me, he tilted so my feet lifted off the floor entirely, and he sped up the rocking of his hips.

We didn't make love, or worship at the altar of one another. This was my pent-up need. This was us coming undone together.

Finally, he followed me off the cliff, moaning his pleasure into my shoulder until his hands eased on me, and he rested along my back.

I breathed, wanting to turn around, look into his eyes, hold him, tell him how much I loved him. All I could do was breathe.

After only a few seconds, with quick, efficient movements, he untangled us, turned me, untied the rope encircling my wrists, and twisted away from me, tying his pants back together, shaking his head.

My heart fell down to the bottom of my toes as I put myself back to rights, and stopped breathing entirely.

"That was so fucked up," he muttered, his head still shaking, and I had to lean against the wall to remain standing.

"Fucked up?" My voice may as well have come from a corpse for all the feeling remaining in it.

"Yes." He threw a hand in the general direction of the room he was beaten in, avoiding my eyes still. "Two people are dead in there and we're out here…"

He didn't finish the sentence, just dragged his fingers through his hair and stalked down the hall toward the front of the house.

I couldn't move. My legs gave out, and if I weren't already leaning against the wall he had me pinned against just a moment before, I would fall. I stared down at the discarded and forgotten piece of rope where it rested across the toe of my boot.

After everything, he thought I was a mistake.

CHAPTER 24

BAD

Tristan

How did I fuck up so badly?

She was never going to forgive me.

That voice…she didn't feel anything for me now. It was obvious in the dead way she spoke.

What was wrong with me?

I attacked her.

All it took was for her to say I was hers, and my grip on myself slipped. Then when she asked me what I wanted…I lost any hold I had.

I turned what was supposed to be something good, something between us, the first time we had been together in so long, into a fucked-up way to dance on those womens' graves.

Once I reached the door to the house, before I opened it and escaped from the disaster I made, I crouched down and knotted my hands on my head.

Pulling on my hair, I curled my body into a ball, forcing all the riotous fire in my blood to slow down.

Fuck, I needed to think. I had to fix this.

Standing up, I looked outside at the night as it swallowed the world, and the hellfire lamps in the house across the road backlit a collection of people with swords at their sides moving down the lane.

Even if she didn't want me anywhere near her, even if I didn't know how to make it better yet, she had to put up with me for a little while longer.

Darting back down the hallway in the dark, she remained in the same spot I left her, leaning against the wall.

"Cinder," I whispered, and she jumped.

"Tristan," she said, her voice devoid of any hint about what she thought. Even in the dark I saw her face was blank.

I swallowed.

"We have to go. Too many armed people are collecting across the lane."

She pushed herself off the wall, and took a step, still not looking at me. But she paused.

"My night vision isn't good in here," she said.

Gods and Goddesses, I couldn't breathe.

"Would it be alright to take your hand?" I asked through a tight throat and an aching chest.

Did she hear it? The question I really asked? The one I was too scared to ask outright?

"Yes." Her voice told me nothing. The look on her face told me less. But she reached out her hand, and I folded it into mine.

Even as we darted down the hallway and toward the side door, my fingers threaded through hers in a way that calmed the raging beast inside me that rode high on fear and thrashed in the heat pouring through me.

She was back to being that warm bath for aching muscles,

that kiss of the sun on a cool autumn day that soaked through clothes and made everything better.

Cinder might never forgive me, but for me there was no going back to that place of searing, white-hot, painful fire where she was concerned.

I was hers. She was right about that. And one day, I would make her mine again.

We made it out of the house and into the moonlight where she let go of my hand, beckoning me to follow her through a tumble of stones covered in moss that ran along a pond off the river behind the stretch of houses on this side of the lane.

Making my way across the stones took every piece of my concentration. Every other step, the moss wanted to shift and send me sprawling. More than once, a stumble forced me to put out a hand and catch myself lest I break an ankle.

All the while, Cinder moved from rock to rock on her toes, no more bothered by the slick, uneven surface than she would have been by walking down the middle of the street.

She paused to let me catch up to her, perched on one small rock at the edge of the field of stones that we navigated through.

When I got there, I stepped off the last rock to stand on the solid ground while she remained in her place, scanning the area.

"Now what?" I asked, no closer to having a guess at where we could go to find the kids, how to deal with Ash, or talk to her about what just happened.

"Did they tell you anything useful?" she asked.

I swallowed and shook my head. "The only thing they even mentioned was something about meeting their fake King at the Carey tomorrow, whatever that is."

"No," she said, her head turning as she stared off at something. "They didn't say that."

"They did. What's a Carey? A town?"

She turned back to look me in the eye, hers still devoid of any hint at what she thought, and nothing about her suggesting we were anything other than two people chatting. Maybe a King and his Fighter. Not a man and a woman who ever loved each other.

"The Carey is the name of the building that still smells like burned flesh."

It was a place of horrors of the last war, and they took the kids there?

The name of the Burnt Market I understood, but the Carey?

"What does it mean?"

"It was an apothecary at the time it was closed up. The people left it as a standing monument to our suffering."

Carey was short for apothecary.

"Do you think the kids are there?" I asked, my voice stolen by a cold wind that blew through, trailing the first snowflakes of what might end up being a lot more.

"If they are," she said, stalking toward the square at the center of town, "they don't have a lot of time left."

A chill ran through me despite the heat in my veins, and it had nothing to do with the snow falling around us.

"Why not?" I asked, hurrying after her, watching as the snow collected on the hood of her cloak.

"Because I thought I saw my brother at one of the houses across the lane from where they took you."

Her voice stumbled over the words to describe where we were, the little house we left devoid of life after I screwed up. Maybe it was a chance for me to apologize, to try and make it better.

Except she saw Ash.

Cinder went from moving through the snow with dangerous purpose, to curling her shoulders, her stride changing from something like a wolf on a hunt to more akin to the deer it chased, and her head tilting so she looked at the ground.

"Where?" I asked, my voice a harsh, grating sound, and my

hands curling into white-knuckled fists at my sides as that heat rose up in me. I wanted to find him and rip him apart before we saved the kids.

"No." Cinder held up a hand, whirling around to face me and planting her feet.

"He deserves it."

"Yes. But we don't know if it was him that I saw. The kids need us. And if it was him, he's got too many people with him." She was shaking. Standing in the winter night, lit only by the soft fall of the moonlight shining on the ever-thickening fall of white, she shook, her eyes wide.

All the rage flowing through me morphed.

It was rage on her behalf from the beginning. Now it shifted to a desperation to make her okay, to protect her.

Part of me still wanted to confront Ash. But she was right. I couldn't do that without Cinder. And for her to be there, for her to face him...I couldn't do that to her. If she didn't want to, I never wanted her to see him again.

Nodding, I reached out for her, to pull her to me maybe? I didn't know. It wasn't a decision, a thought-out action. It was a reflex.

But she turned around and started toward the town square again.

Dropping my hands back to my sides, I sighed and trailed after her.

One day, I would find the words.

Following her to the square, where some people still walked by and more were still loitering around the entrance to the tavern, she held up a hand to stop me.

I did as she asked, and we stood in the shadow of one of the awnings.

Cinder leaned in close, making it even more difficult for me to keep my mind on the task in front of us.

"Go around the back of that building. I'll make my way in through the front here. We'll meet up on the inside."

Shaking my head, I pulled back to look at her, to see if she was serious, but I was too late. She had already run into the darkness and around a corner by the time I figured out she was moving.

Damn it.

I needed to figure out how to focus, or this might end worse than it started.

Making my way around to the back of the building, I took my bow off my back and readied an arrow.

Once I made it inside, I might have to switch to my sword. But out here, the bow remained my best weapon.

The way it sat in my hands was comfortable, and helped my mind pay closer attention to all the details around me.

Cinder must have made her way inside by the time I reached the back of the building, but I couldn't rush it, either. She needed me to make it inside, make it to her, and she would need me to help with the kids, to say nothing of what we might encounter on our way to them.

I already fucked up tonight. I wasn't going to do it again.

At the back of the building, I found the door where it hung crooked in the frame after remaining unused too long.

Pushing it open, I made my way inside, the acrid stench of burned flesh hitting me just as Cinder said it would and making me gag.

But after a moment, I swallowed down the urge to vomit, and moved further into the unknown dark of the building on my way to Cinder.

CHAPTER 25

MEMORY

Cinder

Where were they?

All the trauma this building saw, all the pain and suffering of the living, the dying, and the dead seemed to have permeated the very walls, making it hard to find which direction sounds came from.

They were here. The second I got inside, I heard it, the muffled sound of a child's suppressed sob.

But the building itself conspired against us, and it was too damn dark.

Even if I had a stone light, I wouldn't have been able to use it on the chance that others would see it. The kids would be the ones to suffer if they found me sneaking around. Tristan's warning stayed loud in my mind.

It was so dark, I wasn't sure if I already passed them in this warren of rooms that smelled of the bitter bite of death by fire, and the blast that ripped apart my world.

I breathed through my mouth, trying to keep as much of that torture from my nose as possible, and still failing.

There was a smell to burned hair. Another to burned skin. Yet a different terrible scent to burned muscle and fat. All of those were here. The better smelling of the layered scents as far as my nose was concerned, and still the one that meant the worst, was also here. It was the stench of wounds so horrible I didn't allow myself to remember my people having them. It was the odor of charred bone and marrow.

Nothing about this place was okay. Even deep in the cold place, hiding within it for my sanity, I couldn't entirely push out the memories that assaulted me.

After the last war, when the grounds around my home became a hospital of sorts, and the fields beyond the destroyed walls grew grave markers as plentiful as the crops they used to, even though many of them stood over empty graves of those reduced to nothing, I spent days going through the motions. In a daze caused by more than the impact of the blast, the assault on my lungs from the ashes, and physical change to my landscape, I forced myself to keep moving.

I was the daughter of the last Duke and Duchess, the sister of the new Duke, the one who led the fight for those hiding inside my home even as our fate was sealed by the battlefield too far away to see clearly. I was of service to my people.

For days after the blast, I searched for survivors in the battlefield. Or even just something left to bury.

But eventually I was called back to help with the wounded at home.

The images from those days, ones I could never fully outrun, ones I could never fully drown out, grew louder and more vivid in my mind as the smell of the Carey assaulted me.

My diminished ability to handle this place made me tighten my fists on my spikes and hope that the kids didn't have the same kind of memories I did. That being brought to this place wouldn't dredge up those kinds of horrors for them.

Finally, I stopped in a hallway, and tried to find the cold place, a deeper piece of it.

It took a moment, but I was back there in that washed out space free of my past, the memories pushed back for now.

Refusing to allow my mind to get near my memories again, I prayed to my mother and father on a loop like a mantra, 'Help the kids, find the kids, keep the kids sane and safe.'

Around another corner, through another empty room swathed in darkness, I entered what looked like it might be nothing more than a door to a closet. Every door had to be opened and searched.

And I tripped over someone curled up in a ball at my feet.

Falling to the floor and spinning around, my spikes at the ready, I found myself staring into the deeper darkness that was a person sitting down here with me.

"Queen Cinder?" one of the kids whispered, and I tucked my spikes down toward the floor as they fell on me, wrapping their arms around me as the tears started, and their hiccupping breaths grew loud.

"Shhh," I whispered, this wasn't the time to correct them, or even allow myself a second to wallow in the wave of fresh sorrow that washed over me as they referred to me as Queen. "I'm here now, and I'll lead you out."

"You're here to get us?" one of them said, a sob in the middle that may as well have been an indictment against all the delays Tristan and I took.

"Are there any more of you hidden somewhere else?" How would I find them?

"No. They put us all in here earlier today." The heaviness in the answer told of something else, some unsaid terror in the days before now.

One day soon, someone would need to help them all deal with whatever went on here. But first, we had to go.

I couldn't tell how many were in here with me, which kids were here, or even how big this space was. But it wasn't time to ask any more questions of them. It was time to get them out.

"Let me up," I said, gently extracting myself from their grasps, "and we'll go. Stay behind me."

They helped me up, taking me by the arms, somehow avoiding my spikes, yet not shying away from them either.

Once I was up, one of them grabbed onto the back edge of my cloak, the tug on it as comforting as someone holding my hand, and the others shuffled around until the one directly behind me whispered, "We're ready."

"Hang on tight," I said, making my way out of the little space with my spikes up, leading the way. The patter of feet made our exit anything but soundless.

"Are your captors around here?" I asked, taking the chance that my low voice wouldn't carry any more than the sound of their feet did.

"Somewhere." The answer came with a warble to the voice that made me tighten my grip on my spikes.

In here somewhere, the monsters that took the kids had buried fear deep inside them. So much so that they left them alone together as darkness fell, knowing they wouldn't try to escape.

Maybe I wouldn't be able to make it happen today, maybe it would take me years, but I would make sure that a price was paid for what each of them were put through.

All I could do for right now was try to remember the way out of this place.

Usually, I had a good sense of direction. But that relied on being able to see where I was going. No amount of instinct could lead me through this labyrinthine building the way it could warn me in a fight.

Once, I would have said my night vision was fine. But Tristan proved me wrong about that, too, because his was much better. Right now, I needed his eyes.

Especially because…I took a wrong turn somewhere.

Slowing down so the kids behind me didn't crash into me, I paused to stare into the dark. I tried to figure out where I was, which turn I took wrong, and how I could get all of us out of this.

If I were by myself, being lost in here would just be a delay.

But with all the kids relying on me, I couldn't lead them in circles. And if Ash was expected to meet with some of his people here tomorrow, the night wasn't allowed to stop me. It had to remain my ally. My window.

Capitalizing on that window, getting the kids as far from here and as close to safety with backup for the fight, was the only option.

All I had to do was find a way through despite not being able to see.

"Yeah," I muttered under my breath, sarcasm dripping from my words, "that's all."

CHAPTER 26

SMELL

Tristan

Why was this building built this way?

Every room connected to other rooms and hallways, each door leading deeper in with no pattern I could find.

Maybe I went in circles. How would I know? Nothing about this building made any sense.

And where in this mess was Cinder? Where were the kids?

I gagged and fought back the sick feeling growing in my stomach. No matter how long I was in here, making my way through all the rooms trying to find all of them, the stench tried to make me vomit.

Other unpleasant smells I encountered at different times in my life eventually faded into the background. Not this. This permeated my nose, and made me wonder if I would ever smell anything else. Anything good.

Finally, I stopped, closed my eyes, and tried to think of the best smell I knew…

Cinder's scent bloomed in my mind, perfect along her skin when I buried my face in her neck, and wafting over me when her hair moved in the wind.

Thinking of her protected me from the debilitating effects of this place. I opened my eyes, and set off again into the darkness of this maze.

She was here. She needed me.

And the Shield House kids were here. They needed me, too.

With her and I working together, we could get them to safety, and maybe I could get back here with guard members in time to intercept her brother tomorrow.

Maybe.

Just thinking about confronting him made my blood run hot enough to combust. But if she or the kids needed me after this place, then sending the guards without me would have to do.

Damn it.

Wait… What was that?

I paused, trying to hold my breath and somehow quiet the sound of my own pulse in my ears, straining to hear whatever it was that alerted me again.

There it was.

Some small, muffled sound moved through the building, and I set off in that direction.

Maybe I would find Cinder, maybe I would find the kids, or maybe I would find the human piles of garbage that took the kids and held them here.

But whoever made that sound, I was headed their way.

It came again as I rounded a corner, and I had to adjust my trajectory through the odd collection of rooms.

With my bow at the ready, an arrow nocked, and sweeping it through every room I entered before I was entirely into a space,

I made my way through the building, the scent buried beneath my memories of Cinder.

Turning into another hallway, I almost let go of my arrow. But it was her.

She had her spikes up in front of her, and crept along in the dark, her movements graceful if tentative. A trail of kids were at her back, being as quiet as possible, but they made the sound. Not her.

"Cinder," I said, and she jumped.

"King Tristan," the child directly behind her breathed and she relaxed, although she scanned in front herself like she didn't see me.

"Come on," I whispered, "this way."

She zeroed in on my voice, and made her way to me, her spikes still in hand but to the sides.

Leaning in close, for a second, I thought she came for a kiss, and I closed my eyes as the anticipation of bliss in the middle of this hell flooded through me.

But instead of a kiss, she whispered, "I can't see a thing."

How could she not see at all? It was dark, but I could still see her as if she were lit from within.

I moved my face so my lips brushed along her ear, being as quiet as I could.

"Take hold of my quiver. I'll lead us out," I whispered.

She shivered, but nodded.

Once I had us pointed back the way I came, she gave a tug on my quiver of arrows to let me know she was in place, and we all started to move through the building again.

Near the back door I entered through, with only two more rooms left for us to make our way through, lights poured in from one of the doorways next to us.

I checked that room on the way in, and no one was there. But now someone waved around a stone light by the looks of the pattern dancing along the walls and the floor.

Cinder took the child behind her and ushered him forward, five more coming after in quick succession, before she positioned herself at their back, and nodded to me to keep going.

Part of me wanted so badly to confront whoever was in there that my hands cramped on my bow. Instead, I ground my teeth together, and led them through faster than before.

We got to the backdoor, still open, and I checked the alley behind the building where it butted up against a rock wall that was actually a cliff marking the beginning of one of the mountainsides.

Stepping to the side, I waved the kids out, patting each one on the shoulder as they passed, making sure they each knew I was here with them and soon they would be as safe as I could make them.

Cinder came last, walking backward, her spikes high and her eyes scanning into the darkened maw of the building.

I took her by the wrist even though she jumped, and tugged her to the side of the doorway to stand in our group.

"What do you think?" I whispered into her ear, hoping she would know what I meant, and not wanting to say it out loud lest the kids hear and grow afraid.

"Let me sneak back in and see who it was. I'll meet you at the horses." She looked at me, finally. Her eyes fathomless and every bit of the steel she was capable of alive in them.

The building, with its smell that must have brought back terrible memories for her, waited just as she did for me to say something.

For her to offer to go back inside meant she was serious, and this was more than a half-suicidal mission fueled by her own need to undo the damage her brother wrought wherever he went. But if I said I would lead the kids out, she might never come back to me.

I didn't doubt her ability, her denunciation of her brother, or her denial that she was a traitor. Not anymore. But even she could be hurt. Especially when she couldn't see.

Something in her started to sag as she looked at me and waited. And I couldn't force her decision this time. Not if I wanted her to stay with me if she survived.

Moving my hand from her wrist to her neck, tangling my fingers in her hair at her nape, she breathed in, and her eyes shone as I rubbed a thumb along her cheek, right under her scar.

Here, in the shadow of this putrid hell, I couldn't tell her. I couldn't taint her thoughts with the darkness here. Not if I wanted a shot at forgiveness.

"Come back," I said, my throat tight, unable to say any more than that.

With a nod, she turned out of my grasp, and went back inside.

I shuddered and prayed for the first time I could remember to Gods and Goddesses I didn't even believe in, to the Dragon Kings of old, to watch out for her and bring my Flame home.

Then I turned to the kids, huddled against the side of the building as the snow fell. They shivered in just their clothes, no cloaks except for the youngest, who was swimming in a swath of fabric that must have been the cloak of one of the older kids.

Slipping mine off from under my quiver, I handed it over, and three of the next youngest wrapped themselves in it.

"Let's go. She'll meet us there. We have to be swift and quiet." My voice was little more than the gentle breeze around us, and was swallowed up by the falling snow. But the kids all nodded, and we took off.

Passing the last building in this little town was the most dangerous part, but the kids didn't even whimper. And no one accosted us.

The party at the tavern still spilled out into the square

behind us, and it seemed the noise and the traffic there were enough to distract anyone else that was out tonight.

Steadily, a little bit at a time, we moved through the shadows. The kids were in a tight formation close to me, and my bow never dropped from a ready position.

Finally, we passed the last house, and ran down the path toward the little flat part where we left the horses, our breath fogging in front of all of us.

Every step we took outside of town sent shockwaves through me, shouting that I should turn around, I should get Cinder, I should make sure she survived unscathed. That I should be at her back.

But when the littlest stumbled, I instead put away my bow, picked up the child—who couldn't have been more than four—and ran along with her friends.

Once we got to the horses—who were miraculously still there, and simply lifted their heads at our arrival, throwing their manes to knock the snow away—I put all the kids on their backs.

The littlest, Betsy, I sandwiched between the two oldest. She stretched her cloak out to cover the girl behind her. Jeremiah, the oldest, was up front with the reins, only the horse and the girls at his back for warmth. All I could do was hope it would be enough.

For the other horse, I loaded up the three already sharing my cloak, the oldest of them, Helena, with the reins.

"We have to wait for the Queen," Helena said, sniffing in the cold, but showing no signs she was going to cry.

"Queen?" I asked, and it dawned on me. "You mean Cinder?"

"I know she hasn't had her coronation yet. But she will be. We need to wait for her."

Part of me, the part that still ached at thinking about the plans we made and lost, wanted to explain.

While the part of me that was desperate for that to still be a possibility one day, no matter the obstacles, couldn't tell her otherwise.

But I nodded, and looked down the empty path toward the town. We would wait.

Come back, Cinder, I thought, come back to me.

CHAPTER 27

DESERVING

Cinder

Were they really this cocky?

Making my way through the two rooms in the dark to where the light came through that doorway was easier than searching through the entire building, even if I still couldn't see a damn thing in the dark areas.

After I was done with these assholes, I would take the time to figure out what game Tristan was playing while I made my way to the meeting point. But for now, I shoved it far away in my mind.

I wanted the chance to enjoy this. They would pay.

Even if these people were slaves of my brother, they held children captive. There was no coming back from that.

The hard part was going to be not killing them right away so I could find out what my brother wanted with the kids.

Was it just to lure me out? The same ploy as taking Angeline and Gus? Or did he have some other disgusting reason to target the Shield House kids again and again?

One day, maybe I would figure out how it was possible to hate him and still have so much love for him at the same time. Even as I entered the room where I could see the stone lights dancing through the doorway, I wondered how my brother—the same one who played with me when I was tiny and joked about our parents with me when they were silly or embarrassing—was this person.

No matter what he had done to me, going after kids and buying slaves was so far beyond anything I could have ever imagined.

Crouching down along the wall next to the open doorway so the light wouldn't touch me, I shook off thoughts of Ash, closed my eyes, and entered the cold place. I pushed away worries for Tristan and the kids, and strained my ears for anything going on inside.

Muffled sounds. Something being moved and shuffled around. A thud.

Slipping one of my spikes back into the sheath along my thigh, I tucked throwing knives into each cuff before I pulled the spike again, ready.

"He'll be here tomorrow." It was a woman's voice, concerned and raised.

A grunt in response.

"I'm telling you, though, I saw her. He needs to know she's here." The woman again.

Was she talking about me?

Yes, please. Tell my brother I was here. Tell him his sister hunted him. Maybe that would give him pause. Maybe it would stop him from carrying out his plans.

Even as the thought crossed my mind, I chewed on the inside of my cheek knowing that if I wasn't a deterrent for him before, I wouldn't be now.

How did he expect to keep this all from me forever?

The only plan I could think he had was to have me kill Tristan. And then for Ash to take the throne. Even if he did it with his army, he must have thought he could keep the truth from me. But…then…what? Keep me as an assassin? I couldn't see past that point. He had to know I wouldn't support declaring war on…Amethyst.

Oh, I was an idiot. That was why his plan was to takeover Amethyst right after Onyx. He would say it was in righteous retaliation for the last war and our parents' deaths. Punishing all of them.

And was he planning on lying to me that he would be freeing the Corvid slaves to attack there next?

I shook my head as I tried to make out more of their now-lowered voices and muffled words.

"Paula," a man's voice, familiar enough to send a chill down my spine, made me straighten my back, and open my eyes, "even if Cinder is here, what is she going to do? Not even the terrifying Cinder can make it through all our people to get close enough to him."

His voice was different, dripping in sarcastic condescension. But I knew it.

The last time I heard it was after I killed the people that I thought held him captive.

Brix said someone on the inside, someone who knew which Shield House kid to take along with Gus, told them all about the orphans and my connection to them.

Standing up from my position, too stunned to even try to hide myself, I rounded the corner, and stepped into the light.

More people were in here than I thought.

"Well done," Layton yelled, looking at me from the other end of the room behind six other people who were all unloading boxes full of weapons. "You surprised me."

"And you disgust me," I said, spitting on the ground as the

taste of bile filled my mouth. He truly did nauseate me. "They trusted you."

"They're all better off dead. Just like I was. Your false King isn't a Dragon, and he needs to be replaced."

In the opposite corner, Paula, the slave woman I saw before, cowered behind three large people with the crow burned on their hands.

Other slaves I saw—Fiachra's, anyway, and ones we fought—rarely ever had the burn on their hands. I wondered what it signified. Although it didn't matter.

As soon as one of them moved, they would all die.

"You're wrong, Layton," I said, looking at him now, and wondering how I didn't see it before, that simmering hate that looked too familiar. "My King is more Dragon and more human than yours will ever be. I know more than anyone what Ash really is. Although I'm more than willing to help you remedy that little personal plight, and show you one of my brother's lessons."

Layton's eyes flashed as his lip curled, and he bunched his hands into fists. His entire body filled with rage in a way that left him too open.

Even after training with me at the arena, even after his time in the guard, he was still an amateur, allowing his own issues to get in the way.

I made that mistake myself before.

But now, I knew which side I fought on.

"No one deserves King Ash as a sibling less than you, traitor." Layton's voice rang out in the room. Something in it brought me back to moments when Ash sounded like this.

My shoulders wanted to curl in, my eyes wanted to look down at the ground, my muscles prepared to be hit, and everything in me wanted to avoid a confrontation.

But Layton was not my brother, and I wouldn't be the one getting beaten today.

"Thank you," I said, my voice low and biting.

Layton took a step back, looking toward Paula and the others around the room, and turned into the young man I met at the Shield House.

"What are you talking about?" he asked, his voice wavering.

I grinned and dropped into position with my spikes ready.

"For confirming that I didn't deserve the things he did to me. Here, let me show you some of them."

"Layton," Paula whispered, although if she thought she was just going to run in order to do Ash's bidding, again, she was very wrong.

"She needs to pay," Layton yelled, pointing a shaking hand at me.

His people advanced on me from two sides, pulling short swords and daggers.

Tristan didn't want me to kill everyone. But he wasn't here.

I turned, passing one of my spikes to the other hand, and taking both my knives out, throwing one into the neck of one person coming at me, and one into the eye of another.

While Paula screamed, I readied my spikes in each hand and surged up from the floor, inside one of the attacker's guards and up into their gut, yanking it away with a twist to leave their intestines spilling to the floor.

The coppery tang of blood filled the air, mingling with the screams and gargles in such a way that if there were any ghosts in this cursed building, they would have been awakened.

Another turn, and I slipped my spike between another attacker's ribs.

Behind me, the movement of the air made me drop to the floor and twist, coming up behind another attacker to slit their throat.

Finally, I found myself face to face with Paula, but this time she held two daggers in front of her wide-eyed face.

"Wrong choice," I said with a smile, slamming my spikes into her daggers, the force opening her up.

I jabbed my spike into her throat, the point of it smashing into her vertebrae, and sending a jolt up my arm.

She opened her mouth again and again like a fish, her scream of earlier the only thing haunting this place as the shadow of it leaked out of her.

Yanking my spike away, I turned again, advancing as one of my attackers stepped back while swinging his short sword in front of him. Like that would work.

Crossing my spikes, I caught his sword mid-sweep, and his eyes lit up like now he had the advantage.

But I pulled him in tight, and brought up my knee, driving it home in his balls.

He bent forward.

I used his own momentum to pull my spike from the crossed guard, and impale him in the neck with it.

The next came at me screaming with his sword raised high. I blocked it with one spike, and stabbed him in the heart with the other.

A second later, before I had a chance to move, a blade ran along the leather of my pants on the side of my thigh.

I leapt back, turning to kick it away before it could get to me again.

The woman wielding it stayed low in a crouch, a good grip on her short sword.

With a smile, I launched myself through the air at the other person with us, who raised their dagger in front of their own face in horrified, defensive shock, making it all too easy to slam my spike into their dagger and force it back toward their face.

Another twist of my other hand and they fell to the floor with their abdomen splayed as their wailing joined the dying sounds of the people around them.

Turning back to the woman who cut me, I sheathed one of my spikes, and pulled my short sword.

She circled to my side, and I let her, making note of the practiced way she stepped, and the comfort with which she held her weapon.

In wait, she watched me just as she had as I cut through the room. For once, I actually had someone to fight.

"Come on, then." My voice contained so much joy that she froze for a second, and it was all I needed to come at her with my short sword first, holding my spike back so she didn't think about it.

The woman met my swing with her own, the steel singing as our blades clashed. I led her in a dance clashing blades. But a minute later, as I blocked her sword with my own again, I lifted my spike and drove it home between her ribs, the light in her eyes blinking out before she could register what happened.

Letting her drop to the floor, I looked to the corner where Layton and his stone light were.

But he was gone. Only the stone light remained, sitting on a crate.

SOFTEN

Tristan

It was too cold.

Sometimes snow acted as a blanket, the world frozen, and yet the chill became muted by the way the snow layered over the landscape.

Tonight, though, the kids had long eaten the last of our traveling rations and huddled together, shivering, while I stared down the path and begged the world to give Cinder back to me.

How many people did she confront?

Did someone come upon her in the thick dark that she couldn't see through?

Even blindfolded, she was deadly, but I still broke through more than when she could see.

Just running that exercise through my head made me shiver even though I wasn't cold.

"Come on, Cinder," I muttered into the night, more willing

by the second to drop to my knees and beg, give up everything, or destroy worlds if she came back to me.

She was still an assassin, and I was still a fool.

For her. I would gladly be a fool every day for the rest of my life if I could have her with me.

I dragged my hands through my hair, wet from melted snow, and squeezed my eyes shut before I let the kids know how fast my boiling hot blood flowed through me.

When I opened them again, I sucked in a breath.

The kids muttered in the background, but I couldn't hear them. Her name rang out inside my mind as loud as any explosion.

Cinder made her way down the path, limping.

Running to her side, I checked over every piece of her, desperate to understand where and how bad she was hurt.

She just raised a hand, stopping me in my tracks.

"We have a lot to talk about," she said, no hint of how much pain she was in, "but we need to get the kids to Solaria."

"You're limping." My voice was flat, like there were so many emotions battling for supremacy in me that they blocked each other from coming out.

"It's fine." Cinder gave me a sidelong glance as she moved past me toward the kids, taking off her cloak and handing it to the oldest. "Let's go."

There was no point in arguing, or pressing the issue when the best thing for whatever wound she had was the same thing that was best for the kids: get them to the manor house where her cousin, Solaria, was Lady with an entire guard dedicated to the valley, and connected to the palace and the guard of Onyx.

We made our way through winding paths that didn't really exist, and over bridges that were too small for the horses to be comfortable. They picked their footing carefully after an initial balk.

Cinder brought us toward the valley floor, and she was right about not being able to go through this area without attracting attention.

Every small island we made it to, lights went on in the houses, or people moved the curtains to peer out at us. A few even stepped out of their open doors and stared us down.

The rivers, even this late in the night, still had some people awake on their boats. What they were doing, I couldn't guess. But everyone we passed watched our progress with a careful eye.

Finally, she found our way to a real road. The horses whinnied in response, falling into an easier gait, and we made better time, reaching the manor house before dawn.

Members of the guard acquiesced to our demands as soon as we both introduced ourselves and gave them a good look at our faces, ushering us inside amid the rising cry that the King was there.

Solaria—a woman whom I remembered as breathtakingly beautiful, if thin and small—made her way into the foyer, a sweeping space of wood and stone with a glass chandelier in blues and greens that somehow mimicked the tangle of rivers in the valley floor.

But this woman before me, bent over a cane and taking slow steps, held her head high and her chin sharp, even though she was clearly in pain.

If I didn't know what she survived at the hands of her husband, there would be no mistaking the change in her, or the way she commanded the room and the adoration of the people present.

"Cinder," she said, sagging on her cane and smiling brightly enough to change her back to that breathtaking woman she was when first introduced at court, age and pain falling off of her.

"How are you?" Cinder asked, going to her cousin, and wrapping her arms around her for a moment.

"Better." Solaria leaned back from Cinder, the smile falling from her face. "But what brings you here?"

"Solaria, King Tristan and I need your help." Cinder turned toward me, Solaria following her gaze, her brows rising.

"Forgive me, King Tristan," she said, rather breathlessly, "I did not believe them when they said you had arrived with Cinder and no retinue."

The perfect, formal speech pattern she used reminded me of the world we were on our way back to. One where I was a King first, and a man who wanted to make the woman he loved believe him second.

"No apologies needed," I said. "In fact, please forgive the intrusion. If there had been another way to save the children, we would have taken that path."

She looked past me to the huddled group of kids as they shivered in the remaining cold of the flight from their captivity.

"Children," Cinder and I were forgotten as Solaria made her way to them, showing none of the pain evident when she walked as she crouched down to be on the same level as the youngest among them.

Even in the face of all their trauma, they took to her faster than they had to Cinder, seeing to her core the way only children did.

After talking with them a moment, Solaria began giving out orders.

The assembly of the guard, contact with the palace guard in the area, food, clothing, beds, and turning up the heaters in rooms for the children.

After they hugged us, the children followed after one of the nannies for Solaria's baby, Liberty. Only then did the Lady of Thirteen Rivers Valley turn to me and Cinder.

She wore only a nightgown and robe over it, her hair in a braid, but she was every bit the Lady of the land now. And she wanted answers.

"How bad is it?" she asked, her eyes on Cinder.

Cinder glanced at me, and took a deep breath.

"Ash is a traitor."

The words hung in the air, like a miasma of hate, violence, and the ugliness in us all.

For Solaria, who probably thought her Duke cousin was involved in saving her, even though Cinder wielded the weapon that killed her husband and delivered her to safety, the words must have been a shock.

Mouth dropping open, one fluttering hand went to Solaria's brow.

"Your brother would never...Are you sure?" she asked.

"I'm so sorry, Solaria." Cinder's slip into informal pronunciations made Solaria do a double take my way. But they also seemed to break whatever vision her cousin had of her brother, driving home a dagger into the heart of the person that everyone thought Ash to be.

"Lady Solaria," I said, feeling dawn come closer with every breath we took, and knowing Cinder would suffer in silence until she dropped, "Lady Cinder was wounded in the fight to save the children from Ash's people."

At that, Solaria hustled to Cinder's side, looking over her cousin, who sighed and shook her head at me.

"We will make sure you are informed of all that we have learned on this mission. But we must move quickly if we are to make it back to the Burnt Market in time to intercept him there today."

She nodded and walked away, issuing more orders to her guard and her servants as Cinder came to my side.

"You can't stop me from being in this fight," she said, her voice low and painted in dangerous markers that made me brace myself for a fight no matter what I said. "I need to go with you. And if I need to get my wound seen to, then I don't care if your eye already looks better than it did, I'll make sure you get your wound looked at too."

"Cinder." I dragged my hand through my dripping wet hair, and tried to find the words to explain the way my heart tore me in two.

I didn't want to hold her back, but she was hurt. How would she be able to fight, and avoid a more dire injury? And how could I be sure she could handle being on the opposite side of a battle with not just her brother's forces, but possibly her brother?

"Don't, Tristan." Her voice was strained, and I stared into those eyes, the pain running behind them. "Or are you going to order me to stay out of it?"

How she managed to make her words feel like she slipped one of her spikes into my heart, I didn't know.

As King to his Fighter, I could order her. But she would never forgive me, and I didn't want to be that to her, just another person controlling her life and decisions.

As someone who loved her, I could explain and beg her. But I ran the risk of her rejecting me. I wasn't sure she was ready to do otherwise, and I was *not* ready to let go of my hope.

And as a man, I forfeited all right to ask her to stay back because I did something so stupid that she might already have ceased to see me as anything more than scum.

"I won't order you," I said. She let out a breath, her shoulders relaxing. "But I will ask you, please. If you come with me. Please, be careful."

Her eyes softened, and her mouth curved up a tiny fraction at one corner.

The physick arrived. They fell into conversation as the man knelt next to her and started poking around her thigh.

But even as I turned away to start preparations to make our way back to the Market and whatever we would encounter with Ash, I held on tight to that soft look in her eyes.

CHAPTER 29

LITTLE SISTER

Cinder

Solaria was too good. And this conversation still had to wait.

I hugged her as a thanks for her help, and mounted the horse, my leg wound cleaned, stitched, and bandaged under my pants in such a way that made riding more complicated.

Of course, I carried through with my threat, and Tristan had a pink paste along his eye.

My cousin stepped back, and turned toward the manor. Her steps were slow and careful still, but getting stronger all the time.

The damage Lord Fall did to her body might always have its echoes, but hopefully the wounds would scar over in time. And then, what was one more scar? According to Tristan, it was just a marker of something lived through.

"We're riding directly there?" Tristan asked, mounting up next to me with pieces of armor on that someone outfitted him with, turning his head from side to side as he tried to keep up with the frenetic movements going on around us in preparation to leave.

"No. The main road will only take us so far before it goes in another direction. But with the guard along, they can assist us in getting the locals to use their boats and things."

"Boats," Tristan said, turning to look out at the valley and the increasing number of the flat-bottomed craft dotting the lazy twists of the rivers as we neared dawn.

I couldn't help it. No matter how inappropriate it might be, the skepticism in his voice almost made me smile.

The Captain of the guard gave the signal, and the column began to move, picking up speed once we made it past the gate so we gained some time on the section of road we had.

Riding along next to Tristan, he back in the role of King and I back to being his Fighter, I realized why it felt odd.

Almost every time we went into a battle, side-by-side, back-to-back, or me running headlong after him, it came as a surprise. This time, not only did I know it was coming, but it was against my brother.

My hands tightened on the reins. I forced my legs not to move, and urged the horse to an even greater speed.

I needed to stay with Tristan. My King needed me. But even now, the thought of killing Ash weighed heavy in my mind, and I wasn't sure I could do it.

For years, the cold place welcomed me when I needed to escape. I wasn't sure it would be there for me afterward if I had to be the one to kill my brother.

Praying to my parents would come to an end. Except to ask for forgiveness...

Killing him was heavy, but thinking about the aftermath was even worse.

We made good time, but some distance still from the Market, the first rays of the sun peeked over the edge of the mountain to the East. By the shuffling of feet among the guard as we ran along a bridge from one island to another, I guessed they felt it, too.

Time was running out.

Once we got to the other side of the bridge, I looked at Tristan, at the guards around me, at the pace of every pair of feet in the group. My stomach churned.

Ash wouldn't give us a lot of chances to cut off his progress. This was one of them, and we needed to capitalize.

I might not have been sure of a lot anymore, but I was sure that of all the people here, the only one who was likely to get him to stop and talk, the only one who was likely to be able to buy us time, was me.

"King Tristan," I said, leaning toward him as we climbed into a boat so it could take us across another part of another river.

"Fighter," he said, his voice heavy with apprehension, and his brow lowered.

"This is too slow. We might lose our shot."

A muscle in his jaw flexed, and he scanned the group, assessing the same way I had. But I wasn't wrong.

"Do you have any suggestions," he said, with a gesture to encompass the large mass of people moving through the landscape with us at its head, "because I don't see how to go any faster."

"I can. If I go alone."

He took in a deep breath, and turned away from me to stare toward the rising sun.

Those first rays of dawn alighting on that face made me think of another morning, and I steeled myself for him to tell me to stay, for more anger that I didn't want to carry.

Instead, he turned to me, his eyes a raging green fire as he said, "Come back."

I didn't wait for him to change his mind. I grinned, leapt off the boat as we turned a corner, and ran to the other edge of the little island.

Grabbing onto a swing lift for bringing up large things from the boats, an empty net hanging from it, I kicked off the ground and let it swing me out over the water. Letting go and tucking into a ball, I flew through the air to the other shore, landing in a roll.

Popping up, I had a bridge this time, and I took it at a full sprint.

Running, jumping, even dancing from one boat to the next like floating steppingstones, I left a wake of people yelling behind me as I made my way to the Market as fast as I could.

But even doing that, by the time I was on the lane heading into the square, it was already packed full of people, all of them armed, and all of them arrayed facing me.

I was wrong. I wasn't entering a town. This was a death squad.

My legs stopped running mid-step, and I stood with one foot forward as I pulled the spike on my right thigh and the sword across my back.

"Little sister," Ash's voice rang out over the shuffling of his people standing before me.

"Kids, Ash?" I yelled, hanging on to the list of things he did that might allow me to fight him like I needed to.

"Actually," Layton said, stepping out between two of the people in the line in front of me, playing with the tip of a sword in his hand, a grin on his face and a swagger in his step, "That was my idea."

"Which one of you sick, evil fucks thought it was a good idea to give little Angeline to Brix so he could torture her to death?" I screamed.

The people in the mass in front of me looked to one another, their movements unsure.

"No one knew what Brix was." Ash yelled back from somewhere that I couldn't see.

He might have paid for these peoples' loyalty through lies, manipulation, and all the money he could scrounge up to buy them away from Corvid and Amethyst, but I saw an opening.

"You're a lying coward, big brother. He was a monster, and your best friend since we were small. How did you not know about his mother?"

More shuffling, more disconcerted looks and shaking of heads.

And there he was, my brother, sitting high in the saddle of a horse as the crowd parted for him.

Of course he remained far back, allowing all the bodies of his followers, his fake subjects, to stand between us.

"No one knew. I only learned of what he was from Layton's report." He spat the words at me, the people nodding along when faced with their false King.

"Yes," I yelled, pointing a finger at the traitor in the front as his eyes grew harder and his arms shook, "Layton. The one who told Brix about the orphanage in the first place. The one who *picked her out* for him."

I let these people digest that as I slowly said the words.

Just as they were bought and sold as nothing more than a commodity, she was torn from her home and made a plaything of someone more powerful and more twisted than most of us could fathom.

"He traded her as a way to get to me. Like she was nothing." Every bit of the rage and hate in me poured out of my mouth, and it still wasn't enough to get across even a modicum of the renunciation he deserved.

"But she wasn't nothing. She was a little, innocent soul who deserved better."

The words hung in the air, and finally, the crowd behind

Layton recoiled from him before they shoved him forward yelling and screaming all the same words raging in me.

Raising his sword, he blocked a blow headed his way, but more came at him as he stumbled back.

"King Ash," he wailed.

I darted forward, ignored by the crowd, and grabbed him from behind. I stabbed my spike into his arm, making him drop his sword, and held my short sword at his throat.

"No one will help you now," I snarled into his ear as he thrashed and screamed for my brother.

The crowd stepped back from me but urged me on, yelling for me to kill him.

"Do you hear that, brother?" I screamed and they fell silent, turning toward their coward monarch. "Your own people don't appreciate someone who trades in souls and attacks children."

Cheers. They cheered for that announcement.

Ash, his face only visible between others as the crowd shifted and moved, raised a brow, his mouth twisting in a bitter smile as he nodded once.

For the last time, I followed my brother's instructions to kill.

Sliding my spike back into place on my thigh, I wrapped my hand around Layton's throat and squeezed until he stopped screaming, his hands clawing at my arms, his body bucking and lurching.

Planting my feet, tightening my muscles, I kept up the pressure on his throat, not allowing any of his thrashing to stop me.

"I want you to fucking suffer. Brix went too fast." My rage got the best of me then. I wasn't going to make that mistake twice.

The crowd hushed as I strangled one of their own, whispering the names of the Shield House children, living and dead, into his ear as I did.

Once he turned to dead weight in my arms, a process that took more than a minute but meant he was only unconscious and not dead, I slit his throat and dropped him into the melting snow of the lane.

"Your false King is no better," I yelled, and they stepped further from me, shaking their heads.

"Tell them what you used to do to me, Ash. Tell them what you did to your baby sister when she was still a child."

All hint that he knew how to smile fell from his face as he stared at me through the shifting crowd.

"Maybe I should tell them why you're so loyal to King Tristan," he yelled back.

What was he talking about?

"Because he's a good King, and you're a fraud who beat me and made me kill, told me it was for a good cause. All the while, you didn't use it to help people. You bought them." He didn't get to turn this around on me.

"Oh, a good King. Good in bed you mean."

"Fuck you."

At that, one of his people decided to try for me. I ducked their bad swing, and jammed my sword into their belly, kicking them off the blade when I was done.

"Your King—"

Whatever Ash might have said was cut off as he screamed when an arrow hit him in the shoulder.

The crowd surged, his horse disappeared in the throng, and I slashed and jabbed at anything that moved in front of me, screaming one name over and over, "Ash."

REGENT

Tristan

"Fuck," I muttered, running as I fired another arrow toward Ash on that stupid horse above the crowd. I fired too early, incensed by Cinder fighting one of Ash's people while he looked on.

But now he was in the flat part of the square, and I was still going up the hill, no longer able to see him.

I kept firing. Shooting arrow after arrow into the crowd as Cinder laid waste to any person foolish enough to come within range of her flashing blades. The guard rushed past me, more of them entering the square from the other direction, all focused on decimating Ash's gathered troops.

How many more he had waiting in Amethyst or around Onyx, I had no idea. But for today, the snow ran red in the blood of his people.

My foot hit a body, and a quick glance showed Layton dead at my feet. His betrayal still hurt deep in my heart. But I stepped over him, and kept shooting until our forces were the only ones in the square.

Standing at the edge of the pass to Lehar, Cinder held her sword and her spike at her sides, the blades dripping lurid red onto the melting snow, making it run in little rivulets belying the number of deaths she dealt.

"Cinder," I said, running to her and knowing well enough not to surprise her.

"I can follow him," she said, not turning to look at me, keeping her eyes focused on the gray ashes as they fell on the other side of the pass while the last of Ash's people melted into them.

"Everyone else could get sick if they spend more than a day in Lehar, but I won't."

"No, Cinder, you can't."

Turning her eyes on me, her jaw tight, pain flared in her gaze, and part of me wanted to take it back.

"Lehar needs me," she said. "Ash won't find a warm welcome from our people for his war, and the people would tell the slaves he bought that they're free no matter what he wants. So, they'll need someone to start running the duchy properly, and keep Ash out of the funds. Or are you planning to give the duchy over to whoever your new bride will be?"

"What new bride?" I looked around like the answer to her nonsensical question was somewhere in this square full of the dead and the dying.

"You don't have to pretend. You need an heir to the throne, to the Dragon powers. For that you need a queen. And I need to be Duchess of Lehar. Or are you going to strip me of my title?" She stared at me, her face open and assessing, showing nothing of what she thought about anything she said.

My stomach threatened to paint the snow with the tea I drank with Solaria. Just thinking about marrying for an alliance made my hands shake now that I knew another way existed.

Going the alliance route didn't work for my parents. They were nice enough to each other, but I thought she understood when I made the joke about them having different rooms.

They were never in love. Not really. Just like generations of our Kings and Queens before them, politics overrode any romantic ideas they might have held.

And if she entered Lehar, took up residence in the ruins of her home, and set about the business of ruling it, would I ever see her again, have the chance to make things right?

There was only one way I could think of to keep her with me, and that was a risk.

"I won't find another queen. I meant that. And, yes, you're Duchess of Lehar. But you're also Fighter Cinder, and I need you."

She turned away from me, staring toward her home, and swallowed before she nodded.

Without another word she went back to the square, leaving me at the edge, watching her retreating form move through the blood-stained snow.

Assigning search parties for Thirteen Rivers Valley, and for short trips into Lehar took most of the day, along with updating Solaria on everything happening.

"Can you appoint a regent to begin putting Lehar back together while you are fighting at the front?" Solaria asked Cinder at one point in our unending work.

"Maybe," Cinder said, looking down at her hands that still had dried blood on them. "The hard part is finding someone who has no loyalty at all to Ash. Someone who would kill him on sight and not try to reason with him."

"You do not want to reason with him?" I asked, my voice low, not sure how she would take me even asking the question. He was her brother. No matter what he did to her, she still tripped over his name every time she said it. And choosing to fight next to me did that to her relationship with him. Maybe she blamed me.

She shook her head, turning to look out the window toward the valley.

"If anyone gives him a chance, he could manipulate them into something that could put Lehar at risk. I have no idea how deep his rot spread among the leaders at home. Jocelyn may even fight for him."

Not once had it occurred to me that her trainer—a fearsome warrior according to Cinder, and someone from the Protectorate—would fight next to Ash. But maybe Cinder was right.

"Cinder," Solaria said, placing a hand on her cousin's.

"Meg," Cinder said, shaking off whatever made her seem so far away. "A quick message—the messenger cannot be in Lehar for more than a day—needs to be sent to Meg in the baths at home. I will write it right now."

She got up from the table, and went into the room next to us. I put my hands on the arms of my chair to push myself up and go after her, but more guards came in, forcing my attention away from her.

One of them looked familiar, but I couldn't place him.

"My Lady," he said, stepping up before the others, "I am so sorry, my wife and I just returned. How may we be of help?"

At the word 'wife,' I realized it was the man from the inn we stopped at. He meant his very new wife.

While Solaria asked him some questions, and gave him instructions, I looked to the door Cinder left through.

He had his orders, saluted and turned to go, running right into Cinder as she came back into the room.

"Oh, hello," she said, smiling. "I did not expect to see you here."

"I did not expect to see you either..." he turned, and looked back toward Solaria and I where the guards gave her an update regarding one of their searches. His eyes widened before he looked back at Cinder with his mouth hanging open. "Wait, you are not just Cinder. You are Fighter Cinder."

"Lady. Fighter. I am always just Cinder. And you are my friend, should you or Willa need anything." She grinned and grabbed him to give him a quick hug.

And that was it. The hug. He wasn't just the groom at the wedding we saw. He was the man she was hugging the next morning, and I remained a fool.

I wanted to push everyone out of the room and throw myself on Cinder's mercy, beg her to forgive me my mistakes and foolishness, and love me again.

But instead, she joined us at the table, and we all went back to work, my eyes straying her way far too often.

Finally, after hours of work, we loaded the children into carriages at the edge of the valley. Cinder and I would join them.

The space in each carriage meant that she shared one with half the children, and I shared one with the other half. Even though it left me open to the skies and made the Captain of the guard nearly apoplectic this close to the rest of Onyx and the dangers of Corvids, I watched until the door shut after her.

Lady Solaria, after saying goodbye to her cousin, placed her hand on the window of Cinder's closed carriage door and made her way to me.

"King Tristan, I hope your eye heals soon," she said, and I dipped my head to her.

"No doubt it will. You have any support you need from the crown, Lady." I meant it. All my thanks to her were met with a wave of her hand, but maybe she would be more amenable to some kind of tangible support from the country than my words.

"We appreciate that." She cocked her head to the side and stared at me, direct and unwavering. Whatever else Lord Fall did to her, he couldn't tear her spirit from her. "I want you to know that Cinder loves deeply. She is loyal. And this is hard for her."

"I am trying not to make it worse for her even though she is fighting against her brother. I know she struggles with it."

"That is not what I meant." Solaria smiled a sad version of a smile. "Fighting at your back makes it a challenge for her to forget you."

Solaria turned and walked away to her waiting horse with the canopy of vines on a contraption attached to the saddle, leaving me staring after her with my mouth hanging open.

"My King," the Captain said, hands shaking where they shielded his eyes from the sun. He was unaware of the way his words made my heart ache while I wanted to stop everything and talk to Cinder. "You need to go."

"Yes. Thank you, Captain." I gave him the salute, he returned it, and I climbed into the waiting carriage.

Once we got back to the Obsidian Palace, I needed to find a way to talk to Cinder.

CHAPTER 31

BLESSED AND CURSED

Cinder

Crossing the bridge into the palace, my hands shook.

There was no delaying this. I couldn't back out now and head to Lehar.

It was easier to accept that I lost my friends without facing the spaces in which I had them. It was easier to keep moving if I didn't have to look Gus and Jacquetta in the eye and explain why I protected Tristan and not Madam.

And it was easier not to explain it to myself.

But the light on the other side of the glass went out as we entered the tunnel, and even the fantasy in my head of opening the door and leaping out while the carriage kept going was no longer an option.

Sitting next to me as she had the entire trip, Betsy reached out her little hand and curled it around my shaking fingers.

"Queen Cinder," she said, "don't be scared. Everyone knows queens need baths, too, sometimes."

I smiled and nodded, looking down at the dirt and blood caked all over me as light came through the windows, proving we were past the tunnel.

No matter how many times I tried to remind them I wasn't Queen, they persisted in calling me by that title. And I couldn't bring myself to tell them I would *never* be that.

Words and conversations collected in my body, truths I couldn't force past my lips or allow into the air and outside the raging, bleeding heart trapped in my chest.

Holding onto Betsy's hand, I rubbed my chest with the other as the carriage came to a stop.

The door opened, and, one after another, I helped the children climb out until it was my turn.

Someone reached their hand out, and I took it out of habit. But the second his fingers closed on mine, heat poured through me, and I knew whose face would meet mine when I lifted my eyes from the steps.

My King was back in his palace. The entirety of the people gathered in the courtyard for his return looked on him with the reverence his title commanded, and his character deserved.

And although he wore their attention as he always did, rising to meet it with grace and humility, standing tall and proud even in dirty clothes, in need of a bath, with a split lip and a bruised eye, his eyes were on me.

Eyes that weren't bright green for the first time in too long. Eyes the color of the sun, golden and soft.

I took in a deep breath, not knowing what else to do to keep myself upright, or what it meant that he looked at me that way now.

But the second the air was inside my lungs, before I could say anything or do anything, someone slammed into me, and Jacquetta's scream rent the air, "Gus."

Grabbing on as Gus squeezed me tight, I closed my eyes and let go of Tristan.

"Come inside, right now," Gus said, dragging at me with her odd gait as she made her way up the steps.

Waiting for us inside the massive open doors, Jacquetta stood with her shaking hands over her mouth, her feet shuffling back and forth as she looked between us and the sky and back again.

Making my way up the stairs to her, I tried to formulate what I would say. What could I say that wouldn't make them turn their backs on me?

But once inside the doors, Jacquetta threw her arms around me and Gus, tears streaming down her face.

"Neither one of you is allowed to scare me anymore," she said.

"Star," Gus said, kissing Jacquetta's forehead, "we talked about this. You can't ask that of either of us."

"I can, and I will keep reminding you that the only safe place right now is inside." Jacquetta tugged on both me and Gus, pulling us further into the palace and toward the sweeping staircase to the second story.

"Loving the two of you is going to drive me to an early grave," she muttered, not pausing in her frantic yanking even as the children waved at me while they talked to Tristan.

"Wait," I said, not wanting to pull back and send all three of us tumbling back down to the floor of the foyer, "I need to be here for the kids. And what did Gus do?"

"The kids will meet us all for dinner after they get settled in," Jacquetta said, apparently aware of more than I was about the plan now that we were here.

"And she thinks I go outside too often." Gus rolled her eyes, but her smile at Jacquetta said she didn't mind her fiancée's worry. "You're the one she wants to tie to a chair."

"I didn't think either of you would miss me," I admitted, swallowing as Jacquetta stopped in the middle of the hallway.

Both she and Gus turned to look at me, their mouths hanging open in matching expressions.

"She lost her mind," Gus said.

"Maybe she was in a fight and got hit in the head," Jacquetta said.

"Very subtle." I shook my head and bit my lip, "but I mean it. I didn't keep Madam safe. That was my job. And I saved Tristan instead. I never deserved to be called one of her girls."

"Oh, Cinder," Jacquetta said, a smile tinged in sadness gracing her face as her lip quivered and she took my hand again, hers no longer shaking. "Mom loved you, and you did what she would have told you to do."

"And this is war, Cinder." Gus shook her head at me, her mouth pressed into a thin line. "You can't save everyone no matter how much you want to. She was brilliant. She knew that."

It was my turn for my hands shake and tears to fill my eyes.

"But Madam…and your wedding…and…" I lost control over my tears. They fell down my face in a torrent.

"Shhh, Cinder," Gus said, wrapping an arm around me.

"Mom would tell us not to cry," Jacquetta said, her own tears making silent tracks down her face as she came into the hug as well.

"I'm sorry," I said, my voice thick and wavering, barely getting the words out between sobs.

"No," Jacquetta said, squeezing me tighter.

"There is no reason to be. You didn't force other people to make terrible choices," Gus said, and Jacquetta nodded.

"What about your wedding?" I asked, although it sounded like a little kid whining as I asked through my tears and my hiccupping sobs.

Jacquetta laughed as she cried, and Gus smiled, bumping me with her hip.

"Now that you're here," Jacquetta said, looking at Gus.

"You have a job to do." Gus grinned, as bright as the sun. "Think of it as the last assignment Madam Valentin gave you."

My knees almost gave out. I might have fallen in the middle of the hallway had Gus and Jacquetta not held me up.

I nodded.

"Tell me. I'll do anything she wanted me to."

Gus kissed Jacquetta and wiped the tears away from her cheeks before she broke their hug to keep her arm around me, and pull us all forward.

We got to my old rooms, the Lehar sigil still on the wall, and I sucked in a breath.

"Are you sure staying in these rooms is a good idea?" The room felt both blessed and cursed in equal measure, and I wasn't sure which it would bestow upon me this time.

"Yes. This is our suite," Jacquetta said, her eyes still watery, but her smile soft.

She opened the door, and I was no longer sure if I was in the right place.

Gus pushed me inside, a low laugh she tried to hide behind a hand coming out of her while Jacquetta spun in the middle of a sea of gold fabric to face me, her arms out to her sides.

"Um…" I tried to take it all in and failed.

Every single surface in the room had something gold on it. Flowers. Shoes. Undergarments. Weapons. Swaths and swaths of different fabrics. Gold had spread all over the room like a disease.

"What do you think?" Jacquetta asked.

"Maybe tell me what I'm looking at?" I chose my words carefully, like I was talking to a little kid who showed me their artwork.

Gus lost control of her giggles, passing me on her way to one of the sofas, bent over with that hitch to her gait as she guffawed. Once she reached the sofa, she shoved a pile of fabric to the side and flopped down, some of it still spilling onto her lap.

"I told you she would think this is too much," Gus said between giggles.

"You also told me to do whatever I wanted," Jacquetta said, planting her hands on her hips, and twisting up her nose at Gus, who just kissed at the air in her direction in response.

"And whatever you wanted included redecorating with every gold thing you could get your hands on?" I asked, going to the table where an impressive array of weapons sat, picking up a dagger that I was sad to find wasn't functional, and may well have been for wrapping up hair.

"No, ding dong, this is preparing for our weddings."

She said 'weddings.' Plural.

The dagger dropped from my hand, and clattered on the table as I sucked in a breath.

"Cinder?" Gus asked, leaning forward.

"Rath was supposed to tell you," I said, taking hold of the ring still hanging on the chain around my neck.

"He's been pretty busy." Jacquetta looked back and forth between me and Gus.

"What did he not say?" Gus asked, shaking her head at Jacquetta.

"I...He..." My voice failed me each time I tried to explain.

A deep breath and I closed my eyes, looking at them while I said it made it worse.

"Tristan broke it off. Our wedding, our relationship, everything."

CHAPTER 32

SURPRISE

Tristan

"King," Rath yelled, barreling into my bathroom and tossing a little bag of flowers into the water.

"Rath, man, let me wash off the dirt. And what is this?" I asked, trying not to laugh at him as he boosted himself up onto the sink to sit.

"Lady Jacquetta sent that along for your bruises. And you don't have anything I don't have. You should have waited until after I got to talk to you. Besides, you big baby, I can't see anything from over here." He flung a bar of soap off the counter at my head making me duck and splash water out of the sides. "Spoiled King couldn't stand to be dirty anymore. Just had to take a bath before he talked to me."

I did laugh then, shaking my head, and picking up the bar of soap to scrub off the grime.

"Not my fault you were late. The General caught me up on everything."

"Are you sure she caught you up on *everything*?" he asked, swinging his legs with a smirk on his face like a child with a surprise burning a hole in their pocket.

"Just tell me." The amount of dirt coming off in the water made me question if one bath would be enough.

My friend was silent by the sink far too long as I scrubbed. Finally, I looked over at him and raised my brows in a silent question.

He rolled his eyes and said, "You're no fun right now. Come on, give me a little anticipation. Guess or something."

"Fine. Um, Ash isn't Cinder's brother, and she's free of him completely."

"No, but that would be nice. And I can see where your mind is going, right to your little flame. Just don't get too excited while I'm in here. That might get weird. I'm not into you that way."

I laughed again, moving on to scrub other parts of my body.

"Then...the Corvids lost too many, and are headed home permanently."

He cocked his head, his mouth in a line, and I shrugged.

"A person can hope." I laughed and he sighed. "You didn't say they had to be good guesses."

Moving so he was leaning forward on the counter, hanging on to the edge, his eyes wide, he made me sit up, and give him my full attention.

"Rumor has it that Duke Asshole has a kid."

Of all the things I thought he might say, that wasn't one of them.

"From his wife?" I asked, trying to parse out how long that meant he had been married.

"Damn it," Rath yelled, throwing his hands up and slumping back against the mirror, "who told you he has a wife?"

"Cinder and I met one of his slaves. Remember the man we sent your way?" I scrubbed harder, trying not to think about her or the way that everything she learned that night had hurt her.

"No, the kid isn't from his wife. And the man you sent knew very little I didn't find out other ways."

Looking Rath's way, I kept scrubbing, trying to think through what I knew of Ash.

"She's never said anything about him having a kid."

"What are the chances that he would tell his sister he forced one of his slaves to have his kid, and then sold the baby to the Corvids?"

I dropped the bar of soap with a splash into the water.

"He what?"

"Yeah. Apparently, he thought the kid would jeopardize his investment in his little army."

Surging up from the bath, I sent water sloshing all over the floor. Rath yanked his legs out of the way of the splash.

"Damn, King, that's a strong reaction."

"I…" I was naked. Standing in dripping suds in the bathtub with Rath right there, and there was nothing I could do about any of it. I sat back down, pulling my knees up. "Sorry."

He looked at me from under a furrowed brow, swiping at the water spots on his pants.

"Okay, King," he said after letting me sit a while in not quite enough water while I stared at a droplet making its way down the wall. "Out with it. That was weird."

Partly because it was Cinder's story to tell, not mine, and partly because it made my chest ache and blood burn to tell it, I carefully chose what I said to Rath to explain to him what Cinder endured.

"That worthless pond scum called her his investment as he abused her? His own sister?" Rath's knuckles went white where he gripped the countertop.

All I could do was nod as I turned the tap on the tub, putting more water in. Cold this time.

"So, when are you going to kill him?" Rath asked, crossing his arms over his chest.

He didn't ask when I was going to send him to do it, or when I would attack with the guard. He asked when I was going to kill him.

Everything in me wanted to snap Ash's neck with my bare hands.

The water around me wasn't as cold as I wanted it to be. It did nothing to cool my white-hot blood.

"Rath, if I could, I would drop everything else, and hunt him down like I was Cinder until I could cut his throat. But even that is too quick. I want him to hurt." I dragged my fingers through my hair. They came away dark with dirt.

"Good answer," he said, hopping down from the counter and heading out of the room.

When he got to the door, I finally found the ability to respond.

"You interrupted me in the bathtub for that?" I asked. That could have waited.

He slapped a hand on the door frame, and smiled back at me.

"Nah. I just wanted to catch you off guard so I could figure out if you pulled your head out of your ass yet."

"Rath." I held my arms out to the side and shook my head, my mouth hanging open. What the hell kind of reason was that?

"Good to know you're back together with the little flame," he turned around, and stepped backward into my room.

"We're not." I dropped my arms back down and he stopped moving.

"You act like you are."

All I could do was shake my head, and rub that ache in my chest.

"No." What else could I say? There was too much to explain. Too many things happened on our trip. And if I did have my head up my ass, I only really pulled it out right before we needed to leave the valley.

"Maybe you should be taking care of that, huh?" He raised his brows at me, crossing his arms again.

"I kind of thought it would help my case if I didn't have other people's blood on me." That, and I thought she needed time. There was a lot of repair that I needed to do. I needed to overhaul what she thought of me, and somehow make amends for how I treated her before I even ventured to ask.

Solaria thought Cinder struggled to forget me. Yet I wanted her not only to remember me, but to fall in love with me again.

"You should probably just walk into her room like you are right now." One side of Rath's mouth lifted in a wild grin. "Wet, cock out. What's the worst that could happen?"

I chucked the bar of soap at him, and he ducked, laughing as he left my room.

"Asshole," I muttered to myself as I grabbed another bar, and went back to work cleaning myself.

No matter what Rath said, I needed to do this right. I needed Cinder. I wanted her with me. I wanted her to want me again.

Fucking her with dead bodies in the next room wasn't my best moment, but this next one had to be.

CHAPTER 33

ALTHOUGH

Cinder

I needed Tristan for this. I needed his help, and the comfort of knowing someone supported me as I stumbled through it.

But that version of Tristan didn't exist anymore. Not for me.

There were things I knew, and things I had some kind of grasp on. And then there were weddings.

Ash didn't include weddings in the things he thought were valuable for me to learn, and I always assumed I would never get married. Even after the conversations we already had with Madam about them, I didn't know what my responsibilities were as far as supporting my friends.

Never, not one time, did I think about how much I would need to know to be a good friend when my friends were getting married.

Maybe because I didn't have friends then either.

While I took off my weapons, Gus and Jacquetta followed

me to the bathroom and spoke of weddings and traditions, and what they would or would not be doing. Because without Madam, things needed to be different.

"I wish she were here," I said, slipping off my clothes and starting the bath water.

"Us too," Gus said.

"She is here. She'll be here whenever we need her," Jacquetta said, her smile tinged in grief I wished I had magic to take away.

Gus hitched up her skirts to sit down next to the tub. Her bad leg had a huge boot made of metal on it that looked like armor running all the way up her thigh and curving over her hip.

"What is that?" I asked, pointing to the boot.

"Oh," she grinned and stuck her leg out, turning it from side to side. "This is Jonesy."

"You named a fake leg?" I studied the way this one worked. It was so much more elaborate than Inara's wooden one.

"No," Jacquetta said, giggling and shaking her head at Gus as if they had this conversation already, and she thought her fiancée was adorable. "It's not a fake leg. It's a brace."

"And, of course, I named it. This guy and I are going to be together for a while." Her smile showed no signs that this bothered her at all.

"Your gait, that's why it's different."

"Jonesy and I are still working it out, but without his help I wouldn't be able to walk as much as I do without a lot more pain in my leg. He supports me as I build the muscle back and work through the scar tissue."

"That's amazing." I climbed in the tub, the heat of the water seeping into my bones and all manner of dirt floating away from my skin.

"Duchess Inara's people made it for me at that lighthouse place you all went to."

"You both went to the Lighthouse?" I smiled, but Gus shook

her head, cutting her eyes toward Jacquetta whose own eyes were wide and staring toward my bedroom.

"No. She brought me the boot. We don't…" Gus looked to Jacquetta, taking her hand and squeezing it, "go out much anymore."

Jacquetta shuddered and sat next to Gus, tucking herself into her side, her eyes downcast.

I looked at Gus who frowned, and wrapped an arm around Jacquetta.

"None of us should go outside for a while," Jacquetta muttered to herself.

So she didn't get better while I was gone. If they were never angry with me, if they didn't blame me for Madam's death, did I make Jacquetta's fear worse?

Gus and I made eye contact, and I mouthed, 'I'm sorry.'

With a bite of her lip, she nodded, and leaned her head on Jacquetta's.

The water washed away the stains from battle and the grime of travel, but it didn't manage to wipe away the pain I inflicted on my friends.

After a time, I started to scrub away the deeper dirt.

In silence, Gus and Jacquetta began to help me. They washed my hair, careful to untangle it as they went.

"We need to hurry, and get you ready for dinner with King Tristan," Jacquetta said, finally breaking the silence and letting me take a full breath even if it wavered and stuttered.

"And for tonight," Gus said, wiggling her eyebrows, "this is the perfect chance to fix the broken parts."

"Tristan and I won't be staying together tonight," I said, chewing my lip and holding onto the ring dangling along my chest.

"Cinder? Don't you want to work through it?" Jacquetta asked.

Explaining how complicated it all was to them required the

cold place, and by the time I finished, Gus emptied the tub and refilled it again, the water had gone cold, and I was no closer to being clean.

"So, you are still in love with him," Jacquetta said, slowly, carefully as she washed my hair again.

"And you just need to know if he's still crazy about you, too," Gus said, with a chipper tone in her voice that made me narrow my eyes, and run through our conversation again.

"Gus?" Jacquetta asked, her face mirroring what mine must have looked like, baffled.

"Pretty easy," Gus said, handing me a scrubbing cloth with Jacquetta's special soaps on it.

I looked at the cloth and opened my mouth to ask another question, but she raised a finger in the air, pointed it at the cloth, and then at my body.

Laughing, only because I didn't know what else to do, I scrubbed my skin.

"Flower," Jacquetta said, running her fingers through my hair, "please explain to me what is so easy."

"After dinner, ask him back here to talk war or something, and kiss him. You'll get your answer." She beamed, and I snorted.

"Sure, if I want the answer to be, 'Ew, traitor's sister, go away.'" I shook my head and started in on the rest of the bathing process.

"It would work on me." Gus rolled her eyes. "If Jacquetta and I were in a fight, all she would need to do was kiss me, and I would know I was where I belong."

Jacquetta leaned in to kiss Gus, touching her cheek and whispering to her.

While I kept busy in my bath, my mind remained heavy with the weight of the possibility that Tristan could tell me I was wrong. That he wasn't mine anymore. I wasn't going to be his.

As much as I wanted to follow Gus' suggestion, to just run to him and kiss him, beg him to forgive me for lying, and be with me, the hammering of my heart told me I needed to take it slower than that.

Somehow, I needed to keep up our constant company until he agreed with me, until he realized he was where he belonged, too.

That plan seemed like a good enough idea out on the road, but at the palace...my hope diminished as I thought about the distance between us right at that moment. Distance enough that it was already a barrier.

After I finished with the bath, completely clean, smooth, and soft for the first time in days, Gus and Jacquetta helped dress me as they changed and prepared alongside me. My stitches were re-bandaged with Jacquetta's special herbs and flowers, even though the wound already looked better after my bath.

While they dressed in hellfire green with gold accents—the perfect couple preparing for their wedding—I wore Tristan's crimson red.

My hair was in an intricate, braided style with loose curls hanging down, and the dress had long, velvet sleeves. But the back was open all the way to where scoops were gone from the sides showing the edges of my abdominal muscles. The neckline was high, but the silk of the front made my breasts look as if I wasn't wearing anything on top at all, and the line of silk down the back of the skirt did the same for my ass, while the rest of the skirt was velvet.

It was beautiful with just enough sexy to be exactly what I wanted to wear to see him again this way, as Lady Cinder... Duchess Cinder.

"He named me Duchess of Lehar," I muttered into the mirror.

"And you're just now mentioning that?" Jacquetta asked, dropping her hand from where she pinned a golden star and flower gem-covered comb in her hair.

"What was his other option? Leave Ash in charge of the hell-fire mines?" I laughed without humor and shook my head. "Besides, it's a smart way to keep me in line, and close enough that he can keep an eye on me should I turn traitor."

"Cinder," Gus said, cringing in the mirror.

"You're creepy when you do that," Jacquetta said.

I looked back and forth between them in the mirror. My friends still managed to look like I was scary, but they weren't scared *of* me. It made me love them even more, and wonder how I got so lucky.

"How is that creepy?" I asked, smiling.

They looked at each other, having some discussion with their eyes that made me realize I wasn't going to like this conversation.

"Listen, we love you," Gus said, a statement that, even though the feeling was mutual, made all the hairs on my body stand on end.

"But you remind us of someone else when you do that." Jacquetta's voice was small, and she looked like she was bracing herself for me to take that hard when her words weren't that bad.

I shook my head, still not understanding.

"You get very calculated and creepy," Gus said, lifting her chin and squaring her shoulders, "and it makes us think of what you've said about your brother."

CHAPTER 34

SOON AS POSSIBLE

Tristan

I paced back and forth in front of the door to the dining room, not sure if this was smart or not.

But I needed to see her, gauge her reaction, and maybe even try to…Shaking my head, I stretched my hands out at my sides.

"King Tristan," Second Prince Nevan said, freezing me in place. "You look…" He narrowed his eyes, one hand playing with the lace along his throat, the rings on his thin fingers flashing. "Well," he waved a hand and stepped past me toward the door. "I'm sure jitters are normal before weddings."

He rapped on the door. It swung open as he smirked at me, and I tried to gain control over my brain before I spoke.

"Forgive me, Prince Nevan," I said, stepping to his side as we walked through the door, my strides longer than his because of his heels, "I was not aware you were still in Onyx."

Prince Nevan lifted one corner of his mouth in that smirk that made me stiffen by his side, and wish he were gone.

"My King and Queen believe that it would be prudent to remain here should Onyx need our help. As allies." He tipped his head my way, and I returned the gesture.

Even if I didn't trust his reasons, sending him away without cause wasn't good for our fledgling alliance. And I had questions for the Second Prince of Amethyst.

"We also assume that when the new Queen of Onyx is crowned, the coronation will be the international affair of the year."

"Speaking of international affairs, and our alliance," I said, stopping in my tracks and making him stop as well to avoid being rude. It was an added bonus that it took us away from the conversation about the breakdown of my plans to marry Cinder.

Prince Nevan smirked at me, and raised a brow, conceding the point to me.

"I have come into some intelligence that involves a member of the Amethyst nobility that I must discuss with you."

Everything about his cocky face froze, like he didn't know where this was going, and it made his brain implode as he tried to find the best way to play the situation without any warning of what it might be.

"King Tristan," Betsy yelled, barreling across the dining room at me in a pretty little party dress, clean and cared for. The rest of the children poured in through the open doors, all similarly ready for dinner.

"Hello, Betsy," I said, bending down, and scooping her up into my arms.

Prince Nevan looked horrified. He reared back, stumbling in his heels.

"Are you alright, Prince Nevan?" I asked while his head

whipped from side to side, his eyes widening as he took in the children.

"My apologies, King Tristan," he said, tipping his head, "I must go. Afraid I am not well."

He turned and fled back through the doors we entered through.

"Why did the big man run away? He looked funny purple." Betsy said.

I turned back to her, but she watched Prince Nevan's hasty retreat.

Big man? The Amethyst Prince was a lot of things, but he was not what I would ever describe as big.

Cinder said something was odd about him. And that time he slapped me on the back, he was stronger than he looked.

Maybe Betsy just had the ability to see his hidden strength more than I did. Or maybe anyone would be big to such a small child.

"King Tristan," Betsy said, putting her little hand on my cheek and turning my head toward the other set of doors, "look. Now she looks like a queen."

Near the other doors, crouching down to hug one of the children crowded around her, Cinder looked up, her eyes finding mine.

The smile on her face for the children turned into one that didn't cover the somber look in her eyes. She stood in a red dress that only made her presence feel even more like home to me. The way it hugged her body made me want to take her in my arms.

She did look like a queen.

Every bit of her strength and the way she moved like a blade singing through the air in a perfect swing remained when she was in a gown. But something about the trappings of the finery, the hair, and the makeup made the woman wielding her lethality like a shield more obvious.

Gods and Goddesses, she was beautiful.

"Are you sick?" Betsy asked, putting her little hand back to my face and pulling it away fast, looking down at her fingers. "You're very warm."

I set the little girl down and smiled, "No, I am not sick. But I think you might be a little furnace."

She giggled and we started toward the others, my eyes unable to look anywhere but Cinder.

Betsy called her a queen. My chest ached to have her be mine. Tonight, though, wasn't the time. Not while we were surrounded by everyone. I didn't even think I would get a chance to speak with her.

And this wasn't a conversation I wanted to have with everyone listening, watching, judging. People didn't tend to like seeing their King on his knees, prostrating himself before anyone, even if that person deserved the world.

Making my way to stand before her, surrounded by the kids who didn't notice the thunder happening in my chest as my heart hammered at me, I didn't know what to say. What to do.

Once, being this close to her was easy. Now, it was torture. Not because she was any less perfect, or being around her was any less good. It was because I wasn't allowed to revel in her presence.

With Cinder mere steps away from me, I couldn't reach out and even take her hand to lead her to her seat.

"King Tristan," she said, dropping into a curtsy, looking up at me for a moment before she slowly stood tall again.

I swallowed and gave her the salute she earned as a Fighter, again, marveling that I was so angry and so hurt that I set it all aside, everything she did for me and for the country.

She looked down at her hand where it held something on a chain around her neck.

Augustina and Jacquetta took her other hand, and led her to the table. The General, her face in a perpetual state of something between mourning and shock since Madam Valentin's death, met them there with warm embraces.

With half my attention on the myriad of stories the children were telling me, and half on the way Cinder's hands shook as she spoke in low tones to General Pace, I tried to formulate a plan.

How would I make her my hellfire Queen? How would I avoid losing her to this war, to her duties to Lehar?

But the loudest question ringing in my mind as I smiled and played with the children and found our seats, was how would I get her alone to apologize? And what would she do after that?

"My King," she said, halfway through dinner. My head snapped in her direction, my blood on fire, and every muscle in my body stilled.

"Yes, Duchess Cinder?" My voice sounded too low and too grating to my own ears, but it was only because I didn't know how to speak when she said that. It was one of many things I missed her saying, but now it meant something wholly different. And made my chest ache.

She opened her mouth to speak, closed it, and looked down at her plate.

"Would you still be willing to perform the wedding ceremony for my Ladies?" she asked, the plate in front of her instead of me, and the looks on Jacquetta and Augustina's faces made me smile even as I wanted to drag Cinder away and explain, just so she would look at me.

"Of course. When would you like to have the ceremony?"

They beamed, Jacquetta grabbing onto Augustina's arm.

"As soon as possible," General Pace answered for them.

"But, General, there is so much to do with the guard," Jacquetta said, glancing at the children when she didn't use the word war.

"Love should not wait for the end of struggle," General Pace said, her eyes watery, "not when it is what gets us through."

I still didn't know exactly what her relationship was to Madam Valentin, but I could guess what her feelings were. I recognized the unique pain.

Turning my gaze to Cinder, meeting her eyes as she rubbed the end of the chain against her chest, I said, "You are right, General."

CHAPTER 35

HOLDING ON

Cinder

"Duchess," Tristan called after me as I wandered down the hall toward my rooms after dinner, trailing behind Gus and Jacquetta.

I stiffened. Hearing him call me that would never feel normal, but I turned his way.

Out of the corner of my eye, I took note of Gus and Jacquetta stopping in the hallway ahead of me, waiting for some kind of signal that they should stay or go.

But I couldn't give them one.

Not when I wasn't sure what he wanted from me.

He strode toward me, delicious in his formal jacket with lace, even if he went the way of long pants instead of hose, and flat shoes instead of the heels that hurt his once broken foot. The pants were so tight. Were they painted on? I had to school my face not to give myself away.

Tristan wasn't ready to know how much more difficult this was for me than our days on the road.

Being here, surrounded by memories of us together, preparing to sleep in a bed we once shared, tore into my chest with each beat of my heart.

"Pardon me, Duchess Cinder," he said when he reached me, with that soft smile and his eyes their natural, mercurial hazel that made it hard for me to breathe, "I know I am keeping you from well-deserved rest."

When he paused, as if waiting for some sign from me, I dipped my head in recognition, although I doubted that I would find much sleep. Restful or not.

"I…" he looked past me and smiled, that open and friendly smile he wore most often, lifting a hand. "Lady Jacquetta, Lady Augustina, may I speak with you?"

He didn't want me.

Again.

Turning, Gus and Jacquetta walked toward us, looking at me with their eyebrows high yet smiles on their faces.

"After the conversation at dinner tonight with General Pace," he said by way of hello, "I want to ask you all if you would like to have the wedding the night after tomorrow."

Gus and Jacquetta looked at each other. Gus didn't seem convinced, but Jacquetta beamed.

"Only two days?" Gus asked.

"I thought tomorrow would be too fast to prepare every-thing," Tristan said, an apologetic quirk to his mouth.

"We can do that," Jacquetta said, nodding and almost bouncing as she tightly gripped Gus' hand.

"You can, of course, make any use of the Obsidian Palace you wish. And should you need anyone brought from anywhere in Onyx, let me know, and I will try to make that happen."

"Thank you, King Tristan," Gus said, smiling and shaking her head as Jacquetta made a high-pitched noise in the back of her throat.

"Now we have a lot of work to do," Jacquetta said, "Thank you. Goodnight."

She dragged a laughing Gus toward our rooms, and left me alone with Tristan in the hallway.

"First, Madam Valentin's funeral, and now their wedding?" I turned back to him and smiled. The fact that I missed her funeral hung in the air. It was one more thing I wasn't prepared to think about. "You are going to fast become their favorite person."

"Perhaps who you love matters to me," he said, and I couldn't breathe, the air leaving my body in a rush that left everything in me tensing up.

"Thank you for being kind to them. They deserve it."

"Yes."

Was he still talking about them? Was he trying to say something nice about me?

Oh, I didn't know. I couldn't think.

If I guessed, and I was wrong, how could I recover from it? But if he was doing this for me...could I finally have him back?

"May I walk you to your room?" he asked, his voice low and as liquid soft as the silk on my dress.

Nodding, I turned toward my door, but he stepped to my side and held out his arm, allowing me to tuck my shaking hand into his elbow for him to lead me back to my room.

So many times. We did this so many times in the past. It meant something different before, but the meaning of it this time flitted from my ability to grasp it.

I should have been able to guess, but instead I second-and triple-thought his every move and mine as we made eye contact and walked side by side down the hall.

"Will the children be returning to Shield House?" I asked.

"Yes. They all want to go back. The guards there have very

specific instructions, and there are more of them now. But it will help me sleep tonight to know that at least some of them are here tonight, safe."

At my door, he opened it for me, and I slipped my hand from his elbow, my hand cramping as if it didn't want to let go of him.

Turning back to him in the doorway, I swallowed as I looked into those ever-changing eyes, and tried to lock his image away in my mind. Just like he was. Right then. So I could look at him while I slept tonight.

"Duchess Cinder," he said, my new title still sounding as awkward for him to say as it was for me to hear, "please tell me if you need anything in preparation, too."

"I will." What I needed was him. But that was the one thing I couldn't ask for. "And when will we be meeting again regarding the war effort?"

War. That was, again, the easier topic for me to discuss. Somewhere in the process of the last seven years, I became very fucked up in what I was and was not comfortable talking about, and why.

"Should anything new come up in that regard, I will make sure you are notified." He nodded, sighed a heavy sound that filled the air with defeat, and turned around and walked away.

Closing the door behind him, the second it clicked into place, I sagged, dragging in breaths, my legs going weak.

No matter what happened one minute, the next I didn't understand what was going on anymore. The way he just nodded and walked away, it shattered whatever I thought was happening moments before.

"Cinder?" Jacquetta yelled for me from her room.

"Yes, let me just change into a nightgown, and I will be right there to help." Whatever work they needed to get done to prepare for their wedding, maybe it would at least be a good distraction for a while.

My friends deserved better than me.

While I changed, I held onto the ring hanging from my neck, until I stood before my mirror in my nightgown.

The braids in my hair were undone, leaving it hanging down around me. The ring on the chain was warm from my hand, and I stared at my reflection, trying to tell myself I should do it.

If I was going to be able to focus on Gus and Jacquetta for the next two days with the singular purpose I used to have for my missions, I couldn't afford to think of anything else. I didn't have the ability to think about my own heartbreak while I helped them prepare for the great celebration of their love.

Selfishness needed to be something I changed, regardless of whether or not it would get me any closer to having Tristan back.

He made me the Duchess of Lehar.

And that title came with responsibilities.

Chances were, I would help with their wedding, fight in the war, win the war, and then go home, saying goodbye to Gus, Jacquetta, General Pace, and Tristan.

Pain wracked through my body in shaking, uneven jolts and waves as I slipped the chain from around my neck, holding the ring tight in my fist until I set it all down on the vanity and turned around.

For now, it would remain there, while I spent my time looking after my friends. Before I had to tell them goodbye.

CHAPTER 36

TOO TIGHT

Tristan

I couldn't breathe. The air was too thick. My heart beat too fast, sending the sound of blood rushing through my body into my ears. This damn formal wear was too tight.

Standing in front of the main doors to the palace, the grand foyer festooned in gold and transformed from a place of arrivals, diplomatic moments, and the in-between of people going from one section of the palace to another, into a place of happiness, light, matrimony, and my personal nightmare.

Augustina's family, who were all apparently now living at Madam Valentin's home in Bridgeton, were sitting in the arrayed chairs alongside the Second Prince of Amethyst, Rath, Duchess Inara, and more royals. It was a unique mix.

Part of me wondered if anyone in the room knew that Rath —who actually dressed for the occasion and looked like any other dignitary that came to the palace—was a pirate and a spy for me.

But I could barely look at the people sitting and chatting.

Cinder would be coming out of the hall to the throne room any second.

And I wasn't supposed to turn that direction to watch her.

My role for today was to stand here looking toward the grand staircase the brides would be coming down, and perform the ceremony.

Eventually, I would be able to join everyone in the festivities after. But Cinder and her Ladies had sequestered themselves for the last two days, only speaking to those they needed to coordinate with to make this happen.

I wasn't one of those people.

The Chamberlain, whom Cinder didn't even like, spent more time with her the last two days than I did.

Just the expectation of seeing her meant my blood burned inside my body, and my heart thrashed around in my chest, both waiting for her presence to find equilibrium.

Where was she?

But then I felt it.

Where I struggled to pull in a full breath moments before, I could fill my lungs now.

The riot in my body calmed from the raging of a building inferno to the steady flame of a hellfire water powered furnace.

Finally, the muttered conversations among those gathered around settled into quiet attention.

She was here.

Keeping my eyes forward was an act of will. If she wore the traditional gold, even an accent of it, I might fall over anyway.

General Pace came into my field of vision first as she escorted Cinder, who was on her other side with the box in her hands.

They walked to the bottom of the stairs, and turned to head to the point where the stairs split, one side going to the royal wing, and the other to the wing where Cinder's room was.

I watched Cinder walk away from me, each step the gliding of graceful power.

Her dress from the back had no gold. It was silver. Long and flowing. The skirt of it trailed up the stairs behind her, making her long form seem to go on forever.

The fabric seemed to be layers of sparkling, transparent material, as if she were the physical manifestation of half the dreams I had of her. There were sleeves, off the shoulder, which she hated, and billowing in a single layer of the same fabric. But in the back of the tight-fitting bodice, it laced up with chains, her skin showing between the pulled-tight panels, and in between the delicate, shining silver chains.

Just thinking about dancing with her, being able to feel her skin between the chains, made my hands heat.

Cinder's hair was piled on her head in curls with one long one hanging down on one side, and I wanted to pull it all free, feel the strands run through my fingers.

General Pace and Cinder turned to each other, the General placing a hand on the box and closing her eyes, something that wasn't part of the traditional ceremony. Then she took a ring out of her pocket, kissed it, and put it on her own hand.

She embraced Cinder, who hugged her tightly, before she turned and headed down the stairs to stand to my left.

I wanted to look down and see the ring she put on, to see if it was some kind of representation of what I thought it was.

But my duty was simple, and it now involved doing one thing I would never be upset by: staring at Cinder.

Augustina and Jacquetta appeared at the same time at the top of the two staircases.

Of course, when the Chamberlain asked me if Augustina could use the royal wing's staircase, I said yes.

She was beautiful, her full ballgown a rich gold that made her look like a sunrise when paired with her red hair.

Jacquetta on the other hand, was also beautiful and also in

gold, but she wore a body-hugging dress in pale gold gems that shimmered when she walked. With her dark skin and hair, she looked like the sunset.

Matching each other's pace down the stairs, they met in the middle on either side of Cinder.

Cinder turned around then, sticking out her elbows so Augustina and Jacquetta could each put a hand on one of her arms, holding their matching bouquets of white flowers in their other hands.

If the brides were the sun rising and setting, then Cinder in her silver gown was the moon that filled the sky between them.

They were all so beautiful that it was hard to look at them now.

Here we all were at a wedding, and instead of Jacquetta and Augustina leading Cinder to me to marry, she led them to me to perform their ceremony.

When we all discussed it before, I knew this day would come before our wedding. But at the time, I was still sure that Cinder and I would have a wedding.

After making their slow procession down the stairs and across the foyer to where I waited with the doors behind me, the black covered in massive swaying panels of gold fabric, they stopped.

"Duchess Cinder Ahmya of Lehar, do you know the two people with you?" I asked, my voice ringing out in the room, bouncing off acoustics made strange by the swaths of gold. But I managed to say her name without stumbling on it, so I stood a little easier.

"May I present," she said, turning to look at one and then the other, filling the roll of Madam Valentin and Augustina's parents for the day as they had requested, "the Lady Augustina Rivers of Onyx, and the Lady Jacquetta Valentin of Onyx, two people I personally know."

"And do you know them both to be willing and consenting

to this marriage?" Yes. The entire crowd could see how they beamed at each other. But it was tradition.

From the time of the Dragon Kings, the consent, and the witness to consent, were the most important parts of the wedding in most of Onyx.

"Yes." Her pronouncement was loud, and the waiting room cheered, so her follow up, spoken softly with her eyes no longer on mine, barely registered with anyone but those of us up here. "I do."

I sucked in a breath, taking the ring box from her as I was supposed to. But my hands shook, and I almost dropped it just from the force of hearing her say those words. Even if she said them to the floor.

She stepped to my right side, the mirror position to General Pace who held her hands out for the box.

Turning her way, I gasped and swallowed on air, trying to retrieve my bearings.

Placing the box on her hands, I met her eyes and she smiled. It was the first one I saw form on her face that wasn't colored by her sadness.

Looking down at the ring on her finger, I finally saw what was on it.

Unlike what many in the guard did, it wasn't names. It wasn't rank, which would also be fitting for someone of her place.

And even though Madam was gentry, she didn't have a sigil.

Still, I knew that the bridge of flowers was Madam's symbol, and the sword was the General's.

If General Pace could get through this day, I could.

Lifting my eyes back to her, I smiled back, and let go of the box.

CHAPTER 37

LUCKY

Cinder

After General Pace gave them their rings, and they made their vows, Gus said her 'I do' in gold, lace-covered satin that made her voluptuous curves the star of her side of the ceremony.

She grinned and laughed through most of the vows, but for her 'I do,' she was as serious as her love of Jacquetta.

Jacquetta said her 'I do' in pale gold that made her statuesque frame the star of her side. She giggled and beamed through most of her vows, leaning toward Gus. But when it came time for her 'I do,' the smile was sprinkled with tears of happiness.

They were what everyone was told a couple was supposed to be on their wedding day. Beautiful, thrilled, and wildly in love.

"You may start your path as a married couple with a kiss," Tristan announced, and they flung their arms around each other, their kiss enough to put a blush on Gus' little cousin's face as the assembled guests cheered.

Rath was the loudest and most obnoxious of them all. Which didn't surprise me.

I *was* surprised when he jumped over the person sitting in the chair in front of him, ran up to my friends, and picked them both up in the air as he whooped and twirled them around.

Tristan, General Pace, and I all flailed in their direction.

"No."

"Put them down."

"Don't drop them."

But as he set them back on the floor, Jacquetta and Gus both laughed louder than anything we yelled.

Their laughter was like unlocking the rest of the guests, and everyone swarmed to the space in front of the massive main doors.

Stepping out of the melee of well-wishers, I walked over to the doors to the ball room where the party would happen, more than happy to get out of the limelight, and let it belong to my friends as it should.

Of course, I didn't have to wait long before someone joined me on the outskirts of the loud congratulations.

Rath made his way over to me, and slung a heavy arm over my shoulders.

"Did you just do that so you could get your hugs in first?" I asked.

"Come on, Flame, don't give away my secrets." He winked at me, but I froze when he called me by that nickname.

"You should talk to him, you know?" He squeezed my shoulder, jostling me around.

"Maybe I should get a drink," I said, and he laughed, releasing me. Then he put two fingers in his mouth, and let out the most ear-splitting whistle I had ever heard, making me cringe.

"Time to lift a glass to the happy couple," he yelled.

Everyone smiled. Gus and Jacquetta were somehow pushed

to the front of the group, and they led the way, hand in hand, into their party.

It didn't take long for the servers to get glasses into everyone's hands, including their own as tradition dictated.

"Long and happy lives," we all sang out together, our glasses in the air. "Together as a pair. Well matched, well chosen, and well loved."

Glasses clinked together all over the room. Rath managed not to break either of ours as he touched my glass with his, and the server on my other side grinned when she touched her glass to mine.

"Congratulations." I drank my glass down in one long drink, serious when I told Rath that I needed it.

Whatever possessed me to say 'I do' to Tristan…No. That was a lie I couldn't even tell myself.

I knew what made me say it. The visions running through my head that made me wear this dress, the same ones this dress inspired when I first saw it, Tristan and I in our own ceremony.

Just once. I needed to say it just once.

Now, no matter what happened, if I died in this war, under Jocelyn's blade in a fight against my brother, or even of old age in Lehar as the unmarried Duchess, I would at least have that moment to play back in my mind as the life left me.

As soon as it wouldn't be noticed, I took another glass from a passing server and tossed that one down, too.

But looking up from my empty drink, I caught the eyes of Second Prince Nevan on me.

Shit.

The last thing I wanted to do was go rounds with him through political doublespeak, or worse, things he knew about me that I didn't want him to know.

And I didn't want his sympathy right now. I didn't want anyone to ever feel sorry for me. For him to do so for this, it just made it worse.

"Duchess Cinder," he said, coming to stand in front of me.

"Hello, Prince Nevan. I was surprised you took the time to come to this wedding. You must be very busy." Code for, please leave. Not that he listened. He just gave me that crooked grin.

"Of course. Your Ladies are delightful." He took a slow sip of his glass, studying me over the rim.

I took it as my cue to set my empty glass down on the tray of a passing server, and take another, the wine already starting to make my body lighter. Although, I was a long way from being fuzzy at the edges. Which meant I had a lot of drinking to do.

"Yes, Prince Nevan," I said, turning back to him with a smile, "they are wonderful."

"Since meeting you, I have discovered you are very lucky in your friends."

"That is true." I looked over his shoulder to where Gus and Jacquetta were holding court, sitting in golden chairs that the Chamberlain had assured us the palace possessed. I had only partially believed him.

Not even having Nevan in front of me kept the smile off my face as I looked at my friends.

"Maybe not so lucky when it comes to the family you were born into," he said.

Every muscle in my body tensed, and I slowly dragged my gaze back to him.

"What do you mean by that?" I asked, curling my free hand into a fist around the ring hanging around my neck again and down into my cleavage, my other hand tightening on the glass as I raised it to my lips.

"All I mean, Duchess," he put heavy emphasis on my new title, and I narrowed my eyes, wishing for Fighter Cinder's clothes and her spikes strapped to my thighs, "is that it is difficult for those of us who were not blessed in that arena to deal with the challenges they present to us simply by the accident of birth."

He…spoke as if he were talking about himself. As if he, too, were somehow labeled a traitor because of his family.

I took a sip of my drink and it dawned on me.

Nevan spoke that way because he *was* labeled a traitor due to the family he was born to.

My brother was a traitor to his country. Some people would think me guilty by association no matter what I accomplished as Duchess or as Fighter.

But Nevan's parents, and his brother, as monarchs of a slave trading country were traitors to all of humanity. And some people—I used to be one of them—would think him guilty by association.

The smile on my face this time was for him, as was my nod.

"Well said," I lowered my glass and my fist unclenched from the ring, dropping back down to my side, "friend."

His crooked grin turned into a beaming smile, and he nodded back, his eyes going soft.

"On that score," he dipped his head and leaned to whisper as he walked by me, "I am the lucky one."

Prince Nevan had surprised me more than once, but this was the first time he almost brought me to tears.

I took another drink of my wine, and, when I looked up, I found myself staring at Tristan as he stared back at me.

Maybe I could talk to him tonight. Maybe I was ready.

Rath popped up right in front of me, and I startled back, almost spilling my drink.

"Careful," he said, "that's good liquor. If you spill it and one of my crew found out, you likely would never be allowed on my ships. And I still owe you a sail."

"Yes, you do. Although, I would blame this spill on you if they asked."

He opened his mouth in mock shock, and placed a hand on his heart while I laughed.

"Let's dance, Flame." He grinned, rubbing his hands together like we were going to eat a good meal.

"Dance? With you?" I shook my head, but I threw the rest of my wine back, and put my empty glass down on a tray of a passing server while he whooped.

"What dance are we going to do?" I asked, walking toward the open area of the ballroom. The musicians played the tail end of a valz.

"Have you ever heard of the ancestor's pairing?" He raised his brows, and smirked at me out of the corner of his eye.

"Of course, but that's not a dance." It was one of the regular training sets that any expert short sword user trained with.

"Yes, it is. If you don't intend to kill with it." He tossed me a dagger he pulled from somewhere and twirled one of his own.

I grinned, testing the feel of it in my hand.

"With daggers? You don't do it with short swords?"

He turned around and set himself into the first stance of one of the sides of the movement.

"I do it with any weapon I have handy."

Dropping into a crouch with the dagger pointed down along my side and my other arm extended, I couldn't wipe the smile from my face.

"Good to know."

With a point at the musicians, a kind of shanty started up, one I recognized from taverns.

My laugh was loud as I shook my head.

The steady beat that increased incrementally over the course of the song was the perfect tempo for the ancestor's pairing, and I couldn't believe I never connected the pace of the two before in my head.

Circling each other, our feet landing in time to the music, we went through the first turns, parries, and thrusts, avoiding each other's blades.

But as the music picked up, so did we, and our blades clashed together in perfect time to the rhythm.

He started to sing the bawdy words that went along with the tune, and I laughed as we twirled and lunged, striking our daggers harder and harder against each other.

Finally, the part I was waiting for came, and I picked up my skirts, doing a move that no one but those of us who fought with Jocelyn had ever seen. It flung my skirts into the air while I moved faster than most people ever trained to. It created the illusion that my entire body was twisting through the air in a spiral, and when I stopped, it was still in perfect time, with my blade slamming against Rath's.

My breathing was too fast, but it was worth it. His mouth hung open, and he looked stunned.

"What was that?" he asked as I stepped back and handed him his dagger.

"Just some extra fun. It's been a while. I wanted to see if I could still do it."

But when I turned to the rest of the room, too many eyes were on us.

And Tristan's bore into me with a look I couldn't see into.

CHAPTER 38

DANCE

Tristan

"You are an asshole," I said, whispering to Rath as I grabbed another drink. I couldn't drink fast enough since I couldn't get away from this party.

"I don't know what you're talking about, King." But he slapped me on the shoulder and grinned.

For a spy, he was a terrible liar. Of course, he never actually tried to lie to me.

Everything in me was back to a hellfire water level of heat. But it wasn't angry, or wanting to lash out.

No. Watching Cinder spar, the way she moved, and the power hidden inside that pretty, delicate dress made me want to take her to bed so badly that these damn tight, formal pants nearly caused a diplomatic incident in the middle of this crowd.

Besides, just watching her grinning and dancing with a blade in her hand brought too many moments back to me. I started thinking about her legs around my neck.

"You know, she's as bad off as you are." He lowered his voice, but the grin was still plastered on his face. And if anyone in the room were watching, they would have assumed we weren't talking about anything serious.

Maybe he was a fantastic liar.

"Rath, I'm asking you, please stay out of it."

"And I'm telling you, you're being stupid. Put on your big boy crown, act like the damn King, and go to her."

"Fuck."

"Well, like I said, if you want that, you're really going to have to talk to her."

"Damn it, Rath."

He slapped me on the back again and laughed, holding his other hand up in the don't-hit-me gesture as he walked away.

But my eyes strayed to Cinder, sitting with Duchess Inara, chatting while they watched Gus and Jacquetta dancing.

It was good of Duchess Inara to come, even if she were heading back to Breakwater tonight because of everything still happening along the coast.

After another hour I spent talking to everyone but Cinder, Duchess Inara said her goodbyes, and Cinder wandered over to the food table.

She traded out another empty glass for another full one, and I looked down at what must have been my hundredth.

Was she just as bad as I was?

Did that mean she would forgive me?

Or did it mean there was no way to get her back?

Part of me wanted to grab Rath from where he was menacing the Chamberlain, who looked a strange shade of purple in the cheeks, and force him to tell me exactly what he meant and why he said it.

But, instead, when I started to move my feet, I went in Cinder's direction.

The closer I got to her, the more at home I felt, even as my heart rate picked up and my blood grew hotter.

When I reached her side, she looked up at me and froze.

"Duchess Cinder, that was an interesting dance."

I didn't even know what I was saying anymore.

She smiled and the muscles in my back relaxed.

"Rath suggested it." She shook her head and took a drink, staring out at the dance floor where he was pulling Augustina from her seat.

Her hand strayed to the chain around her neck that disappeared into her cleavage. She pressed it against her chest, rubbing it.

"May I have a dance?" I asked, my voice low and hoarse.

Cinder sucked in a breath, her full, cupid's bow lips parting.

"Of course," she said, omitting the 'my King' that I so badly wanted to hear her say that it rang in my ears as a phantom bell.

She put down her drink and placed her hand in mine. I threaded our fingers together, and led her to the dance floor.

The first few notes of a quartanza were playing. Rath and Augustina danced to steps of something completely different that he was trying to teach her.

But Cinder fell into the proper step of the dance for the place we were in the music, and I followed suit.

It wasn't the dance I wanted to have with her when I walked out here, but soon, the twisting, dipping, spinning and jumps had us both breathing hard.

Her chest rose and fell, faster and faster. Her breasts pushed against the fitted bodice of her dress, and I wanted to tear it off.

No matter how much wine she drank tonight, she still moved with grace and precision, her body an art form, and I its biggest fan.

We moved together. Every time the dance called for us to touch, even fingertips, the contact sent ripples of sensation through my entire body.

By the time the dance hit its last twist, turn, dip and jump, we found ourselves facing each other with our hands touching. Both of us dragging in frantic breaths.

She locked eyes with me, and I didn't know what to say. I couldn't even think properly.

Her eyes were soft. But there was a sadness in them that I wanted to be able to take away for her. Even though I didn't know how.

The music changed to a valz with only seconds between.

Wrapping my hand around hers, I moved us into the position for the valz.

It started off as the traditional dance. We even turned our heads at the appropriate times. And from the first night we were in this ballroom together, we always struggled with the moments that required us to look where the dance dictated.

But now, we both did it without question, and without saying a word to each other.

Of all the stupid things to worry about, performing a valz correctly wasn't one I would allow to keep me from using this chance to the fullest.

Finally, I gave up the pretense of the correct moves, and pulled her to my chest, wrapping my arm around her back, and pressing my fingers into the skin between the chains like I wanted to.

I stared down into her wide eyes, and rubbed my thumb along the back of her hand in mine where I held her palm to my chest.

"This dress is beautiful," I said, trying to find anything safe to say.

She hitched a breath, her mouth opening and closing.

"And you did a lovely job at the ceremony," I said, wanting to mention her impromptu 'I do,' and not sure if I could speak about it without breaking down and begging.

"You…you look very nice in your formals," she said, her voice a stumbling whisper.

"I remember how you like them." I smiled, splaying my hand out along her back, holding her closer while the music went on.

Cinder swallowed and said, "And you performed the ceremony perfectly. Gus and Jacquetta will never forget how well it went."

"Good." I bit my lip, and she shuddered in my arms, which made me furrow my brow, not sure if I should let her go or keep talking.

"Tristan," she said, her voice so quiet I wouldn't have heard her say it if she was anyone else.

But I could pick her voice out of crowd, I wanted her to say my name again. I closed my eyes, and took a deep breath before I opened them again.

Rubbing my thumb over her hand, and my fingers along her back, I waited for her to say whatever she wanted.

"Tristan, I…" she squeezed her eyes shut, the shudder worse.

And the music stopped.

She opened her eyes, pulled away from me, and a tear fell down her cheek.

"Cinder, you're crying." I didn't know what else to say.

"It's a wedding." She stuttered over the word. "I need to go."

And she turned around, fleeing the room.

No matter what I was supposed to do, no matter what everyone expected of Cinder and I tonight, I went after her.

Because I was hers. And she was mine. And she needed me.

CHAPTER 39

STRIKE

Cinder

I didn't want to do this tonight. It wasn't supposed to happen. It wasn't supposed to be like this.

Fleeing from the party was the last thing I wanted to do, but I couldn't make my legs slow down. Even as the stitches along my leg screamed, I sped up, trying to outrun the tears streaming down my face.

Why did I wear this stupid ring? I knew better, but my pathetic, sentimental heart made me put it on.

And then I went and almost told him in front of everyone. Seconds away from just blurting it all out, and inviting the whole room into the shattering of my heart all over again—I was an idiot.

Grabbing onto the frame of a doorway, I flung myself around it, and tumbled to the floor of the receiving room.

No light pierced the complicated patterns in the window

glass like last time. No phantom dragons chased across the room, waiting to attack me.

Instead of glass dragons, I stared at the place where Tristan once wanted us to sit side by side. Propping myself up to my knees, I stared at another thing I lost.

Sniffing, I wiped my chin and my cheeks, but tears of silent mourning wouldn't stop falling.

Rubbing my ring against my chest, I took in shuddering breaths, and tried to make sense of what just happened.

I said 'I do' at the wedding. Because my brain stopped working while looking at him standing there. Those words were the only thing left in my mind.

He asked me to dance. First, it was hot and sweaty, full of heavy breathing and moving with him. That was bad enough, but when he wrapped me up in his arms…

Why? Why did he do that to me?

"Cinder," his whispered voice echoed through the room, and a sob ripped me in half, tearing me apart from the heart out.

Scrambling to my feet, I lurched up and ran for the open door on the other side of the long room, trying to outrun the way he haunted me.

I needed to pull myself back together, and get back to the party. I needed to be there for Gus and Jacquetta.

What if they noticed I ran out?

They shouldn't be forced to deal with my mess on their day.

Making my way through another room I had never been in, I was assaulted by visions of Tristan and his family along the walls.

Paintings of him, as a baby, a child, a teenager, and as a young King were prominent in the royal gallery. The look on his face, that sober expression too old for his years, tore at me.

Running again, my dress in my hands to stop it from tangling around my legs, I stifled a scream that threatened to break free of the cage my body had been transformed into.

I knew what I needed to do, but I didn't know how to do it here. In this place.

None of the rooms I sped through even came close to a place I could shove it all back now that it was breaking free.

Somehow, in the giant maze of the palace, I needed a place that would allow me a focus that I only ever found with a blade in my hands.

Around another corner, I found what I was looking for.

One of the smaller, arched doors to the outside hung in the obsidian wall. I slammed into it.

My shoulder ached where I flung myself against it, but I had to take a step back and look.

With frantic, uncoordinated movements, I managed to finally yank the door open, and dart out into the night.

The few guards in the courtyard all looked to the skies, as so many people did now.

But the last thing I wanted was for them to even notice me as I ran through the dark in my silvery gray dress like a wraith toward the open arch under which I knew a wall of weapons sat waiting for anyone who wanted to train.

No lights were on out here tonight, so no one would see me. The guards didn't notice when I ran under the arch into the shooting range. No one blinked when the ceiling, the palace itself, blocked any light at all from reaching me. Not a single soul cared when I collapsed to the ground.

My knees hit the stone with a force my dress did nothing to mute. My hands followed a second later, tiny bits of dirt on the stones digging into my palms.

The point of coming here, to this spot, was still too far from me, hanging on the wall. I wanted to train, to stop thinking, stop feeling. But I didn't run fast enough, and it all crashed down on my head. Days of suppressing everything for the kids, for Gus and Jacquetta, days of pent-up misery and confusion all slammed into me as I kneeled on the stones.

Once, a long time ago, my brother taught me to force all my feelings away.

He said it would save me.

When he made me kill the first man I ever thought I loved, he said it was for my own good.

Ash lied to me about so many things. I thought he lied to me about that, too. But the pain in my chest made me wonder if he was right. Just thinking about Tristan ripped through me in such a way that it made me a bad friend.

Maybe it was better not to feel at all than to feel this.

I choked on a sob, and bent my head, slipping my eyes shut, allowing the darkness and the chilled winter air to cover me.

Somewhere along the way I became addicted to feeling.

Like I was loved.

As if I belonged.

Home.

But I couldn't do it anymore.

The last two days, I managed to keep it all at bay. The last two days, I shoved it back into the corner, painted over it with the cold place, and managed to stay in the moment with my friends, focusing on their feelings.

Somehow, right this second, right fucking now, I needed to do it again.

Instead of succeeding, chasing the pain through my mind to try and seal it off only gave it bigger claws to attack me with.

One day, maybe, I would be able to shut it away tightly enough to ask Tristan how. How did he unlock this ability in me to feel his loss even as I stared at him, touched him, danced with him?

How did he make me love him?

Because I never wanted this.

I never wanted to be so out of control of myself that I would do anything, give anything, endure anything for someone.

Not after I did it once already.

My feelings for Tristan even managed to break through the hold Ash had on me.

"How?" I wailed, tilting my head up at the ceiling I couldn't see in the dark, and looking into a future just as murky.

The thought of breaking myself permanently—not just setting aside my love for him long enough to get through something, but one day not feeling it at all—made my whole chest heave with a sob.

Now that I knew what it felt like, I was incapable of letting it go.

"Cinder," his voice came to me again, this time stronger, a touch of panic in it, and it sent a line of fire scorching across my icy skin.

Surging to my feet on legs I barely felt, I whirled around, and sucked in a breath as he lifted a hellfire lantern, the low light of it casting his face in deeper darkness and flickering light.

My Dragon King found me at the same time the scaled, terrible thing he turned my heart into smashed through my chest.

CHAPTER 40

FLAME

Tristan

"Cinder, please don't run," I said, my voice low. She stood as still as the stones under our feet.

My lantern's small flame flickered and burned, green at the center, orange and red at the edges, casting dancing shadows over her, turning her shimmering silver gown into an ethereal cloud of smoke, and her tear-streaked face, with her piercing eyes into the fire at the center of it.

"Tristan," she said, her voice a mere breath of air as formless as the shadows undulating around her.

"Why did you run?" I asked, wondering if this place, the archery and throwing range, was the place she always meant to end up. The first place we spoke to each other.

Her face crumpled on a silent cry, and I stepped toward her.

But she scrambled backward, almost tripping on the train of her dress while she held her hands out to stop me from advancing.

She righted herself and screamed, a primal, guttural scream that shook every bone in my body, and stole my ability to move.

"Why did you make me feel?" Her voice was raw and ragged, and my heart ached as she put words to what I felt so many times since the cells.

"You made it come alive." She grabbed at her chest, her fingernails digging into the skin. "Now my heart is a dragon as big as this palace, and it's destroying me from the inside out."

"Cinder," I said, choking on her name, desperate for her to stop, but still unable to move.

"Don't." She shook her head, one more curl falling from the pile of her hair and trailing down her shoulder. "Don't you dare say my name like you still love me. I can't do this anymore, Tristan. This game you play."

"It's not a game." I managed to break free enough to set the lantern down on the ground, but her feral rage left me shaking in place, making it impossible to go to her like I wanted to, wrap her in my arms like my whole body screamed for me to do.

"No? What do you call it?" she laughed without humor as her tears continued to flow. "You called being with me fucked up."

"Oh, Gods. That's not—" I took two steps her way, shaking my head. She couldn't think that's what I meant.

"It is." She swatted at my outstretched hands, lifting her dress out of the way as she backed up further. "It's what you said. And now..."

Her hand waved as she backed against the wall and sagged.

"Now you act in there, in front of everyone, like I matter to you."

"Of course you fucking matter." Even as she waved me away, I ran to her. Even though she hit my arms and pummeled my chest, I grabbed on tight and didn't let go.

"Cinder, stop."

"I can't." She punched me in the shoulder, a blow too ineffectual to be from her. "He said I shouldn't love. He said I shouldn't feel."

"Who?" I tried to wrap my arms around her, and she turned from glancing blows to hits that would leave marks.

"He was right." She managed to kick my legs out from under me. My hold on her forced us to topple to the ground, but I kept her from taking the brunt of it.

I grunted with the impact, but still hung on.

"You said he lied. But he was right." Tears fell from her eyes, sprinkling my cheeks as she shoved at me beneath her.

"Cinder, who?" A dread seeped into my gut, followed by the rising of the heat in my blood as if I called it.

"My brother," she said, the shock of it knocked loose my hold on her long enough for her to pull back, her necklace hitting me in the face.

I grabbed onto her again with one hand, the soft fabric barely a barrier to her skin. But it was the necklace, as I folded my other fist over it, that froze us both.

She sucked in a shaking breath, the necklace pulling taught in my hand.

Even without opening my fist to look at, I knew what it was. The shape of it, the imprint of the sigils on it, was etched on my soul.

Looking into her eyes, my heart skipped a beat.

Unwrapping my hand from her arm, still holding on to the ring in my other fist, I touched a tentative finger to her tear-streaked cheek, right below her scar.

"You kept it. You wore it." My voice didn't sound like my own, even to me. Because it wasn't anymore.

My voice, my body, my heart, my soul, my everything belonged to her.

"You made me promise," her voice was so small that it reminded me of when she curled in her shoulders. I hated myself for making her feel that.

Surging up from the ground, I slid my hand around to the back of her neck and captured her mouth with mine.

The noise she made, plaintive and desperate as she opened her mouth to me and I slipped my tongue past her teeth, sent my entire body into a state of hyper awareness.

I felt the stone beneath me. The way her legs parted so she could straddle me. Every tiny hair at the nape of her neck. Her hands tightening their grip on my shirt. And her heart beating as fast as mine against the back of my hand where the ring remained in my fist, pressed between us.

Breaking from the kiss, she whimpered and dove at me. I pulled my head away and looked her in the eyes. She needed to hear this. I needed to tell her.

"Cinder, I love you. Nothing about being with you has ever been fucked up. It was the bodies in the next room. You deserve better."

She closed her eyes, slow and soft, as a tender smile bloomed on that perfect mouth, and tears still traced down her cheeks.

Opening her eyes, she said, "I love you."

My mouth met hers. It wasn't crashing together as we had so many times. It wasn't wild, and rushed.

It was careful, and reverent.

Pulling back, I touched my forehead to hers, and held her close.

"Why did you do it if you thought it was fucked up?" she whispered, holding her breath as if she really thought she needed to brace herself for the answer.

Maybe she did. I wasn't sure how she would take the truth of that moment.

"As soon as you and I…As soon as *I* ended…" I didn't want to say it. I didn't want to think about that moment in the cells when I threw it all away.

She nodded, letting me off the ledge I created for myself.

"Well, I couldn't let go. Not enough. And I thought you

wouldn't…" Looking into her eyes, into those unfathomable depths that I got to explore when no one else did, I found home. It let me take a deep breath and tell her. "You said, 'He's mine.'"

One of her eyebrows rose, and her mouth broke into a cocky grin.

"You like that I call you mine?"

"I am yours."

"And we belong together."

She kissed me, sweet and gentle, and full of the love we denied ourselves for too long.

Deepening the kiss, she rocked her hips against me, and need rose within me as hot as hellfire.

"By the way," she said, pulling back and looking at me from under her lashes, "I would still fuck you on top of bodies."

A hum built up in my chest, the kind only she caused, and I growled as she pressed her pussy against me, my cock as hard as the stone beneath me.

She bit her bottom lip which sent my blood temperature rising.

As soon as she released that lip, I reached out with my teeth and trapped it, caressing it with my tongue.

Cinder made that little whimper noise, and I let go of the ring hanging from her neck to grab her hard ass, pressing her against me as I released her lip.

"Don't bite that," I said, kissing her bottom lip with a quick touch of my lips, "it's my job."

"Get to work," she said, and I fell on her mouth, kissing, caressing, nipping, and biting.

My Flame turned molten in my arms, rocking her pussy against me through those thin layers of skirts and my too-tight pants. Still, she wasn't close enough.

"Let me take you inside," I said into her neck, kissing my way down to her collarbone.

Writhing in response, which turned my need of her into an ache, she said, "No. I want you."

Picking her up by her ass, I kept her pressed to me as I stood and started to walk out of the target lanes. But she crashed her mouth down on mine, tightened her legs around me, and bent her body until she could press herself against me harder.

"Cinder." I wanted to take her to a bed, worship her like she deserved, and make her cum so many times her legs never stopped shaking. "I won't make it to a bed without needing to be inside you if you keep doing that."

"Tell me what you want, Tristan," she whispered into my ear.

"You. Now." Always.

"I want you to make me yours. Here. In bed. In every room of that palace." She moved her hands from my chest to wrap them around my neck, playing with the hair at the nape, sending tingles through my body, and making that growl come out of me again.

My cock throbbed, but there were guards in the courtyard, people at the party.

"No one wants to see the King lit on fire by his flame in the target lane on the range," I said, claiming her neck with my mouth, and speaking around the soft skin there.

"I want the man. Not the King. Not tonight. What would the man do to make me his?" She pulled my face away from her neck, and pressed her mouth to mine with the same abandon she had in that house, her body yielding in my arms.

The burn inside me ignited, and I couldn't wait anymore.

With a turn and two steps, I leaned her against one of the targets, slipping my hand between us.

She sucked in a breath when I made it past the thin layers of her skirts and pulled her panties to the side.

A moan followed when I found and rubbed her clit, her hips rocking against me.

Kissing her, feeling her tongue on mine, I pressed my throbbing cock against her pussy. While my hand massaged her clit, I rocked against her, my movements begging for her to shake and scream for me.

"I want you to cum for me," I whispered into her moans, the words sent her over the edge, her body quaking in my arms, and I lost all ability to think.

"Tear them off," she panted.

"What?" I didn't stop rubbing. She threw her head back, her hips rocking, her lip between her teeth as I fell on her cleavage with my mouth, still watching her face.

Cinder shuddered and writhed, her foot twitching where it pressed into my back, and she broke apart again, calling out.

She lifted her head and met my hungry gaze with one just as ravenous and said, "I need you."

CHAPTER 41

PROMISE

Cinder

The dragon in my heart had transferred to his eyes as he devoured me with his gaze.

He pulled back from me, and even though I wanted him to, just for a second, I still made a sound so close to begging it may as well have been.

But he didn't waste time.

Tristan twisted my panties in his fist, the delicate fabric tearing at just that amount of force, and yanked them off me, shredding them.

While he undid his pants, I met his eyes and licked my hand before I wrapped my wet palm around his cock. It throbbed in my hand, and he made a noise in his throat that almost undid me.

Stroking him made me even wetter. But he took my hand away from his cock, claimed my mouth with his, and rubbed against my sex.

"I want to feel you cum again." he said into my mouth, his voice like a hungry moan. "Your pussy throbs, and I love it."

Every word thrummed inside me, entered me like I wanted him to while he rubbed his cock against my clit and drove me toward the cliff.

"Please," I said, squirming as my muscles began to shake.

"Cinder," he moaned, his cock throbbing with me.

I called out as he drove me up the side of that mountain, my entire body shaking. Being with him again made every touch more sensitive, rocking me to the marrow in my bones.

Winter existed outside of us, the cold not making it through to my skin as his heat and the building inferno in me melded together.

"My Flame."

I broke again, losing all control of my muscles, and he moved, tilting me so he entered me a fraction. My shattering increased.

Slow, languorous, he took his time working his way inside me as he suckled, nibbled, bit, and kissed my neck and the top of my breasts.

My hands tightly clenched around the soft lace at his collar, I let him stretch me and rock his hips until he was deep inside me, moving in me.

He held my ass in place against the target behind me as he drove us both, closer and closer.

"Tell me what you want, Cinder," he said, kissing along my jaw as I throbbed around him. Rocking. In and out.

"You. All of you." I would never get enough.

A hum went through him, sending my shaking to a new level. The heat of him against me, inside me, radiated out to every bit of my flesh.

He moved one hand from my ass and pressed it between us, rubbing my clit, making me cry out.

With his other hand he adjusted my ass again, and moved his legs so he pushed himself inside me even deeper than before.

This time when I came, I screamed his name. He moaned with me, following me into that exquisite breaking apart to come back together as one. A bond stronger for all we put it through.

But when he was done, he didn't put me down, he pressed me to him, breathing, "I love you," into my ear, again and again.

Wrapping my arms around him, holding him tightly, the strength in my arms slowly returned.

Finally, he pulled away enough to do his pants back up, keeping me pressed against the target.

I watched his face, the soft smile that just seemed to exist there now, never dropping from him.

Even as I pushed my skirts down to cover my exposed sex, I was distracted by that grin. I never wanted it to leave again.

He finished with his pants, and looked at me from the side of his eyes, one brow high.

"Why are you covering up something so pretty?" he asked, with a flick of his gaze to my hand pressing my skirts down.

"Because we need to go inside." I tried not to grin back at him and failed.

In swift movements, he wrapped my legs tighter around his waist and picked me up off the target, carrying me from the range.

"How about I take you inside like this?" He leaned his head back, and I crashed my mouth onto his.

"Everyone will see you," I said, smiling and snuggling into his chest anyway.

"They'll see a man who loves a woman. They won't even notice the King." He kissed me, never once missing a step as he carried me across the courtyard.

Maybe they would have, maybe they wouldn't. But when we

got to the bottom of the main steps, I jumped down and stood in front of him, one hand on his cheek.

"Promise me," I whispered, the smile falling from my face, and his turning concerned.

"Cinder, I'll do whatever you want." He turned his head and kissed my palm, running his fingers through the few tendrils of my hair that hung down.

"I believe you. But all I want is for you to promise me that you know now." His brow furrowed, and he kissed my forehead, wrapping me in his arms before he shook his head.

"Flame, I'm sorry," he said, and I braced myself, unable to breathe, "I don't know what you mean."

Letting my breath out in a whoosh, I nodded and tried again.

"Promise me that no matter what, you will always know," I moved my other hand from around his neck to the inferno of his heart, "in here, that I love you. I don't even know when it happened. I tried to figure it out, the moment. And all I can think of now, when I look back on everything, is that I am in love with you."

He took in a deep breath, his heartbeat picking up speed, his eyes turning golden and soft. That look I wanted as much as Lehar wanted the ashes to stop falling made everything in me calm in a way that I didn't know I could be. That love on his face welcomed me home to where I belonged.

Touching his forehead to mine, wrapping his arms around me and holding me close, a shudder ran through him. He pulled back and looked me in the eye, his still with that gold-covered look.

"I promise. But you need to promise me, too." The look changed as his mouth tightened, and he bit the side of his lip, running the lightest of touches across my cheek.

"Anything." And I meant it. I would give him anything, swear to anything. Just as long as I could hold on to him.

"Promise me that you will trust me, and not keep things

from me." He looked so serious, that gold in his eyes still tinged with the stale taste of my lies.

"Tristan, I trust you." He nodded and swallowed, the strong lines of his jaw sharpening as he tightened his mouth.

"Don't hold back," he said, rubbing along my cheek again, "I can hear the 'but' coming in your voice."

He was right. I wanted to tell him everything, to keep nothing from him. And I did trust him. He looked into the darkness deep within me and loved me anyway.

"Just know that I trust you. It still might be a challenge for me." Seven years, all of them during a time when I turned from child to adult, all of them while my soul formed into its present tempered steel from the roughhewn ore it was, wouldn't disappear overnight. No matter how much I wanted them to.

The breath he let out made the air around me taste like relief, and I held onto it, tucking away the feeling somewhere deep inside me to use when I needed to tell him something I didn't want to in the future.

"Cinder, I wouldn't expect you to be a different person. I love you as you are. I just want you to try to talk to me."

He kissed me, claiming my mouth with his, and I clung to him.

Pulling back, he smiled and kissed my forehead, but I had to break the spell of his relief.

Maybe it was my first foray into telling him the truth. Maybe it was something within me trying to sabotage the happiness washing over me that still seemed foreign, and was something I struggled to believe I deserved. Or maybe it was just morbid curiosity. But the question burned inside me as hot as his skin on mine.

"Why do you love me?" I asked, trying to only show him the curiosity.

He tilted his head back and turned, looking into the sky, a soft smile playing on his lips.

"Did you look at the stars a lot as a child?" He glanced at me, and I nodded, watching him as he watched the stars shining in the winter night.

"I used to wonder what they were made of, and if I could find magic. If I became the Dragon King, would I have magic enough to hold one." Turning back to look at me, he ran his hand along my back and studied my face.

"The answer is, it would be impossible for me not to fall in love with someone who shines like those stars, and makes me just as curious to know what she's made of. Especially because I get to hold her in my arms while I search for the answers." He smiled, and my heart flew out of my body to join those stars he loved as he leaned down to kiss me.

CHAPTER 42

IMPATIENT

Tristan

Walking inside the palace, I was ready to drag Cinder to my bedroom, but she tilted her head and pulled me back toward the ballroom.

"Not too long," I whispered in her ear, wrapping my arm around her, and nibbling on her earlobe as she laughed.

"Are you impatient for something?" She leaned away from me, grinning.

"Maybe I need to show you what my impatience feels like."

Her eyes danced. Slowly she opened her mouth, her tongue appearing with a caress of her bottom lip before she trapped that lip with her teeth.

"Now you're just being mean," I said, my voice low.

"It's not mean," she said, leaning in to play her lips along my jaw, "if it's a promise."

"Wait," I grinned, "does this count as flirting?"

"This counts as starting that show of impatience." She pulled free of me, and walked into the ballroom so fast that all I could do was groan. I promised myself that she would pay for that little trick.

I shouldn't have pointed out what her little movements with her mouth did to me. Cinder with knowledge of what got to me was obviously just as dangerous as Cinder with a blade.

As soon as I walked in, Rath descended on me, circling me with a gleam in his eye that made me check who was in ear shot.

"Spit it out, Rath," I said, trying to keep my voice neutral.

"King," he said, brushing something off my back, and slinging his arm across my shoulders to cover his move, "everyone wondered where you went. Don't worry, I covered for you."

"What, exactly, did you say?" Oh, Gods and Goddesses, this could be bad.

"That there was nothing to worry about. You had to go handle a little flame," he said, and I choked, "you know, putting out all those fires going on with the war."

I looked to Cinder, sitting with Jacquetta and Augustina, and wondered how many fires would take me away from my Flame.

"Rath, we need to find some way to end this war," I said, something I repeated often, but with even more urgency in this moment. With the involvement of her brother, it felt like the longer it went on, the more likely it was to hurt Cinder more than it already had.

"Already working on it." He nodded, his face lapsing into a level of seriousness that was so seldom there it made the fire inside me rage hotter. I wanted to hide Cinder away, keep her safe.

"What do you know?" I whispered.

"Nothing yet. But I have some ideas. You just take care of getting your Queen, and I'll find out more." He slapped me on the shoulder, and wandered off toward Prince Nevan.

Getting my Queen…

Hours slipped by and finally, Augustina and Jacquetta retreated to their rooms for the night.

Cinder watched them go with her hands covering the giant smile on her face until they rounded the corner down the hall, and her brow furrowed.

"Tristan, I just realized," she said, turning to me, "I don't have a room for the night."

Shaking my head, I threaded our fingers together. Pulling her hand so she followed me up the stairs, I smiled.

"You have a whole palace." I squeezed her hand, and she laughed.

"My King does."

Those words, on her lips, may as well have been welcome home. They helped me prepare to say what I wanted to.

At the turn in the stairs, I led her toward the royal wing, and debated how I would ask the question, how I would get her to agree to what I hoped for.

"For tonight at least," I swallowed, "will you share my room with me?" We had talked about it before, but she had no idea what it meant. And I had no idea if she would say yes.

Her free hand strayed to wrap around her ring hanging on its chain, and her eyes softened along with her smile.

"Yes."

My heart grew weightless in my chest, making me want to fly. Instead, I got her to the top of the stairs and scooped her up in my arms.

Cinder was heavy when she was unconscious or hurt or fighting, but when she wanted me to carry her, she was as light as ashes. It was part of the magic of her. And right now, she felt so insubstantial in my arms, it was as if I carried the myth of those stars that I dreamt of rather than the very real woman I loved.

"Tristan," she said, tucking her head under my chin, "if I'm being honest, I find this wing kind of terrifying."

"You're scared of something?"

I turned the corner to the staircase we needed, and adjusted my hold on her to open the door at the bottom of the winding stairs.

"Do you want me to walk?" she asked.

"No, I don't want to let go of you." I kissed her forehead, and inhaled the scent of her—vanilla, roses, and just a hint of ashes. Warm and rich.

She sighed and we started climbing, the door swinging shut behind me.

"What has you scared?" I asked.

"Honestly, I'm not really sure. Your private office I love, but this wing doesn't feel like a place someone like me should ever be allowed." Her hand played with the lace along my collar.

"This wing," I said, reaching out to the door at the top of the stairs, "and any other place in the palace is as much where you belong as where I do."

Her smile was soft as she watched my face, and, finally, she nodded.

I swung the door open to the darkened interior, the only light the moon shining through the windows.

Cinder's mouth fell open as I closed the door behind us, and I let her down so she could move to the windows that looked out over both Bridgeton and the palace's courtyard at the same time.

"This is your view? Why did you spend so much time in my room?"

My laugh was small, but my smile wasn't.

"Did you really just ask me that?"

She waved her hands as if to ask the question again by pointing out at the scene displayed before her.

"I would rather never see that again than miss a chance to be with you."

Cinder went still and turned slowly to face me.

"You should come here then," she said, her voice husky and low, full of command.

"Maybe we should start that conversation about impatience again." I took a step in her direction, the light of the moon falling over her, and shining through her shimmering gown.

Looking her up and down, I committed every bit of her image to memory. One day, I would commission an artist to paint this for me. A painting not for the gallery, but to hang in my private office so I could keep the secret of my Cinder to myself.

"Tristan," she said, her voice edged already in that throaty impatience.

"Are you going to tell me what you want?" I took another step, close enough to see her chest hitch as she breathed in deep, but not close enough to watch as her breasts pressed against the tight bodice like I imagined they did.

"You. Always."

I took another step, and she pressed her hand against her chest.

"Tell me." I wasn't going to let her get away that easy. Not tonight.

She took that breath again, but instead of saying anything, she tugged at something behind her. The dress fell loose along her front, and now it was my turn to take in a shuddering breath.

With one hand, she slipped the gown off, letting it fall to the floor, and taking one step toward me.

"Now you really are being mean," I said, my voice low.

"But you said, I needed to learn what your impatience felt like." She grinned and tilted her head.

"You do."

Her swift intake of breath made me tuck my arms behind me, and hold one wrist with the other, forcing myself not to go to her.

"Please," she whispered, that delicious, plaintive noise heavy in the word that made my cock press against the confines of my pants.

"Tell me what you want." Hopefully she couldn't see me hold my breath in the dark.

"I want you inside me, touching me, making me scream."

A humming built in my chest, my cock throbbing.

"What does it feel like, what you want?"

Cinder shuddered, her breath coming faster. She ran one hand along her chest, her breasts moving as she did, with the other she touched her thigh, and ran it along her skin until she dipped it toward her pussy.

"Perfect," she said, begging in her voice, and I couldn't hold myself back.

I darted forward and scooped her up, her mouth claiming mine in a passionate kiss that made all the heat in me turn into liquid fire running down my limbs as I carried her to the bed.

CHAPTER 43

MORE

Cinder

Tristan ran a hand along my body as he laid me down on the bed. In the dark, his eyes were the only thing I could see.

"Come here," I said, the throbbing in my body matching the desperation of my voice.

"Not yet." Those glowing, golden eyes met mine, and I grabbed the lace at his collar, pulling his mouth to mine.

His tongue played with my mouth, languid and slow as he made a noise like he tasted something divine. I was molten, transformed by his heat from the thicker hellfire source into the flowing hellfire water.

While he kissed me, his hand ran along my body, those clever fingers in the dark turning every piece of my skin into a place as sensitive as my fingertips that felt the pattern of the lace in my hands.

Pulling my leg up, he turned my calf and then my thigh into

the most important parts of my body with his touch. He placed my legs so I was open to him with my feet planted and my knees bent.

But even as he ran those fingers along my inner thigh, even as I ached for him to bring them higher, to touch my sex as it grew wet in wanting, he only brushed along the edge.

Just that tiny brush of his fingers made me whimper.

My need grew worse when he broke the kiss and pulled back, unlatching my hands from his collar.

"Stay still," he said, that delicious growl making my breath come in gasps.

His hands returned to me, his mouth trailing the lightest of brushes, his hot breath running along my skin right behind his fingers.

The sensation made me moan, and shivers shot through me.

When he moved on from my stomach to my arms, I turned my head and watched as his golden eyes stared back at me.

Slowly, so slowly, he moved his fingers up one arm, his lips brushing along behind them. The heat of his breath set my body ablaze, and tingles ran through me.

He reached my breasts, and the feel of his hands barely caressing them made me writhe.

"Don't move, Cinder," he reminded me, that deep growling sound still there, but married now with a smile that I could hear. A lascivious grin that made me want to kiss him until he struggled to breathe.

Not giving me a break, he followed his fingers along my breasts with his mouth. This time he included his tongue. The first wet, hot contact making me cry out as a ripple of sensation ran through me in a towering wave that built and built.

"Tell me what you want, Cinder," he said against my skin. A mewling sound came out of me, words beyond me as I tried to hold my shaking body still.

"Do you want me to touch your pussy?"

"Yes." Oh, Gods and Goddesses, his voice alone came close to undoing me.

He moved his hand, slowly trailing his fingers down my stomach until he got to my sex.

With one hand caressing my skin just above my sex, sending shivers through me, he used his other hand to push my legs further apart, settling between them, kneeling.

Just having him there, the sides of his legs pressing against my knees, made it all so much worse. I wanted him to touch me.

"Tristan," I said, my voice breathless. "I need you."

Sounds of fabric moving in the darkness left me imagining his beautiful, naked body and expecting a blanket. But it was his hands that finally returned to me. The first touch of his fingers along the bend where my inner thigh turned into my sex made me gasp and moan.

"You didn't move. Good girl."

No, but the shaking in my legs made it more difficult not to move. I whimpered.

He paused his fingers, holding them steady with the lightest touch on my tender skin.

But a second later, his mouth followed them, and I cried out, throbbing.

Trailing hot breath along the edges of my sex, his heat made me grip the blankets of the bed in tight fists. My feet pressed harder into the mattress.

"Please," I begged, my muscles quaking.

"Are you impatient?" he whispered, his breath tickling along my clit, sending me skirting that cliff, moaning.

"Are you impatient, my Flame?"

"Yes." The word barely made it out of my mouth through my moans as he teased his breath along me.

His fingers brushed closer to the center of my sex, and I arched toward him, wanting his touch right there.

"Don't move, Flame. Now, I'm going to make you wait longer."

I moaned as he went back to teasing his breath along my sex, his fingers just beyond where I wanted him to be, making me need him more.

Running the whole of his hands from my spread knees up my legs in that torturously light touch, I shivered with every new bit of flesh under his hot skin while his breath tickled along my sex.

Finally, his fingers ran along the sides of my center again, his mouth still brushing the slightest breeze against the point of my aching need.

"Tell me what you want," he whispered, the words running across my clit, making me quiver and cry out. I lifted my head from the bed to look down the length of my body, hidden in the darkness, to his golden eyes.

"I need you to touch me." My words were frantic, pushed out between short, ragged breaths.

"What kind of touch? Like this?" He ran those barely-there touches right along the sides of my throbbing center, and my legs shook. My hands kneaded the blankets in my spasming fists.

"Your fingers, your mouth, your cock. I want it all."

"And patience?" he asked, his breathing speeding up, driving me closer to breaking apart.

"Gone."

He made a growling humming noise that curled my toes.

"Not yet," he murmured, and I whined. But he ran those gentle fingertips right along the opening of my sex, and the whine turned into a moan of his name. All my breath left my body, replaced by heat that rose up to meet his.

"So wet, my Flame," he said, his mouth so close to my clit that it wasn't just his breath running across that sensitive spot.

It was the vibration of his voice, and it sent waves through my body that made me pull up on the blankets and cry out.

Moving his fingers just along the edge inside of me, he pressed, the touch more solid than before. My cries grew, my shaking uncontrolled.

Trying to hold still, I turned my head, and bit into the blanket bunched up by my face.

He moved his mouth away from me, and I whimpered into the blanket. A second later he closed his mouth over my thigh, teasing me with his fingers, and the whimpers changed.

Keeping his mouth on me, kissing and nipping along my leg, he moved one hand to make room for his mouth.

Pressure built from him into me as his mouth neared the throbbing center of my need.

But he pulled his mouth off me, and I whined into the blanket, thrashing my head to the other side.

"Hmmm," he made that satisfied sound again as I remained a being of pure need, "do you like that?"

"Yes, please." I wasn't sure if the words made it out of my mouth, I was so far beyond words.

"Please, what, my love?" There was a smile in his voice, and promise in the way his fingers kept running along the line of my sex, driving me closer without getting closer to me.

Words failed me. I wanted to tell him to fuck me, to make love to me, to finally put his mouth on me. But I just thrashed my head and made a plaintive noise while my limbs shook. My whole world shrunk down to the feeling of his fingers running along the edge of my wet, throbbing center.

"Do you want me to finally put my mouth on this little, wet pussy?" he asked, pressing along the edge, just the tiniest fraction of one of his fingers slipping inside. I moaned.

He lowered his mouth onto my clit at the same time he pushed that finger inside me, and I broke, all the pent-up pleasure of his attentions pouring through my body in an orgasm so strong I screamed and grabbed his head. My fingers laced into his hair as I bucked and writhed while he fucked me with his mouth and his finger at the same time.

All the other touches were light, teasing, and barely there. But now his mouth clamped down on me, sucking my clit to rub along his teeth while his tongue massaged it.

Unending waves of pleasure crashed through me, tearing apart my control of my own body, until I quivered and shook and couldn't hold onto his hair anymore.

Falling back on the bed, I writhed under his mouth and his finger inside me. His other fingers still massaged along the outside of my sex.

He moved his hand and replaced his finger with his tongue, moving it inside me, continuing to batter my senses with the unending waves of my pleasure and desire.

Even as I broke around his mouth, I wanted more.

CHAPTER 44

ROSES

Tristan

Cinder tasted divine, her pussy so wet, so throbbing, I couldn't tell when one orgasm ended and the other began.

She spasmed around my tongue, then again around my finger when I sucked on her clit. Her orgasms seemed never-ending. Her pussy either clamping tight, or shaking with a tremor that quivered down her legs.

No amount of her would ever be enough. My cock ached and pulsed, a very real manifestation of my desperation to be deep inside her.

In her screaming, she yelled my name, and it shook through me, calling all the heat in my blood to burn hotter.

Finally, I couldn't hold back.

Moving my mouth off her, I shifted my fingers to play with her clit, rubbing it in those slow circles she loved, before crawling over her, claiming her mouth with mine.

She moaned into my mouth, and I moved my hips, dragging my stone-hard cock along her pussy. She shuddered, her legs tightening against my hips.

Adjusting the pressure of my finger on her clit, she threw her head to the side, and crested the constant, breaking waves of her orgasms.

I slipped the tip of my cock into her tight pussy as it spasmed around me, so wet, so welcoming.

Her back arched, her hands scrabbled at the blankets, and her legs wrapping around me.

"Cinder," I moaned, closing my mouth on her neck as she shook and stretched, allowing me deeper inside her tight, throbbing center.

Moving a fraction at a time drew out her orgasm. I didn't ever want it to stop.

She shook and moaned, her pussy clamping down around my cock, releasing, throbbing, clamping down again.

Her exquisite orgasms, and the feeling of being inside her, sent shocks of pleasure through my body. Again and again as I moved inside her, shivering desire shot from my cock down my arms and legs.

I found her breast with my mouth, and she cried out again, her voice sending another wave of sensation through me. I couldn't stop it.

Biting down on her shoulder, I moaned. She screamed my name, and I finally came. Her pussy clamped around my cock, throbbing, sending me off the cliff of my own pleasure into a sea filled with her.

When it was done, I collapsed to the side of her, and scooped her up, bringing her with me, unwilling to pull my cock out of her. It was impossible to be close enough to her.

Her frantic breathing slowed, even as the occasional shudder still rocked her body. She didn't seem to be able to hold me back, her arms weak.

"Tristan," she finally said, the sound of my name in her mouth making me hold her closer and kiss her forehead.

"Cinder," I said, moving my head to kiss her mouth, "I love you."

"One day," she said, "I love you, too. But one day I'll be able to move again. And if you think that is going to stop me from making you even more impatient when I get the chance, you're wrong."

I laughed, and she smiled when she kissed me again.

"Good." I kissed her, deepening the kiss, never wanting to stop.

But she pulled away, and placed a hand on my cheek, staring into my eyes.

"My King," she said, her voice soft and full of the same devotion that swelled in me at hearing her say those words.

"My hellfire Queen," I whispered, looking into the eyes of the future I thought I lost, unable to hold back from asking her now, "will you marry me?"

She closed her eyes, a shudder running through her body, shaking me even as I held my breath.

Her hand on my cheek moved to caress my jaw, and still I waited for her answer.

"I love you," she said, opening her eyes, the look in them full of that emotion, no doubt showing. And yet I heard it, the caveat and hesitation that waited in her mouth.

Swallowing, my breath left me in a whoosh, and she closed her mouth over mine.

Kissing Cinder back, pressing her as tightly to me as I was able, I tried to find the reason in my own mind, but it wasn't there. I couldn't see it. And as much as I had promised to try and understand her, in this I found a bigger struggle than waiting for her to tell me all the details she kept buried for so long.

When I broke the kiss and looked at her again, a piece of my heart turned to flames. Unshed tears collected in her beautiful eyes.

Unwrapping one of my hands from around her caused a physical ache, but I ran that hand along her jaw.

"Please tell me," I said.

"My brother is a traitor. More than I ever guessed. Maybe it would be better to wait until after we defeat him. I don't want you to be the King with the traitor Queen."

The hand at her jaw trailed down to pull up the ring, still hanging on the chain around her neck, so I could look at it.

"When this is over, when he is defeated and you've proved to yourself as you already have to me, that the country will never think of you as a traitor, will you wear this?"

"Yes," she said, and I closed my eyes, kissing her. Every bit of my soul was relieved, and I hoped she felt how in love with her I was.

Pulling back this time, she smiled and closed her hand over mine around the ring.

"At the ceremony today," she said, looking at me, her eyes softening and her body melting against me, "I imagined us there. That's why I said the words. Please never think that I don't want you. All of you. Forever."

I kissed her again, and she held me as I held her.

Maybe patience was something I would have to learn no matter how much I hated it. I would do it gladly if, at the end of it, I got to stand next to Cinder and call her mine, out loud, to the world.

"You know," she said, tucking her head into my chest, and snuggling like I was her security blanket, "I wish we could have a small, private ceremony when it comes time."

Looking at the pile of her hair, I pulled back and started to undo it for her.

She sat up, and I followed, taking all the pins out, and running my fingers through the strands as I freed them, just as I wanted to earlier, tossing them to the side table as I got them loose.

"Well, if we have a private ceremony before some big, ridiculous international affair, I can vow to make you impatient all the time."

Cinder laughed and I kissed her shoulder, continuing the methodical undoing of her hair.

"Have you thought about it?" she asked, a measure of hesitation in her voice that made me run a hand down her arm, and kiss her shoulder again, softer this time.

"Thought about what, my Flame? You beside me as I make you mine? Yes. All the time."

"No, I know you thought about that." She dipped her head toward mine, and took a deep breath. "I mean, have you thought about what you want a wedding to be like?"

"A wedding? No. Have I thought about what a wedding with you would be like? Yes. I want whatever would make you happy and comfortable. I know that marrying me is a lot for you to agree to."

She turned around, grabbed my face, and pulled it close to her.

"Listen to me. Never, not one damn time, was it ever too much to think about marrying you. From the moment you gave me that ring, I have thought about everyone knowing you're mine, and it makes me happy. The only hesitations I have ever had are the throne, and who I am." She dropped one hand to press it against her chest, keeping the other on my cheek. "I love you."

"I love you, Cinder, and I know that."

"Good," she said, giving me a quick kiss before turning around again so I could keep pulling out the pins.

Smiling, I pulled another pin, and ran my fingers through that section of her hair.

"Now tell me what you thought about a wedding with me," she said, and I stifled a laugh.

All it took to make Cinder more comfortable was to make her angry. I filed that bit of information away to help me at some point in the future.

"The only thing I've really thought about is that I would like to use my mother's favorite flowers. She always said they were the Dragon King's roses, that they were planted by the original Kings of Onyx when they founded the kingdom, and forged the Obsidian Palace."

I pulled the last pin out of Cinder's hair and ran my hands through it all before she turned around and climbed onto my lap, smiling.

"My thing is flowers, too," she said into my chest as I laid us back into the bed. "When I spoke to Madam about it, I wanted the roses that used to grow at home. She said she would try to find them."

Running my hand down her back, my fingers through her hair, I nodded.

"We should find them and rename them Valentin roses then."

She placed her hand over my heart and sighed.

"I think she would like that."

CHAPTER 45

CHALLENGE

Cinder

Heat ran along my jawline in the morning, and I smiled before I even opened my eyes. Having Tristan back gave me the best sleep. Just another gift from him that I didn't even know he gave me.

Opening my eyes, I found the molten gold of his staring back at me before he leaned down and claimed my mouth, his hand trailing down my body, cupping my breast, rubbing it and playing with the nipple.

"Good morning," I said into his mouth, pressing my breast up against his hand.

"Hmmm," he made that noise of satisfaction that made me bite my lip before he sucked it into his mouth, nibbling it as he climbed over top of me, settling himself between my legs, his cock hard and pressing against me.

A ring sounded from across the room. He broke the kiss,

burying his face in my neck, and muttering a long litany of curses.

I laughed, not able to help it, and having a pretty good idea what that noise was.

"Do you have a ring for when someone needs the King?" I asked.

"Yes. And laughing makes your pussy rub against me, which is cruel right now." He kissed my neck, pressing his cock against me, and the ringing came again.

"Fuck," he muttered, planting a quick kiss on my mouth before he climbed from the bed and stomped across the room to pull a cord hanging by an alcove in the wall.

While I covered myself with a blanket, chilled without his warmth beside me, he grabbed a pair of training pants and slipped them on.

His room was smaller than mine downstairs, but not by much, which meant the tower we were in was one of the big ones. Above me, the ceiling soared toward the point, a vine with flowers on it growing along a crossbeam of the same Obsidian as the exterior. Up there with the low light of morning, it was hard to make out which plant it was.

I sat up in the massive, four poster bed, keeping the blanket against my chest, and followed the vine down the wall to where it ended in a specialized planter with hellfire water shining through the clear glass bottom, bright green.

And the plant…no. I couldn't be seeing what I thought I saw.

The rest of the room disappeared, ceased to matter. I barely noticed General Pace knock, or Tristan let her in.

Getting out of the bed, I dragged the blanket with me, and started toward the planter.

"Cinder?" Tristan asked, coming behind me, and wrapping the blanket around me so my ass wasn't hanging out in the back. But he didn't stop me as I reached the planter, and touched a little crimson bud, not yet opened, resting among the hellfire green leaves.

"It's the rose," I said.

"The one my mother called the Dragon King's rose," he said, and I turned to look at him, my mouth hanging open, tears pressing against the backs of my eyes and a smile forming on my face.

"No. This is the same rose that used to grow in Lehar. It snaked up the walls at home before the war. This is the rose I was talking about last night."

He smiled, his brow furrowing for a second and then clearing as he shook his head, looking past me at the flower.

"My mother's favorite," he muttered.

"And my mother's favorite."

Tristan pulled me to him with soft hands, wrapping me in his arms, and kissing my forehead before he turned us both toward General Pace.

"She asked me where she could find it for you," General Pace said, her face with that sad veil over her features that didn't go away anymore. At that moment, it was paired with a tiny, wavering smile.

"Madam Valentin asked you?" I whispered, afraid saying her name would make it worse.

But the General just sighed and nodded.

"I told her about King Tristan's roses, but she never had the chance to ask him." Her voice snagged on the word chance, and I went to my friend, wrapping my arms around her and holding on as she stiffened and then relaxed into me, hugging me back.

"We're renaming the rose," Tristan said, and the General looked up at him. "The Valentin rose."

General Pace's mouth trembled, and she nodded, pulling away from me to give the salute to both of us.

She didn't need me crying, so I held my tears back by sheer

force of will. Madam wouldn't want me to make it worse for the General.

"Excuse me," she said, turning toward the door before she stopped with her hand on the knob and said, "we'll be down in the office."

The door opened and shut, and General Pace was gone, leaving behind a pall of sadness that hung in the air and stole the warmth from me, even wrapped in the blanket.

But Tristan put his arms around me, and chased it all away. His heat fueled me, and reminded me there was still life. Madam would be angry if I didn't take this as a sign of her blessing to marry my King.

"I don't want to let you go, but I need to get dressed and go to this meeting," he said, kissing my neck. "But you can stay here as long as you want. Put in an order for something. Whatever it is. Food, books, weapons. Anything you want. Even clothes."

"Even clothes?" I asked, running my hands along the skin of his strong back.

He pulled back and looked at me, trailing a fiery touch along my arm, his eyes hungry, as if I was his favorite meal.

"You could stay naked up here all day, and I'll come to see you whenever I can get away." His grin turned mischievous, and I laughed, pushing him toward a wardrobe on one curved wall.

"Maybe I would do that if I thought you would be able to get away at all." Instead, I tossed the blanket back on the bed, and picked up my discarded dress.

"Cinder," he said, making me look over my shoulder at him. "I love you, but as an assassin, you really should have known that the best way to kill me would be to walk around like you are right now when I can't do a damn thing about it."

"Oh?" I held the dress up to my front, and leaned against the bed post, running the fabric along my body as I arched my back and bit my lip. "You mean, if I want you to live a long time, and fuck me a lot, then don't do this?"

"Gods, no." His breath came faster, and his hands splayed out as he watched me.

I dropped the dress in a pool at my feet, and ran my hand up my body instead, "What about this?"

"There isn't time." He said it like he was arguing with himself.

"Or this?" I asked, and dipped my fingers between my thighs, rubbing a small circle on my clit.

"Fuck," he muttered.

"Yes. Please. I would much rather you fuck me."

He growled low in his throat and darted to me, picking me up and throwing me down on the bed. Tristan yanked his pants off, and climbed up me, crashing his mouth into mine.

"Not enough time," he said into my mouth as I gasped at his cock rubbing against my sex.

Pulling back from my mouth, he kissed my neck and rubbed his thumb against my clit, making me need him more.

"I want you," I said, licking my hand and reaching between us to wrap it around his cock, making him slick, and lining the head up right where I wanted.

He pushed into me, slow and unhurried as he kept rubbing with his thumb, but I pressed his ass with my feet, urging him on.

A moan left him. It poured into my shoulder from his mouth and reverberated down through my body to settle in my heart.

The press of him, swift and insistent now, stretching me, left me gasping in every breath and moaning as I breathed out.

"Cinder," he said.

I made a whimpering sound, and tilted my hips up, wanting more.

"Tristan."

Rubbing his thumb in that perfect way that sent my legs shaking as I climbed the mountain of pleasure, my body beginning to come undone, he pressed himself all the way in. All restraint was gone.

He slammed into me, thrusting deeper, harder, and wilder than last night. His thumb never left me as he sent me shattering apart, tumbling down that mountain, crying out.

A desperation came over both of us, scrabbling at each other with mouths, tongues, and teeth, our hands grabbing and scratching, we crashed into each other and broke at the same time, crying out the other's name.

Tristan collapsed on top of me, and I ran my shaking hands along his back, my legs still quivered, locked tight around him, and my hips still bucked as my sex throbbed around his still-pulsing cock.

Wrapping me tight in his arms, he rolled over and brought me with him until I was on top, neither of us breathing normally.

"I love you, and that wasn't enough," he said, burying his face in my neck, and kissing the soft skin there.

"Never enough. And I love you, too." I moved his face so I could kiss him, and he grabbed my ass, pressing me against his cock, sending another wave of sensation rippling through me.

"My Flame," he pulled his mouth from mine as he smiled and looked into my eyes, "I meant, I didn't make you cum enough."

"Hmm," I mumbled, running a hand along his cheek, "let's say you owe me some attention tonight then."

The smile he gave me was full of promise, and he claimed my mouth with his as he lifted me up, pulled out of me, and gently laid me back down on the bed, his body hovering over me through another kiss.

"I love you. I have to go. Send word what you're doing, and I'll come to you when I can." He looked in my eyes, his soft, golden, and shining with a thousand more declarations of love.

But he was King. And part of the reason I loved him was because he was a good one.

"Go." I pressed on his chest, smiling back, hoping he saw in my face all I saw in his. "I love you."

He jumped up, threw on clothes in rushed and practiced movements, proving what I already knew was true. My King never shirked his duties before I came into his life. He always got up and answered the call when he was needed, and I should remember that the next time I chose to distract him.

Wrapping a hand around the ring hanging from my neck, I smiled, knowing that would be hard for me.

CHAPTER 46

ROYAL FAMILY

Tristan

"What are you saying? You have no idea where he is?" I rubbed my hands over my face and through my hair, trying to press down the rising fury inside me.

It wasn't their fault. Not the General's. Not the Chamberlain's. And not Rath's.

All of this was his fucking fault. And my need to see him dead for what he did to Cinder—if for no other reason among the thousands—made my vision blurry as it clouded everything else.

"Sorry, King. I can't get anything on him." Rath chewed on a piece of jerky, not biting into it and tearing off a chunk to chew on, just biting down on one end of it over and over again.

I clenched my teeth so hard that my own jaw hurt.

"What about the Corvids?" I needed something positive on one of these fronts. "Do we need to go back to Breakwater?"

Part of me wanted to go back to Breakwater with Cinder so we could relive the happy moments. But with everything going on, most of me didn't want to go anywhere near those cells, and risk all that negative energy seeping into anything. Especially if it would cause a problem between me and Cinder.

No plan that allowed even a shred of additional possibility that I would lose her was a plan worth trying.

"Duchess Inara and Rathmoreland's people all report the same thing," General Pace said, "much of the challenges with Corvids on the coast have resolved."

"I don't trust it, though," Rath said.

"We cannot trust that they are not coming up with some new way to attack," General Pace added, nodding, "and we cannot rule out that they may try to attack inland again."

Tangling my hands in my hair, I looked up at the ceiling while keeping them on top of my head. It forced my jaw to loosen, which managed to get some of my headache to subside.

But fuck.

"How did we lose track of Ash?" I asked, not specifically to them, but just to the world at large. If one of them had an answer, I wanted to hear it. "He has a whole damn army, and we know he was in Lehar after Thirteen Rivers Valley. That is more than a start on finding him."

"All we know is that he is not in Lehar and not in the Valley," the Chamberlain said, looking down at the notes of what we covered already. "And we warned the Twins in Mariposa that his initial plan was to head that way to get to Bridgeton."

"I heard that part," I said, trying to keep the rage out of my voice, and only partly succeeding. "What I do not understand is where he went with his huge army of slaves."

"Maybe they travel through the country the way those who attacked you and Duchess Cinder did—in small groups, not attracting attention," General Pace said, her brow furrowed, and her gaze focused on the middle of the table as if she was staring at a puzzle.

"Possibly," I said, thinking it through. It was a decent plan for part of his goals. The other part, though… "But eventually they will have to meet up in one place."

"Yes, and maybe they haven't done that, yet." Rath raised his eyebrows at me in the same scolding look his father used to give. I had to look away so I didn't punch him.

If he expected me to be fine waiting with no word at all about where the greatest threat to Cinder was. He didn't have a…

I turned my head to the side, looking toward the door and hoping for her to walk in.

Cinder didn't have a title in my life that was large enough for what she was to me. Not officially. Even without the crown, she was already my Queen.

And Ash running around the country, making his plans to attack when it might destroy her to fight him was enough to make my blood so hot that sweat beaded on my brow. My hands itched so badly for weapons. Cinder and I would need to spar soon.

"They will soon, if they have not already." I looked back at every person around the table, trying to convey to them how damn important this was. Defeating Ash and protecting Cinder as much as I could in the process was everything.

"When I know," Rath said, staring back at me, leaning forward with his face as serious as he was capable of being, "you'll know."

Nodding, I looked toward the door again. I needed to see her. I needed to hold her. I needed to feel her in the same room.

Just talking about it all with them made the need to be in the same room with her flare higher within me. She would tell me not to get distracted.

I turned back to them, about to tell them I would be right

back, but the General had a faraway look on her face. She looked stern, with a furrowed brow, her lips a fraction tighter than usual.

"General?" I asked, bracing myself for one of her brilliant battle plans or insights.

"There is one place we could still look," she said, taking a long breath and putting her face back to the impassive mask she usually wore, even if there was a tinge of sadness always there now, "but it might blow up our alliance with Amethyst."

"Where?" I asked, trying to imagine how some place in Onyx would cause a problem with Amethyst, but too much of my brain was taken up with the urge to run down the hall and demand answers from Prince Nevan.

Fuck Amethyst. Fuck the alliance, too, if it kept Cinder safe from her bastard brother.

"The area inside Amethyst where he kept his slaves may be where he fled to."

Her theory made sense. And pissed me off all over again.

"After everything," I said, rubbing my hands over my face and hair again, "his whole careful process of bringing in his people, why would he go through it all over again just to flee because he lost the element of surprise?"

"King, there's something else." Rath's voice was low, ominous.

"What else?"

"None of us can rule out the possibility that he had more friends than just the former Lord Fall."

"Fuck," I said, shaking my head and almost laughing even though I didn't find any of this funny, "how many of my own people want me dead?"

"Come on, King."

"I'm serious, Rath. My parents never had people rebel against their rule. Especially not to this extent—plotting together, declaring a false king, raising an army." Somewhere along the way, I did something very wrong to make my own people hate me so much. It was the only answer that made any sense.

"Your parents had each other and an heir," the Chamberlain said, trying for neutral, and yet I still heard the 'I told you so' waiting in the statement. "Even if the very same people wanted to overthrow your parents, it would have been a bigger challenge to do so."

Hanging my head, I twisted my hands into fists on the table.

"Point taken. I was not ready, and neither was she. Seven years ago I was only twenty-one and she was only fifteen." All the Chamberlain's pressure over the years since I became King went through my head again.

For years, the regular arrivals of young noble women for their presentation at court were all I had to delay the potential bride search that the Chamberlain eventually forced us all into. Everyone had so hoped I would finally fall for one of them.

I never even got close after my parents died.

Of course, Cinder didn't come to court. And I stubbornly wanted more than my parents had. More than the arranged marriage I almost agreed to when I was eighteen that my mother talked me out of. More than assuming a pretty woman I got along with would make a good enough relationship.

My mother made me understand that what I almost agreed to so many years ago would never turn into what I hoped for. I wanted to love my Queen. I didn't want to have the cold, professional relationship with her that my parents had with each other. I didn't want years of distance between me, my wife, and our children because of the lack of love. The thought of breakfast being a diplomatic event for the rest of my life made everything in me run cold.

More than once I wondered if my father's distance from me was because of his distance from my mother. I didn't want that for my future, or the future of my children.

They finally broke me down. When Rath heard that rumblings of discontent and disbelief of the Dragon Kings were growing, I finally agreed to the Chamberlain's stupid scheme to search for a potential queen.

Now that I found so much more than I ever thought I would, I would never regret the wait. Even if it left us vulnerable.

"I know everyone wishes we had a royal family to secure the succession, but I cannot, I *will* not, force Cinder to take the crown before she is ready."

General Pace nodded. Rath raised a brow, and his smile grew a wicked edge like he was thinking inappropriate things. But the Chamberlain's mouth opened.

"That is even truer of children, so do not even think about bringing it up to her."

Everyone nodded, but I didn't trust that they would all listen. Not when it came to this. And the last thing I wanted causing a problem between Cinder and I was the issue of children. That damage could be permanent.

"Let me make this plain: if I find that anyone pressures her in any way about children, then they will be removed from their position."

With widened eyes, they all put on more serious expressions, and got back to work, talking of other things.

My mind was back on Cinder. All I could do was hope that we would both live through this war just so that we could have that conversation. But I had the largest target on my head, and my Flame burned bright enough to make her a target, too.

And part of me worried that her brother wanted her dead even more than he wanted to kill me.

CHAPTER 47

COMPETITION

Cinder

"**G**ood," I yelled at the guards sparring in the center of the circle. "Next time, use your other blade for the killing strike."

They tried again, the block, the fumbling pull of the dagger. It didn't work, and the attacker got through using the distraction to their advantage.

"A death to you. Well done." The guard who tried to pull the dagger stepped back, and rubbed their shoulder where their opponent's wooden sword hit.

"Listen, pulling a secondary blade is a good way to secure the kill, but only if you are comfortable enough to do it quickly and accurately. Otherwise, it leaves you more open in the process." I swung my wooden practice sword in a quick attack on one of the guards who managed to block my swing with little effort. At the same time, I pulled my spike, and held it to their neck.

"How did I do that?" I asked, holding the position, the

guard frozen in front of me, eyes roving over me trying to work through it for themselves just as the crowd of watchers did.

"You used your own movement during the swing to sweep your hand along your thigh, and pull out your spike," Tristan yelled as he walked through the gathered guards, smiling. I stepped back from the guard, smiling with him, "Because you are always aware of where your blades are, and are comfortable with pulling them."

"Exactly." I kept my voice raised for the benefit of the watching guards, but my focus was all on my King. "That is a good thing to practice, pulling your second blade in combat."

"Maybe break out into pairs and practice that now," Tristan yelled, coming to my side, and picking up my hand with the spike still in it to kiss the back of it. "Hello, my Flame."

I stepped closer to him, the grin on my face impossible to wipe off as I thought about stealing away with him while the guard trained.

"Show us first," one of the guards yelled.

Laughing, I looked out at the assembled guards, none of them left the circle to pair up and practice. All of them had glee in their eyes as they looked at us.

"What do you say, my King?" I asked, my voice low.

"I say," his eyes shone, and he wrapped an arm around me pulling me closer, making my heartbeat ratchet up, "keep calling me that, and I might just tell everyone to fuck off because I need to go make my hellfire Queen moan those words while I make up for this morning."

"Fight me for it." I leaned in closer, and let my lips brush his ear as he made that humming noise.

"Fight you for what, exactly?" he whispered, a thrill going through me as his hand on the small of my back pressed me closer.

"Let's say whoever wins the fight gets to tell the other what to do." I bit my lip as he pulled his face away, his eyes going right to my lip between my teeth.

"Keep biting that lip. I'll just drag you away right now, and you can tell me to do anything." The hunger in his eyes made a ripple of sensation run through me that settled low in my core.

"Aw, poor King Tristan, he's afraid he'll lose, and then I'll make him hold still until *he* screams."

Tristan turned my hand and guided it until my spike was put away, at the same time he leaned into my ear and whispered, "Promises, promises. But, remember, I'm loudest when you scream."

"Come on, spar for us," a guard yelled, and they started to chant, "Spar, spar, spar."

"One hour," he said, "best out of ten gets the winner one hour of anything they want."

His grin as he stepped back from me turned that ripple into a wave, and I wanted him so badly it was hard to remember what was happening.

"Why only one hour?" I asked as he equipped himself with two wooden swords.

"Because I am impatient," he said, and lunged at me.

The guards cheered as he crashed his wooden sword into mine, lifting the other to my ribcage.

"A death to you," I said, stepping back and taking an additional wooden sword from a guard's hand as they held it out to me.

Fighting Tristan with two blades each made us better matched in a sparring circle. I let him get ahead by two deaths, planning to strip away his win at the end.

"Come on, Fighter Cinder," some guards yelled when it was five to three, and I needed to move faster.

But I had a problem.

Every time I looked into his eyes, he held his ravenous gaze to mine. I didn't want to be in the sparring ring. I wanted to be with him. The way my body called for his distracted me from my goal here.

"Ready?" he asked, his eyes roaming across my body like a physical touch.

"Only one more and you win," I said, twirling my swords in my hands, and dropping into a crouch.

"Motivation," he raised a brow at me, his smile widening.

Running toward him, I made a pass that he parried easily, but he didn't turn as fast as I did, catching him with a tap on the back of his neck.

"A death to you," he yelled over the cheering of some of the guards.

"King Tristan," other guards cheered in response, their warring cries making me laugh.

He came at me, dropping low at the last second, and surging one of his swords up to clang against mine as I swiped down toward him.

With a swift move, his other sword caught my downward swing.

Dancing backward from him, he kept on, relentless in his swings and parries, putting me on the defensive.

Swords clashing against each other, we smiled while the guard cheered at every well-delivered thrust and move.

Finally, as I crossed up all four of our blades, I dropped to swing around him, and he tossed the blades away, snatching me up from the ground, supporting my knees with one arm and my back with the other.

His grin turned feral.

The guard went wild, but if they thought this was a win, they were wrong.

I flung one leg up, wrapping it around his neck, twisting in his arms, and landing on my hands. I secured my legs around his head while he grabbed at them, yanking him off his feet and over my body, letting go at the right time.

Tristan tucked and rolled out of the flip, and I was on him, grabbing a fallen wooden sword on my way by.

"A death to me," I said, breathless as I straddled his lap, his mouth hanging open, eyes wide, and my wooden blade held to his side.

His chest heaving, he shook his head and smiled as the guard yelled.

"New moves?" he asked, his voice low and just for me as his face went from shock to something more like appreciation.

"So many moves," I said, grinning and helping him up.

"You're going to have to show me that one again." His eyes shone, his gaze grew hungry, and I knew he didn't mean now when he couldn't do a damn thing about it.

"Impatient, yet?" I asked, leaning in.

"Always." He stepped back, picked up one of the fallen swords himself, spun it, and raised a brow at me. "Five to five."

"To your posts," General Pace's voice rang out over the cheering hum of the guards as she broke into the circle and announced, "an army marches on Bridgeton from the North."

Dropping my wooden sword, I ran alongside my King toward horses being pulled from the stables. Our fun competition was quickly forgotten as we prepared to fight in the much bigger one. Not against each other, but side by side.

KALEIDOSCOPE

Tristan

"Cinder, please put on some armor," I said, holding my breastplate so the groom could strap me in.

"This is armor," she looked down at herself as she strapped on even more blades.

But the bustier she wore with the other pieces of her outfit was the only metal, and it didn't cover her shoulders, her arms, or her legs in any way.

"Leather does not give a lot of protection," I said, pointing to her arms and legs.

"Fine," she sighed, and strapped on greaves and forearm guards that didn't cover as much as the vambraces and pauldron I wanted her to wear.

"What about your thighs?" I asked, moving so the last piece of my own light armor could be attached.

"Can't. No time, and I need my spikes." She kissed me, and ran to the horses.

"Fuck. Thank you," I called to the groom as I ran out after her.

"How far north? Where were they spotted? Corvid or Ash?" She asked rapid fire questions of General Pace as I swung myself into the saddle, and we started moving out of the palace.

"Not far enough," the General said, her face in the hard lines she always wore during a fight. "They will be at the border of Bridgeton by now, and we need to go down to the East bridge. The West one is full of guard from the training grounds crossing toward the fight."

"Other guards in the city are meeting us there, right?" I asked as we entered the tunnel out of the palace.

"The other guards in the city are already fighting."

"Fuck," I muttered under my breath, hoping the horses crossing would stop my voice from carrying to everyone around us, but Cinder turned her head. I cursed myself for not keeping my stupid mouth shut.

We made it across the bridge, and Cinder, my personal group of guards, the General, and I all urged our horses up to speed through the city.

Not many people in Bridgeton spent much time outside these days, and still there were a few who had to move their carriages aside or run out of the way to avoid us as we charged down the street.

The East bridge crossed the river that divided north and south Bridgeton. No one knew why the Dragon Kings created the palace in the center of the river with only one exit to the south. But the East bridge wasn't far from the palace, and we barely slowed to take the turn onto it.

Looking to the skies, I still wondered which force we were about to confront.

Part of me hoped it was Ash and his army because traditional warfare felt more comfortable. But part of me, especially the part that didn't care about anything except the woman who rode next to me, hoped it was Corvid troops just so she didn't have to see her brother on the opposite side of a battlefield again.

But there wasn't time to ask questions of the General, not as our horses thundered through the streets of the capitol city, headed to fight an unknown foe.

There was only time to wonder if it would be enough. If the training the guard received was enough. If the guards we already had at the front would be enough to hold them back until reinforcements arrived. Until we arrived.

Fighting in the streets of Bridgeton already proved to be a deadly gambit our enemies would use. After the deaths of far too many civilians in those attacks, and the atrocities committed afterward on those captured, any horror seemed possible.

I urged my horse to move even faster. I needed to see the battlefield. I needed to know what we were up against.

Cinder kept pace with me. Her riding was like her fighting, focused and all-out, sure of herself, moving with a grace belying her power.

Looking at Cinder beside me, my heart hurt for her.

Turning back to focus forward, I tried to tell myself that everything would be okay. That anything Cinder suffered because of what her brother was doing would be something I could help her through.

She wasn't alone in this the way she was when she survived his abuse for all those years.

But no matter how hard I tried, unease seeped into my bone marrow, and my hands tightened their grip on the reins.

No matter what happened, and no matter how long it took, Cinder would be alright after all this. She had to be.

We rode hard, our horses heaving deep breaths by the time we slowed at the edge of the city. The duchy of Mariposa's kaleidoscope fields—a riot of color and beauty in the summer when all the flowers and herbs bloomed—lay frosted and devoid of flowers now in deep winter. Instead, they had a fresh crop of the dead, dying, wounded, and the rest of two armies standing off on the north and south ends of the fields.

Bodies were being collected from the middle of what was now a battlefield, the kaleidoscope of beauty and life transformed into a mosaic of death and suffering.

General Pace slipped ahead of Cinder and I, leading our group to the captain of our side.

He stood with a small group of others, conferring.

Across the battlefield, the other side looked like a ragtag collection of people, with only a few in purple armor.

It was those in armor whom I studied, trying to make out whether Ash was there while keeping an eye on Cinder's reaction to everything.

She didn't flinch, but she scanned everything as closely as I did. And she would likely spot her brother before I could.

Once we reached the group of commanders, I dismounted, and stood closely enough to take Cinder's hand when she followed suit.

Looking in her eyes, I searched for any sign that this was hurting her, but there was nothing beside hellfire-forged steel, and determination.

I squeezed her hand and suppressed the heat rising inside me at the thought that she was even here, in harm's way. I couldn't force her off this battlefield, no matter how much it tore at me for her to put herself at physical risk. And, in this case, even worse emotional risk.

"Update," General Pace barked at the group as we arrived.

"General, King Tristan, Fighter Cinder," the Captain said, all the guards in the group gave the salute. "This was a mess."

"Tell me," I said, "Details. What do we know, and what do we still need to determine?"

"We got word that the guards in Mariposa were attacked while they slept."

"All of them?" Cinder asked, her voice harsh, and I imagined that tally of pain her brother caused her just grew.

I rubbed my thumb over the back of her hand.

"No. Some of the guards escaped the attack, and some were not at the barracks when it happened. But…" the Captain's voice trailed off and his gaze jumped around, not meeting any of our eyes.

"Everyone needs to know," the General said.

"One of the Twins turned traitor, and killed his brother." His voice was hard, bitter, like he took it personally.

He had no idea.

Cinder reached across herself to hold my hand with both of hers, and I tamped down on the emotions roiling within me.

Mariposa was comprised of two duchies, Imago and Instar, that functioned as one under the governance of twin siblings for generations. Everyone called the dukes who ran Mariposa the Twins.

"We know where they have been at least," I said to General Pace, and she nodded.

How long did they plot all this? How did Ash manage to find Lord Fall and one of the Twins to turn to his side, how many more traitors were there in my Kingdom?

"And this battle?" I asked, looking out at the field as the last bodies were cleared off it.

The Captain turned to look out over the field with a baleful eye on the enemy on the other side.

"Once we were told of the slaughter of the guard, we set out, but found them already lined up here. The fight was immediate, and I wouldn't call them organized, or even especially skilled, but they are…almost crazed with bloodlust and keep attacking even after they are terribly wounded." He shook his head and looked back at us. "I have never seen anything like it."

I swallowed and looked to Cinder. This was her brother's army. Our forces already crossed blades with her brother's.

But she just shook her head and squeezed her eyes shut for an extra second before staring back at me. Nothing in her eyes suggested she needed me to take her away from here, or even to ask if she were okay.

Hopefully I would be strong enough for that.

"Why did the battle stop?" Cinder asked, her voice giving no hints either. "It looks like both sides still want to kill each other."

The Captain gave her a wry grin.

"Of course we do. But, apparently, somewhere along the way they started using the same horn blows we do during a battle."

Cinder looked at me, a line forming between her brows in silent question.

"Horns are used to signify things in battle," I whispered to her.

"They sounded the humanitarian retreat horn, and our people followed the same instructions."

"We need a new way to communicate to our side," Cinder said, and everyone nodded.

"Yes. And we need to know why they called for the break." I ground my teeth, and wondered if Ash was among their wounded or dead. Would they continue fighting, or would they give up?

CHAPTER 49

BEAST

Cinder

"Because Ash is not here yet," I said, looking across the battlefield, hanging onto Tristan's hand like it was the only thing keeping me from throwing myself across the field, and killing my way through my brother's army.

Maybe it was.

"Why would that matter?" General Pace asked, her voice serious, brooking no bullshit, but not unkind.

"If Ash were here, he would never let them collect their dead or wounded. He believes that getting wounded during a fight proves you were not good enough. Getting killed is worse." How many times did he warn me not to bring anything with me that would trace back to him? How many times did he tell me not to worry, because, if I died, he would put a marker next to the others who we never recovered from the blast in Lehar?

And how many times did I think that was a sign he loved me?

Taking in a shuddering breath, I looked to Tristan while the General and the commanders kept talking about specifics and battle plans.

My King would move the Protectorate Mountains to reclaim my body if I died. So would all my friends.

Part of me was no longer sure my brother was capable of love. Part of me wondered if he ever was.

But it didn't matter anymore.

When Tristan looked to me, his eyes glowing hellfire green, his jaw tight, none of what Ash thought mattered.

The man in front of me, the country he represented, and my friends were what mattered. So, whatever the fuck Ash managed to convince himself of, and whatever the fuck he thought was going to happen, he would be disappointed.

A quick squeeze of my hand, and Tristan engaged again in the conversation. I turned back to study the opposite side of the field.

More guards arrived on our side, the reinforcements from the training grounds, but more were arriving across the field as well.

I let go of Tristan, wandering down through the lines of the guards, my eyes trained on all the people coming through the trees to mingle with the loose tangles of the people facing us.

Somewhere in my body an alarm sounded, clanging loudly in my head, slowing my blood as it moved through me. My feet didn't feel connected correctly to my legs.

By the time I stepped onto the open, frozen ground of the field, puddles and lines of blood turning strips of it into mud, I saw a familiar head of hair and a familiar body, seated atop a prancing horse as he came through the trees.

I gasped and sucked in a long breath.

My brother was here.

No matter how sure I was that he wouldn't want to miss

this, no matter how much I knew what he was now, seeing him like this, on different sides in a war, would never be easy.

The child still inside me that clung to him with everything I had left of me after our parents' deaths would never cease feeling the horrible shock of his betrayal. Never.

Seeing him with my own eyes, truly seeing all of what he chose to become, tore open that raw little hole in my heart that he created, not just making it larger, but more jagged and painful.

He stared across the field, scanning the army behind me. Finally, he jerked in his saddle, the only signal I needed to know that he saw me.

I was too far away to see if he smiled. But I did as I turned on my heel and looked back at my King making his way through the crowd to my side, joined by General Pace and the commanders.

"You okay?" Tristan whispered when he reached me.

"My brother is here," I whispered back.

His head snapped up, and a second later he narrowed his eyes. He found Ash in the crowd.

It wasn't hard. The asshole was the only one over there on a horse.

But...no he wasn't.

As I stared at my brother, another horse emerged from the woods. This one had a rider dripping in purple, including her long purple hair flowing with the movement of her horse.

"Tristan?" I asked, my voice low.

"I see her." His voice had the same curious edge mine did.

From here, I wasn't sure who she was.

Until she reached my brother's side, and he lifted her hand to kiss the back of it. Her hair changed color.

Sucking in a breath I looked to Tristan who only lifted his brows.

"Marquessa Ziya," he said, that same note of curiosity in his voice.

"The Marquessa married my brother. But she was just at Breakwater trying to marry you." All the curiosity was gone from me. Now I was just disgusted. "Perfect match for a snake."

"I'm no longer sure which one you're referring to.

"Neither am I."

Ash apparently didn't get the reaction he wanted, he reached over and grabbed her, pulling her into a kiss.

But if he thought that would do something more than put a bad taste in my mouth, he was wrong.

Making a face at them, Tristan turned to me.

All my brother's terrible choice in a wife managed to really do was make me thankful she wasn't married to my King. She could have her false one.

"Now we know who his ally in Amethyst is," Tristan said, and I gave him a wry smile.

"What's your plan?" Tristan's whisper now had that otherworldly quality to it, and I closed my eyes, knowing he wouldn't like what I was about to say.

"Ash won't be at the front. He'll sit on his horse all the way at the back with a team ready to extract him and the Marquessa."

Tristan made a scoffing sound and nodded.

Yes, Tristan, my brother was a coward who was more than happy to have everyone else fight his battles for him.

I knew that better than anyone.

"My plan is to fight through the lines of his army until I cut his escape team out from under him. My plan is for Ash's scheming to end here. Today."

Looking at Tristan then, meeting his wide eyes, and watching as a muscle in his jaw clenched, I knew I was right. He didn't like this plan.

"You don't have to do this, you can cut off his escape route and leave him to me," he said, his voice tight.

"But I should do this. We need to end this." Even if I had to lose every blade in the bodies of his army on the way to him, once I got there, he needed to die.

Even if I had to skip over the part in my mind where I did it, I knew it needed to happen.

And when he died, I would make sure he was buried far from Lehar in an unmarked grave so he could go on unmourned forever.

"Just let me deal with him directly. He's your bother, you shouldn't have to." Tristan grabbed me and pulled me into his chest, ignoring the people all around us, the blood on the field, the dead waiting nearby for someone to bury them. He kissed me, and I melted against him.

When he pulled back from me, looking into my eyes, and moving one hand from my back to cup my cheek, he sighed.

"Please be careful," he said, his voice struggling around the rage choking him, "I need you to come back to me."

"I will always come back to you. You are mine, and I am yours, and I love you."

"And we belong together."

Nodding, I closed my eyes, and he kissed me again.

We pulled apart and stepped a distance enough from each other for him to pull his bow and nock an arrow, and for me to pull the short swords strapped to my back.

The horn sounded from the other end of the field. Ash waved a sword in the air like he thought he was impressive.

Everyone surged forward.

I ran faster than Tristan, but every arrow that shot past me as I sprinted toward the screaming onslaught of humanity told me he was there. With me. Fighting for me.

Before I reached the fastest of their army, a cry went up from my own forces.

"Crows!"

Fuck.

How Ash managed to get them to ally with him when he was planning to take over Corvid, too, was a problem to solve after we killed as many of them as possible.

A quick glance to the air, and there they were, Corvids flying out from behind the tree line. Along with them, more forces streamed onto the field, these in black, feathered uniforms.

One day, I needed to thank the Corvids for marking their ground troops by wearing feathers. If they didn't, we would be a lot more likely to attack our own thinking it was them.

Knowing the crows were coming didn't slow me down.

Especially not when they started to topple from the sky as our archers—including my King—targeted them.

We prepared for this, I reminded myself as I held on to the chill in the winter air, let it fuel my cold place, and imbue my body with force.

The features of Ash's fastest fighter came into focus, and I readied my swords in my grip. I blocked their swing and sliced their head from their body in one move, not slowing down.

More people came at me, and I destroyed them as fast as my arms and legs could move, some of them never getting their swing started.

Within seconds, I was in the thick of their advance, hacking and stabbing, blocking and slicing my way through body after body. The cold place allowed my body to rebound from impact after impact as they reverberated up my arms.

I might feel it all later, but I used it for now, allowing the yanking of my sword from one body to propel it into someone else.

As it had all along, the cold place made me more than a sword-wielding woman, more than a Fighter. I was an exten-sion of my blade. I was a weapon. My muscles absorbed the shock of my sword hitting bone only to return the same energy into my next strike.

My brother might have created an assassin, but I was more than that now.

I was a conduit for the death and destruction of all he hoped to accomplish.

A shadow fell over me from above. I stabbed my sword into the chest of one of Ash's people only to shove off the ground, let go of the sword, and use the strike's momentum and the still upright body of my victim to launch myself into the air.

With my other sword, I gutted the Corvid flying at me, sending a torrent of hot blood spraying over the frozen field.

Between the jump into the air and the power of the bird's panic before it died, I sailed high above the fray for a moment.

My eyes went to Ash on his stupid horse, an arrow coming for his heart.

But even as I braced myself to see my brother skewered again, a familiar flash shot up and blocked the arrow.

In front of Ash, her armored cloak catching the muted rays of the winter sun, Jocelyn fought to protect him.

Crashing to the ground, the cold place temporarily wrenched from me, I slammed into three of Ash's people from behind, sending them sprawling in the blood-soaked, frozen dirt that was fast turning to mud.

Snatching a sword from one of them as they laid stunned, I pulled one of my spikes and stabbed all three of them as I struggled to get control of my breathing and find that place again.

But the hot blood and bodies of the fallen acted as a sacrifice to the land, turning it from a frost-covered, fallow field to a steaming beast resurrected from somewhere between life and death as it stole soul after soul from the dead and the dying.

The beast fought me for control over the cold place as I sliced and stabbed every enemy around me, my muscles screaming.

My forward momentum through the advancing army ceased as I flagged, my breathing ragged.

What was happening to me?

I needed to pull it together. I needed to get to Ash. I needed to end this.

Even if getting to Ash now meant certain death at Jocelyn's hands, no matter what Tristan said, and no matter how hard it was for me to imagine, I wanted to be the one to make this right.

Screaming an incomprehensible wail of frustration, I managed to get some of my strength back as the first of our guards to catch up to me appeared on either side of me.

As soon as they reached me, I took a deep breath and let their advance buy me a second to adjust my grips and look to the ice-flavored sky, letting it return me to that place.

It only took a few seconds, but that was enough time not only to get me there, but also to spot a formation of Corvids, tight together, flying right for our front line. Right for me.

"Help me jump," I yelled to one of our guards, grabbing him by the collar.

With a gesture and some more shouting, in the few seconds we had, the guard—who was used to me by now as all the guards were—cleared a circle and two more crouched down for me to run the four steps to them.

Leaping onto their shoulders as if it were another step in my run, they shot to their feet and threw me into the air, right at a Corvid's face.

It squawked that strange, half-human, half-crow sound, rearing back, wings flaring.

But no matter how fast it tried to adjust, it didn't get away from me as I rocketed through the air toward it.

With one hand, I reached out and stabbed my spike into the bird's shoulder, ripping it apart as I swung onto its back.

The crow fought to maintain flight, but it would fail.

Yanking my spike out as I jumped from its back to the next one assured me of that.

Landing on the next one's back, I grinned as the bird lifted almost straight up in the air, thinking that would help it.

A swift stab into its eye, and I let myself fall through the air toward the next one.

Two down, a lot more to go.

Maybe I could get one to drop me on my brother's head.

CHAPTER 50

FALL

Tristan

"Cinder," I screamed, firing another arrow at a Corvid careening toward her as she jumped from one crow to another, killing as she went.

It was as if she danced along the crows and the air like she did that night with Rath, blades flashing.

"Arrows," I yelled, grabbing one of the last in the quivers on my back.

One of the guards set another quiver at my feet without a word, tapping me on the leg.

Seconds later, I snatched it off the ground as I flung my empty one backward toward where the resupply would come from behind me, sweeping the full new quiver onto my back, and moving as fast as I could to keep my pace up as I shot another.

"Please," I muttered on a loop. To whom, I didn't know and couldn't guess. But watching Cinder fly through the air made the heat rise so high in me that I wondered if the winter air turned to steam as it hit me. Although, it was probably the blood seeping into the ground that made the air hazy. Not hazy enough to block my view of her meting out death to anything she could reach as she went from bird to bird, sometimes allowing them to bring her higher, and sometimes falling out of the sky at another with her arms and legs sprawled out.

Relying on the guards around me to knock any Corvids out of the sky as they got near me, and keeping the forces on the ground off me, every fraction of my focus was on my Queen as she laid waste to the enemy in a way that I didn't think possible. I shot at anything that tried to target her.

One second, she defied gravity, as much a creature of the wind as the magical birds she rode upon. The next, she stabbed another in the eye, wrenched her spike free, and there were no other crows for her to land on anywhere near.

"Cinder," I screamed, forgetting all about my bow, the fight happening around me, anything but her as she rode the bird dropping out of the sky. I ran as fast as I could in her direction.

"Get out of the way. Out of my way. Move. Go." I yelled orders at the people I passed, orders that got shorter, sharper, less coherent, louder, and more fully imbued with mind-rattling panic with every step I wasn't there.

Something happened around me. People moved and shifted in ways I didn't understand, couldn't properly look at, and didn't care about as I screamed her name while she and the falling Corvid corpse disappeared from sight.

"Cinder, Cinder, Cinder." Every inhalation grated against my searing hot rib cage, and every exhalation was her name. Each more desperate and hoarse than the last.

The people around me cleared, and, somehow, I found her.

My Queen, my home, lay atop the shattered and broken corpse of a Corvid reduced to a mass of bloody feathers and bones.

Falling to my knees next to her, I looked at her chest, my shaking hands touching her cheek and her stomach, afraid of putting pressure on her even as I stared at her, looking for breath. Begging for it.

But nothing moved her chest. Her eyes were closed. There were no signs of life.

Fuck being careful. I needed to try. Tears flooded my eyes, and I scooped her up in my arms, tucking my face against hers, listening for that breath.

"Please, Cinder. Come back to me." I cried and held her limp body tighter.

Finally, she coughed and wheezed in a breath.

"Tristan," she said, her voice weak and barely there.

"You came back." I didn't know what I was saying, and it didn't matter. My Cinder, my Flame, my Queen was alive and in my arms.

Burying my face in her neck, my tears didn't stop.

"Always will."

Those two words, not audible but for my ear where it pressed along her jaw, sent a wave of rage through me at those who would have stolen her just when I got her back.

Looking up, the last of Ash's troops were leaving the field, dragging their wounded with them, leaving behind a swath of bodies that littered the field as if they were nothing more than the normal refuse of an army on the move.

He was still there on his fucking horse, too far away for me to make out his face. I hoped someone hurt him during the battle.

Shifting Cinder in my arms, I grabbed an arrow, knocked it, aimed at his heart, and fired.

It flew toward him while I dropped the bow and clutched Cinder tightly to me, my eyes never leaving him.

A second before it would have skewered him, a flash of what looked like metal came out of nowhere and blocked it.

Someone stood in front of his horse. They blocked it. I should have aimed for them.

"You are dead!" My voice carried, louder and with more weight than it ever had before, not entirely sounding like my own. It was a promise. A vow. And it rang out over the battlefield with all the weight of the blood soaking into the ground around me.

Before this war ended, I would see him dead.

Ash and the person with him turned and fled into the forest.

Cinder's hand gripped my jacket—the first sign that she could move—and I gasped, my tears still falling.

"It's going to be okay. You'll be fine," I muttered kissing her still-closed eyes, pleading with the world that what I said was true.

"King Tristan," General Pace said, sliding to her knees in the blood-soaked mud next me, "We need to go. She needs to be seen to."

"Jacquetta," I said, lifting my head and searching the General's face. "We need to get her to the palace and have Jacquetta attend to her."

She nodded, and I lifted the limp body of my Flame in my arms as I got to my feet.

Once, I would have said carrying her at a time like this, as I had in the past, meant she was heavy and difficult to lift.

Not now. Now she was a part of me. The only pain I felt was hers and the aching of my heart that she had it at all.

We rode in a carriage someone borrowed from somewhere, Cinder still in my arms. The only sign of life was her steady heart beating, her chest moving air in and out of her lungs, and her one hand gripped tight on my jacket.

Eventually I would ask about the carriage, and about what happened at the end of the battle. But right now, my brain could only keep one thought in it for more than a second.

Cinder.

Bringing her into the palace, taking her up the stairs, Jacquetta waited in the doorway with Augustina beside her.

I expected Jacquetta to cry and Augustina to hold her up. Now, though, Jacquetta was all focus and precision, reminding me of her mother. Augustina did everything Jacquetta asked of her, but tears poured down her cheeks and dripped off her chin.

They checked Cinder carefully, treating her with herbs and flowers made into the medicines I watched Madam use before, and, eventually, a bath filled with all manner of things floating in it.

And not one time during any of it did I let go of my Queen. Even as they took her clothes off, I remained dressed in mine, my arms around her. When they said she needed to be in the bath, I climbed in with her, holding her. Even when they declared that she would be fine, that she needed rest, I tucked blankets around her and laid in the bed with her, allowing only General Pace in at first to give me updates and work.

Because if I lost Cinder, keeping the country together would cease to matter.

Plus, everyone else was better equipped to deal with things than I was right now.

Not when she needed me.

My place was with her.

Because I was hers. And she was mine.

CHAPTER 51

WAKING UP

Cinder

My brother blew the retreat horn when I fell from the sky.

That's what the General explained to Tristan. They didn't know why he did it. It didn't make sense to either of them.

"Because he got what he wanted," I muttered, my voice thin and hoarse, exhausting me in the effort to say the words, leaving me gasping and unable to keep my eyes open.

"Cinder," Tristan said, his lips fluttering the lightest touches along my cheeks.

"What did he want?" General Pace asked, more focused on the problem at hand than my beautiful King—who seemed unable, or unwilling, to pay attention to anything other than me for more than a minute.

"He wants me dead…He thought he got it."

They lapsed into silence, a shudder running through Tristan that transferred to my aching body.

"Your brother will not get that," the General said.

"No, he won't," Tristan said, his voice with all the authority of a ringing vow.

"I have too much to live for," I said, allowing my mind to wander from this room, and the pain surging through my muscles and bones.

Sometime later, I didn't know how long, I woke up to the heat of Tristan wrapped around me, one hand running along my cheek, trailing a path of fiery glory.

"Hmm," I muttered.

"Oh, Cinder," he said, pressing his forehead to mine, "you're awake."

"No. Not really. I'm enjoying the way that feels when you run your hot fingers along my skin."

"Umm, that's fun to know. Remind me to use that against you later," Rath said, and I popped my eyes open.

He sat on a chair at the foot of the bed where I was still wrapped in a blanket with Tristan holding me.

"Welcome back to the world of the living," Rath said, grinning at me, leaning forward, and resting his elbows on his knees.

"I didn't die."

"Only almost," Tristan said, holding me a fraction tighter, his breath hitching. "Please don't try that again."

"My King," I said, and Tristan hummed, managing to make me smile in spite of myself, "I will do what I need to do to keep you safe."

He pulled his face back, and I opened my eyes, looking into his, bright green now.

"The only way I am safe is if you are."

So much of my body hurt, and even with that, I pulled his mouth down to mine and kissed him.

"Ahem," Rath said, as if he was speaking the sound of a cough.

We broke the kiss and I said, "Subtle."

Tristan laughed while Rath looked at him funny.

"I may have some news that might help us as we try to keep *both* our King and Queen safe."

Looking at Tristan, not only did I look forward to whatever intelligence Rath could give us, but I couldn't wait to be his Queen.

"Tell us," Tristan said while I tried to think up a way to ask my King to marry me.

AFTERWORD

Thank you for reading!
If you enjoyed this book, please leave a review at your favorite
bookseller.
Don't forget to go to jdarleneeverly.com and sign up for the
newsletter to be the first to know about all the updates on this
series. The fifth book, After Glass Shatters is coming September
2022.
As a special exclusive for those who sign up for the newsletter,
the author is giving away an exclusive prequel in this series, as
well as an exclusive free book in another story world and more.

ACKNOWLEDGMENTS

A whole hearted thank you to Bean, the Rottens, and all of my friends and family. A big bag of thanks to Jupiter Alley and Krystal for their help in making this happen, Heather Cardona for all she does, Miblart for the gorgeous cover, as well as the team at Wishing Well.

The great team at Miblart continues to amaze me with their beautiful work while their country is fighting for their lives. They are Ukrainian designers, so this is a special thanks to them, and a plea to the universe that peace returns to Ukraine soon. Glory to the heroes. I stand with Ukraine.

ABOUT THE AUTHOR

J. Darlene Everly is an author of fantasy stories. The Cinders in Midnight Glass series will wrap up in 2022. Her serial, Crossroad Inn, is available on Vella. Her debut trilogy, The Grimm Star Saga: First Light is available everywhere, and two more series will begin in 2022. Keep an eye out for Major Arcana to go on preorder this fall, and The Grimm Star Saga's first release this summer. And keep reading for all of Cinder's story. There are a lot more stories to tell in this same story world. They will be coming soon.

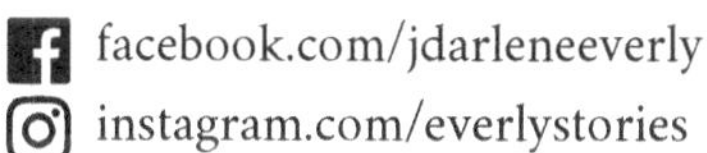

facebook.com/jdarleneeverly
instagram.com/everlystories